I0573164

REVOKED

CAPTAIN DARING, BOOK ONE

BLAZE WARD

KNOTTED ROAD PRESS

Revoked
Captain Daring Book 1
Blaze Ward
Copyright © 2022 Blaze Ward
All rights reserved
Published by Knotted Road Press
www.KnottedRoadPress.com

ISBN: 978-1-64470-289-5

Cover art:
ID 483374688 © prometeus DepositPhotos.com

Cover and interior design copyright © 2022 Knotted Road Press

Reviews
It's true. Reviews help. Even a short one, such as, "Loved it!" So please consider reviewing this book (and all of the ones you've read) on your favorite retailer site.

Never miss a release!
If you'd like to be notified of new releases, sign up for my newsletter.

http://www.blazeward.com/newsletter/

Buy More!
Did you know that you can buy directly from my website?

https://www.blazeward.com/shop/

This book is licensed for your personal enjoyment only. All rights reserved. This is a work of fiction. All characters and events portrayed in this book are fictional, and any resemblance to real people or incidents is purely coincidental. This book, or parts thereof, may not be reproduced in any form without permission.

ALSO BY BLAZE WARD

Captain Daring

Revoked

Returned

Reborn

Hunter Bureau

Mirrors

Latency

Pleasure Model

Inhuman

First Centurion Kosnett

Encounter at Vilahana

Consensus at Aditi

Hegemony at Dalou

Princes at Ewin

Empire at Gloran

Domain at Yaumgan

The Jessica Keller Chronicles

Auberon

Queen of the Pirates

Last of the Immortals

Goddess of War

Flight of the Blackbird

The Red Admiral

The Lazarus Alliance

Escape

Return

Rebellion

Revolution

Liberation

Retribution

Alliance

Shadow of the Dominion

Longshot Hypothesis

Hard Bargain

Outermost

Dominion-427

Phoenix

Princess Rualoh

The Handsome Rob Gigs

Can't Shoot Straight Gang

Can't Shoot Straight Gang Returns

Hunting Handsome Rob

Handsome Rob, Assassin

CHAPTER 1

Joie put her one good eye, the left one, to the keyhole, even as someone kept banging on the other side of her door with an angry fist. She had to grab a handful of long, black hair and flip it over her shoulder to get it out of her way.

Today was supposed to be her day off. Nobody should want to bother her. Nobody she wanted to see, she amended herself.

The image that greeted her through the fisheye lens just reinforced that.

There were two of them standing in the hallway. Once upon a time, she would have been able to read their thermal signatures through the wood itself, using the IR camera that had been built into her right eye.

Back before it was destroyed.

The man in the fancy suit was the one knocking. Three-piece, gray with white razor-thin pinstripes.

Money. As always

He'd been the one to destroy her eye. And her life.

The woman standing behind him and to one side stood like a bodyguard. Looked like one, too. Joie had done the same thing enough in her time to recognize it. Even for the asshole pounding on her door in the middle of the afternoon.

Still, she took a moment to study the woman.

Tall, sleek, muscular. Dressed like a westerner in slacks, blouse, and light jacket, but East African by ancestry, with that long, lean look that you frequently got from athletes from Ethiopia or the Masai.

Fierce face. The close-cropped black hair had what almost looked like speed lines carved horizontally in it. Something of a visual signature, but Joie didn't figure the two of them were on a mission today.

She wasn't important enough for that. Not anymore.

At least she hoped not.

Joie undid the top bolt noisily enough that the man in the hallway would hear it and stop banging. Then she undid the second bolt as well. Unhooked the chain. Unlocked the door itself.

She opened it and stared a hard scowl at Mr. Taylor Kehoe and wondered if she'd died and gone to hell. If she had, somebody had forgotten to mention it to her.

He still had that same sneer she remembered.

Joie hadn't seen it in almost two years. Didn't miss it.

The tall, black woman amped her fierceness up another level, but Joie wasn't a threat.

Couldn't be a threat anymore.

She stepped back now and walked deeper into her apartment, door still halfway open but ignoring the two of them as she stepped into the tiny kitchen and started the faucet for some water.

"Not going to invite us in like civilized folk, Daring?" Kehoe called after her, still in the hall.

"If I hadn't opened it, you'd have just had your pit bull kick it in," she half-yelled back. "Don't want to see you, Kehoe. Nothing I can do about it, though."

Joie glanced back to see him step to the threshold, careful, like she might have left booby traps for burglars. Men like him had trained her in those sorts of things after all, once upon a time.

But nothing exploded and splattered the man across her neighbor's door.

Joie didn't even know the people around here, since she wasn't particularly sociable much of the time.

Too many people stared at her for her to want to talk up strangers. Something about the dead cybernetics where her right eye had once been, which she usually covered with a simple black patch. There was also the right arm, which ended in a stump about ten centimeters down from her shoulder.

The rest of the damage was covered, unless she felt the need to go out in a bikini. That had been more than two years ago, too.

The water kettle was electric. She hung the top part from a hook she'd added to the faucet so she could fill it with her one hand. Done, she shut off the water and put the pot on the electric stand, flipping the switch to start heating it.

Once upon a time, she'd kept frozen beans for her coffee, but in those days, she'd been able to hold a hand grinder with both hands while she worked. That needed two hands, after all. Today, she pulled out pre-ground stuff and measured a couple of spoons into her AeroPress. Joie had almost given up on using her AeroPress, in spite of the personal reasons she kept it, before she'd learned all the tricks and built a few things to help her hold it when she needed to empty it. Too much like admitting defeat.

Kehoe had come as far as the dining space next to her tiny kitchen, standing about two meters into her apartment. He was over on the far side of the battered table she'd picked up second hand when she moved in, while his pet killer was on the end in the open, where she could get to Joie in about two steps if she wanted.

Assuming that the woman didn't have any sorts of cybernetic weapon implants that she could use.

Joie missed her old Mark I cyberarm. Or the other two that she had routinely worn, depending on the mission. The ones with fusion pulse rifles built in.

"You live in a dump," Kehoe offered, like that was a surprise.

She glanced over just long enough to convey her disdain for the man, then made sure everything was ready when the water got hot.

Nice part about the AeroPress was that it only made one cup at a time. Not like she was going to offer him any. Or his deadly bodyguard.

She glanced at the tall, black woman again and wondered how many cybernetic parts she'd had added. None were visible, but that meant exactly zilch in this game.

"Dump?" Joie finally replied. "Well, I got my RDR as an O-3 with bonus time added. You know, *Revoked, Demilitarized, Retired.* At least they pay Captains with twenty-year-equivalence enough that I don't starve, but it is still at the top of lower middle class, Kehoe. Maybe you should talk to whatever pet Congresscritters you have on the payroll these days about improving veteran pay."

He left that provocation alone.

They must want something good from her, not to react to the kinds of insults she was throwing at them, verbal as well as social.

Joie ignored him, as the water was close.

She'd gotten pretty good at doing this, since she only had one hand. Her mind had even gotten mostly over automatically expecting her right hand to be able to do things.

Thirty-six was too damned young to be washed up, but without all the old cyberware, there wasn't a lot she could do about it. And no way she could afford to replace any of it, even with cheap Vietnamese crap. Not with what she lived on.

She poured hot water into the column with the grounds. Stirred it with the flat stick.

Because she bought a pretty coarse grind, it would drain fast enough. She watched it, but her two visitors remained silent as she worked.

Neither of them had even closed the front door, so they weren't here to do anything where a random civilian walking by might become an inadvertent witness. Joie was just glad she didn't have a cat who might have chosen to make a run for it right about now.

She pressed the grounds instead. Dumped them into a composting trough by the sink next to the toaster oven, a task which was always a little hairy to do.

Didn't spill anything on herself today, wonder of wonders.

Cream from the fridge just to draw all this performance out a few extra seconds.

Finally, she turned to find Kehoe sitting at the table, directly across from her.

Joie decided that they weren't leaving until she dealt with them.

"Close the door," she said to the woman.

The stranger didn't rate a *Please*.

Joie sat opposite the man as the killer backed up a step and shut the door quietly.

Kehoe hadn't changed in the last two years. Tall and slim. One hundred eight-five centimeters and about eighty kilos. Hair slicked back with something that made it look wet.

She'd heard him referred to as part of a group of politicians that you could still insult by calling them "cookie pushers in striped pants," even though it had been more than a century and a half since the capitalists lost China to the Reds.

Back when that had meant anything.

Joie stared at the man. Dared him to say something.

Wasn't that her nickname, after all? *Captain Daring*?

She'd been born Josefina Dearing, but everyone called her Joie. *Captain Daring* had been because of what she used to do, back when she still had all her cybernetic abilities.

"Do you even care why I'm here?" Kehoe asked her, starting in the middle of some conversation like he'd been here for a while.

"Only because at some point I'm likely to want some dinner," Joie replied. "Don't plan on inviting you to join me. Or joining you."

She watched him take a deep breath and swallow some level of personal anger.

Joie had never been particularly close to a snake like him, to say nothing of intimate, even when he'd asked. She could still tell someone was jerking his chain. Someone with enough power or authority to do that.

She approved of whoever it was.

"The Secretary would like to bring you in from the cold," he said simply.

Joie considered his words for a couple of seconds, just to make sure she'd heard him right the first time.

She had.

"Go fuck yourself, Kehoe," she enunciated slowly. "*RDR*. Remember? You should. You were the one that triggered all those overrides that shut me down that day. You were even laughing when you did it."

"Mistakes were made…" he began, but she overrode him.

"The fuck they were, you stupid fuck!" she snarled, loud yes but perfectly still so that the killer next to her didn't have an excuse to backhand Joie across the room.

Oh yes, Joie knew what that woman was.

Her, a few years younger. Type Three model, maybe, with everything they had learned from building Captain Daring as the original Type One.

Joie focused her ire on Mr. Taylor Kehoe.

"Boom, my arm goes numb and falls off, sliding right out of my sleeve, you prick," she snapped.

"Then listening to my own electronic eardrum destroy itself. You know how you can top something as disgusting as that, Kehoe? Watching smoke come out of my eyeball when you caused my right eye to cook itself."

Just because, she reached up with her left hand to pull back the eyepatch she wore all the time.

She knew what he'd see. She saw it every morning in the mirror.

Black hair from her Meso-American grandparents, long because she hadn't bothered cutting it once she got demilitarized. Pretty face, with some good plastic surgery to cover up the scars from the original explosion that had destroyed her eye and her ear, at the same time it had broken most of her ribs and cooked off her right arm.

Miracle she'd ever made it to the field hospital alive. Miracle number two that they'd kept her alive from there.

Miracle number three had been volunteering to be a cybernetic test dummy, with new parts that were better than the old ones.

Kehoe would see the blackened eyeball that didn't work anymore.

Didn't track. Didn't anything. Dull gray center where the camera had been fried by an override keyed to the switch he'd held in his hand.

She let him see it today. Then, to be a shit, looked up at the woman.

Let her understand what her bosses might do, if they decided they didn't like you anymore.

Kehoe had accused her of being a double agent at the time. Nobody had ever proven anything, because there was nothing to prove. Instead of an Article 32 and a court martial, they'd pensioned her off, rounded up to twenty years' service so she would keep her mouth shut.

She'd wondered if he was here to read her her rights, since she wasn't about to go with him willingly.

"Mistakes were made, Daring," Kehoe repeated in a quieter voice, talking like she was a wild animal that might attack him.

Like she was still Captain Daring, scourge of terrorists, pimps, and criminals that the US government wanted quietly or loudly eliminated.

She'd been good at that.

Up until two years ago.

"Why the fuck are you here?" she demanded. "What stupid thing did you dumb fucks do that you had to go all the way to the Secretary and get his blessing on something?"

She'd been part of Special Operations Command, once upon a time. Even before getting blown up. After they rebuilt her, she'd moved into a quieter role, officially attached to the 389th Military Intelligence Battalion as a cover for what she really did. Those folks were supposed to be experts in HUMINT, SIGINT, and GEOINT.

Joie had specialized in the first part: Human Intelligence. The robust kind. Signals Intelligence and Geospatial Intelligence involved really smart computers studying images and cell phone networks, then assembling clues.

She'd talked to people. And occasionally killed them.

"There is a situation, back at Bragg, Daring," Kehoe said now, still calm, like he could just convince her to overlook everything.

"*RDR*, Kehoe," she growled at him. "*Revoked, Demilitarized, Retired.* You offering to undo that?"

"We can rebuild you, Captain," he said with a helpful smile.

"What? So you can blow me up again when you're done with me?" she asked in a hot, sharp voice. "Like last time? The only parts you have on the shelf would have the same overrides as before, because I cannot imagine you didn't install them in all of us, including your little princess here."

That got a growl from the woman, but nothing more. Well-trained soldier. Hallmarks of West Point, and not all that long ago. Not enough time in the field to understand what men like Kehoe did when they got angry at you.

And he'd been angry.

"We can replace your eye, ear, and arm," he continued, like she wasn't yelling at him at all. "I have a new-in-box Mark I cyberarm down in the car if you want it. You still have all the internal armor and Argenite bone implants that you had before. Those are still cutting edge."

"What possible thing do you think you could tell me that would cause me to suddenly forgive you and the entire Technology Research Command, Kehoe?"

"Your old partner has disappeared, and nobody knows where she's gone," he said. "Romana Pham."

"The one who started sleeping with my ex-boyfriend after I got tossed into the gutter by you slimeballs?" Joie sneered. "That one?"

She liked the way his eyes held an instant of panic. Like maybe he'd missed something in the file.

Sure, maybe she was overplaying the situation a bit. Joie knew she'd been depressed and lashing out at everyone after Kehoe had destroyed her and her career. Mitch had finally given up trying to help her, when it became clear she wouldn't allow it. Same with Romana.

She wasn't even sore at them that they'd found solace in each other.

It had taken Joie more than a year to find the strength to get out of bed some mornings. To try to find purpose in her remaining years. Decades. Whatever.

Except that there was no way in hell she was going to eat a bullet, if only to make sure that this punk didn't get the satisfaction of beating her.

Nobody had ever beat Captain Daring.

Nobody.

Nobody was going to start now.

Her coffee tasted good enough to shut her up, so she sipped it instead of measuring the trajectory to throw it in his face.

Warrior Princess might be fast enough to stop her. And she might not.

Kehoe apparently realized that he'd come at her all wrong. She watched him reach into a pocket and pull out a business card, laying it carefully on the table between them.

"I'd like to talk at some point," he said, rising and moving to the door. "Or you can reach out directly to the CG at Bragg, or even MacDill. The Secretary cleared it."

He opened the door and exited like it was a Shakespearean play. Warrior Princess scowled at her for a long second before she backed out and pulled the door closed behind her.

Joie picked up the card and let her fingers feel the texture of it.

Commanding General, 1st Special Forces Command (Airborne), Fort Bragg, NC.

What the hell had Romana done this time?

CHAPTER 2

Taylor went down the stairs with deliberation. Behind him Freya Malik followed on silent feet.

He was always surprised at how quietly those people could move, even when the Argenite implants made them weigh so much more than they appeared. Malik had at least eighteen kilograms on him, though you would never know short of trying to pick her up.

He got down to ground level and went around a corner to the side street opposing Daring's apartment, just so she couldn't see him leave. And maybe open fire from a window if she'd been mad enough.

Never discount Joie Daring. She might be the textbook definition of a woman scorned right now, and would need time to get over herself.

Instead, he approached a blacked-out SUV parked in a fire lane with special diplomatic plates that would cause any cop to simply keep walking. Especially in the DMV, the District of Columbia–Maryland–Virginia Greater Metropolitan Area.

Malik opened the rear door while watching the street for non-existent traffic to suddenly turn into threats. Taylor slid in and then across. Malik joined him a moment later, pulling the door shut behind her.

This vehicle had been gutted and rebuilt at the factory, with a rear seat facing forward and the middle seat turned around aft.

Taylor was next to the only occupant in back.

General Valmy Youri Bouchard smiled at him as he settled.

"How'd she take it?" Bouchard asked with a grin. He spoke with the slightest trace of a French accent, acquired in his youth, before a teenager had decided that the French Army wasn't going to be interesting enough and immigrated nearly thirty years ago to transfer flags and citizenship.

Taylor reached into his pocket and pulled out a ten-euro coin, handing it to the laughing man.

Bouchard nodded. "Thought so."

Taylor studied the man as the SUV rumbled into motion, almost as heavy as a tank with all the armor and equipment contained in the innocent-looking shell.

The general was fifty, so seven years older than himself. Tall and lean. Trim from constantly working out rather than sitting behind a desk. His wide forehead and prominent cheekbones made his face look like an inverted triangle, except for the iron jaw.

He wore his Army Blue Service Uniform without a hat today, and only a few of his awards and ribbons. As he'd said more than once, four stars on the shoulder said everything that you needed to know. From the back, you might mistake the man for a corporate executive.

Also not an entirely wrong assessment.

Bouchard turned to Malik now.

"How would you rate her, Lieutenant?" he asked the woman.

"Broken, sir," she replied in a quiet voice. "Still dangerous, though."

"Oh?"

"She understood who I was, and what, General," Malik continued. "Measured all of her actions to remain exactly short of provoking a reaction from me, though I might have responded had I not been forewarned."

"Joie Daring was the best, Malik," Bouchard nodded. "Kehoe can tell you more about her, now that you've met the woman."

"Sir, if she betrayed all of us, why wasn't she thrown in prison?"

Malik asked. "And if she didn't, then why was she tossed to the curb with an RDR?"

"Need to know, Lieutenant," Bouchard growled. "Well above your pay grade. Your job is to work with Technology Research Command and do whatever Kehoe tells you."

Bouchard waited for the woman to nod, then looked over at Taylor. He could almost feel the man weighing his soul.

"Will she take the bait?" Bouchard asked.

Taylor shrugged.

"It was probably a mistake to send me, unless you wanted her that angry, General," Taylor said. "A lot of rage there she still hasn't worked out, most of it with my name attached."

"I'm aware of that, Kehoe," Bouchard nodded. "That was part of the reason I did send you. Daring has, as far as we've been able to tell, given up completely on every part of her life that existed before she was demobilized. She has turned into a quiet person, almost completely unknown to her neighbors and coworkers."

He paused to glance at Malik, as if warning her to keep her mouth shut. She would. The woman was smart, which was why Taylor had selected her for the program in the first place.

"Had she started up on her investigations again, we would have known immediately, and dropped the full might of the US military on her ass in a heartbeat," Bouchard continued. "She has not."

"And the kick in the ass to put her back on the playing field?" Taylor asked.

He was the top civilian in TRC, the Technology Research Command, but only a civilian, and soldiers didn't always like talking about things. Especially not with someone who had been promoted up and over by the civilian intelligence structure.

Right hand, left hand, and all that.

"Nothing in Pham's personnel file suggests that the woman would vanish from the middle of an Army post, Kehoe," Bouchard said. "If she was assassinated by someone, they would have crowed about it somewhere, even on what they thought were secret channels. Had they taken her alive, there would be either ransom demands or taunting videos before we got the one showing her being executed. Even for barbarians, they have a particular style."

"Was Pham sleeping with Mitch Graydon?" Taylor asked.

He was going to be badly handicapped if the General was withholding critical information on this mission.

"At one point," Bouchard nodded. "About a year ago, though the physical relationship didn't last long. They have remained in touch, but nothing more over the last six months."

It was Taylor's turn to nod.

Messy. Complicated.

Waving him in front of Daring was like a matador with a red cape in front of a wounded and angry bull. Adding in a man who had slept with both of them was just going to further muddy the waters, at a time when Taylor was trying to see through whatever conspiracy had been revealed by Pham's disappearance.

He supposed that bringing Daring in from the cold might be one way to handle it, as she and Pham had been partners for several years. Daring might know things that had never been committed to any files.

Still, the woman was a loose cannon, even without the fusion pulse rifle arm she'd worn on some of her missions.

He couldn't help but wonder if reactivating the woman was a bad idea.

CHAPTER 3

Joie didn't need Kehoe's shit. Any of it. He could fucking rot, for all she would get involved.

Today, her only task was sweeping the floor at the coffee shop during an afternoon lull. Biggest coffee chain corporation in the world got bonus points on their annual taxes by hiring a disabled veteran like her, but she didn't mind.

Her retirement pay, as she'd told that asshole Kehoe the day before yesterday, was enough to live on, if she was frugal. Even at minimum wage, this addition was enough to let her splurge a little. Maybe a trip from time to time, or dinner someplace nice.

She had lost count of the number of propositions for dates she had turned down over the last year. Maybe she needed to just admit it and start rescuing cats from the local shelter or something.

The store was always clean. Part of that was Joie constantly moving around to empty trash, sweep corners, restock from the back, and check the restrooms. Occasionally, she even felt friendly enough to work the drive-thru window, but Amy the manager understood that those days were rare and didn't push.

Instead, Joie just moved around and kept things organized. Amy liked that. At twenty-three, the girl was too young to be managing a store like this, but she was also really smart and a six-year veteran of the industry at this point.

And ran a good crew.

Amy was smiling at Joie when she looked up from pulling the trash from next to the door, except that the smile turned to utter and complete panic in the blink of an eye. Joie let the trashbin slide back into place as she turned to look behind her.

Big. Freaking huge. Two damned meters tall. Built like a tree. And not one of those willows, either. No, the man gave you the impression of a sequoia someone had planted in the middle of the store when nobody was looking.

Joie was tall for a woman at one hundred and eighty centimeters. Shorter than the killer who'd stood in her kitchen with Kehoe.

Still looked the guy in the chin. Grizzled jaw that hadn't been shaved in a few days. At least it wasn't that artfully crafted stubble that some guys thought looked good. The ones that spent at least an hour each morning in front of a mirror getting everything perfect.

No, this was just three or four days of not bothering. The blond hair on top was short enough that the guy could run his hands through it a few times damp and be fine. Impossible blue eyes a girl could fall into. Face that was rugged instead of pretty.

Worse, she recognized him.

She scowled up at the man, standing one step inside the door. Two steps away from her. He stopped walking. Held up short like someone had just jerked his leash hard.

Joie wondered if her face had gone all the way down into a snarl. It felt like that from the way her cheeks suddenly hurt.

It almost felt like a movie scene, where the background music suddenly stops. Around her, conversations fell to nothing. Nobody in line for coffee, so the crew was mostly looking this way, save for Andy at the drive-thru window.

Joie fell into a defensive combat stance.

"No, not like that," he said, raising both hands in a non-threatening manner.

Like she could hurt him.

"Why aren't you in prison, Carter?" she rasped.

"It's a long story, Daring," he said.

"Joie, do I need to call the cops?" Amy yelled across the space, loud enough that every head turned towards her.

Twenty-three years old and in charge. *In Charge.*

One hundred and sixty centimeters. Fifty kilograms soaking wet.

Not about to take any of your shit.

Joie scowled up at Carter.

"Well?" she demanded sharply.

"I'd rather not," Carter replied carefully, like maybe Joie was about to bite him or something. Or Amy would step in and do it.

Last time they'd fought, she still had all her cyberware, including the arm with the light fusion pulse rifle that fired out of the palm when you needed it.

She'd needed it that day.

Needed everything she had and an extra dollop of luck to take this man down. To bring him in.

And what had it gotten her?

RDR, when Taylor Kehoe had been expecting the dead part of *Dead or Alive*. They'd assumed she'd turned or something, made a deal with Carter somehow, instead of merely beating the man bloody and unconscious.

Beating him.

Bringing him in alive.

Joie turned back to Amy and straightened.

"Boss, I think I need to clock out for about fifteen minutes to deal with some personal issues," Joie said in a hard, quiet voice.

She spoke barely above a whisper, but the room felt like a pin would be a loud intrusion.

"Stay on the clock, Joie," Amy said firmly. "He can behave himself or I'll toss his ass out into the parking lot."

The weight differential between the two of them was probably one hundred and sixty kilos, considering the amount of Argenite alloy inserted into the man's arms and legs to reinforce them against breaking under extreme conditions. Just like hers. And the way his muscles had been artificially augmented with all sorts of experimental viruses over the decades until he had the overall density of concrete, everywhere except his skull.

Nobody had ever accused Carter Faulkener of being dumb.

Joie considered revisiting that opinion now, looking up at him.

Carter actually smiled at her sheepishly. And Amy.

"Go get some coffee then sit your ass down," Joie snarled quietly. "I need to empty this can, then I'll come deal with you."

You maybe could have knocked her over with a feather when he nodded and walked over to where Amy was behind the counter. And ordered two mochas with extra caramel.

Son of a bitch hadn't forgotten, then.

She heard him pay in euros as she walked out the door, but that didn't mean much these days. Dollars used to be a powerful currency, according to history. Constant inflation meant that most folks dealt in euros instead.

She grabbed the can with her one hand and hauled it out the door to where the dumpster was. No way in hell she could delicately empty it into a larger bag right now.

Not the way her hand was shaking.

Joie leaned against the wall of the store outside for a few seconds and just tried to breathe calmly. Around her, the breeze was just enough to ruffle her hair and bring her birdsong as vehicles were six deep in line for their fix.

Two days ago Kehoe. Today Carter Faulkener? What the fuck was tomorrow going to bring?

She sucked a last breath all the way to her toes and stood ramrod straight again. Just like West Point hammered into your bones and your soul. Shoulders back. Head up. Feet apart.

You are a soldier. Act like one.

She grabbed the empty can and returned to the store. Got it under the hole in the counter where people dropped things.

Turned around and found Amy personally delivering two covered cups to a six-top table as far away as you could get from a pair of hipster moms with precocious kids already packing their shit up to hit the door at a dead run.

Not that Joie could blame them one bit. She'd like to do the same thing.

Carter smiled shyly. Amy looked like an apocalypse warlord surveying her domain. Even seated though, Carter was taller than she was.

Amy surprised her by stepping close and putting a hand on Joie's bad shoulder.

"Tug your ear and I'll call the cops. The phone will be in my hand," Amy said to her. "Then remember that hot coffee burns the eyes."

One of those little things that women shared when men weren't around. When you had to deal with some manner of sexual assault, because nobody ever held men accountable for their shit.

No, they always blamed the woman for it.

Joie nodded and stepped over to Carter. She was taller, so he was looking up at her.

She suppressed an angry growl and sat down across from the man. Took a sip of her caramel surprise.

Waited.

"A little birdie told me where to find you," he began quietly, also sipping, like two old friends meeting to catch up.

"You haven't answered my question, Carter," she replied. Not snarling. Not friendly, either.

Up close, he'd at least put on some cologne. Or found a better antiperspirant than he used to wear in the old days. Musky and tough, but masculine. Went with that ruggedness of a jaw.

Almost made you think lumberjack thoughts, assuming you didn't know anything about the man.

He opened his mouth to say something. Closed it immediately. Thought about it for a second, then spoke.

"You and I both know that no prison was going to hold me for long, Daring," he replied. "The Department of Defense spent a lot of money and a lot of years teaching me how to escape from any situation. Same as you. They just didn't expect to have to use it on me."

"That why Kehoe wanted you dead?" she asked.

"Partly," he agreed. "Joint Chiefs of Staff still had some allies on it at that point, such that nobody would make the President sign the serious paperwork for one of their own, so they only listed me dead or alive."

"And now?"

"I've been a fugitive for twenty months, Daring," Carter said with a nod.

"So you show up in a coffee shop in Arlington, Virginia, in the middle of the afternoon, two days after Kehoe and the TRC knock on my door?" she pressed. "I'd ask how stupid you thought I was, but the answer to that's pretty fucking obvious."

Give the man credit, he at least grimaced.

"They don't actually watch you here," he said. "The folks paid to narc on you in your building are a different matter, but nobody here is on the government's payroll."

"How do you know that?" Joie demanded, not surprised at her neighbors, but amazed if nobody in earshot had been given a business card to call in certain situations.

But then, it was Amy's shop.

"I still have friends on the inside, Daring," he replied. "Not everyone thinks I'm a villain, in spite of the arrest warrants and rewards. Same as they don't think I somehow turned you from being a loyal soldier. Again, in spite of scuttlebutt here and in various posts and bases around the world."

"So you showed up here to make sure I get arrested for harboring a fugitive from justice?" Joie asked, pissed.

Way pissed.

Chewing nails pissed. Punch enhanced warriors in the mouth pissed.

"What did Kehoe want?" he asked, changing the subject.

Except that he hadn't changed the subject. It was all one big, gnarly mess.

"Help tracking down Romana Pham," Joie replied.

If asked later, Kehoe hadn't said anything about keeping the conversation quiet. And Joie had half a dozen witnesses right now, not counting the two moms who were pulling out of the parking lot.

And possibly calling the cops anyway. They had the look about them.

Not that Joie would mention that to Carter. If he hadn't figured that one out, he wasn't as bright as she thought.

"Because she's vanished," Carter said. It wasn't a statement.

"So Kehoe said," Joie noted, neither agreeing nor disagreeing.

"When was the last time you talked to her?" Carter asked.

It was probably an innocent question. Carter wouldn't know the truth. Couldn't.

Not if he'd been in prison for a while and then on the run since.

Right?

"About a year," Joie replied, taking a sip of coffee and wondering if his augmented reflexes were fast enough to keep her from throwing hot coffee with caramel into his face. "We didn't part on good terms."

"Yeah, I'd heard that," Carter offered offhandedly.

"How about you, Carter?" Joie asked, mostly just to toss this mess back into his lap.

"About four months ago," he said succinctly.

Joie nearly dropped her coffee.

Four months?

Miss Spit-and-Polish Romana Pham hanging out with a wanted fugitive?

What the hell had the world come to?

Something in her good eye must have shown. The bad eye was covered, as always, with a simple brown eyepatch that didn't stand out too much against her olive skin.

Carter took a breath, lips pressed together like he'd been sucking on a lemon. Finally, he came to some decision.

"Unlike you or I, she's still human, Daring," he said quietly. "No cyberware. No Argenite bone implants. No kevlar underlayer to her dermis."

He took a drink and watched her for a reaction. Joie was too stunned to actually have one.

"She's never, to the best of my knowledge, had any of the viral transformation treatments to grow extra muscle like my kind. Never had pieces cut off or blown off to need mechanical replacements like you. Human."

"Agreed," Joie managed, letting the extra sugar and cream try to warm that cold spot at the center of her stomach.

The one that wanted to turn to ice right now.

"Not all that long ago, everyone was human," Carter said next, apparently intent on dragging her off on some stupid-ass tangent while somewhere a clock counted down to the moment when armed SWAT teams surrounded the place.

Amy would throw his ass out at that point. Carter might even let her. He'd never been a terrorist, regardless of the stories promulgated about the man. Just another agent like her. Different research program. Same purpose. Maybe the same outcome, since she was *RDR* and he was running from the law.

Failure.

"So?" Joie asked. "Technology Research Command exists to push the boundaries of science. Creating advanced soldiers like you, or combat cyborgs like me."

"Very little advancement was made for most of the twentieth or twenty-first centuries, Daring," he replied. "Then thirty years ago, all that changed."

Joie shrugged. Thirty years ago she was in first grade. Carter actually looked younger than her, but she knew better.

"How old are you, Carter?" she asked abruptly.

"Fifty-five," he smiled. "One of the side effects of the original set of treatments was that I would grow old extremely slowly, relative to everyone else. Downside was complete sterility. No kids unless I wanted someone to clone me. Early on, they were afraid of creating a superior species of humans, and watching folks like us take over the world in some bizarre eugenics war or something. Fear is still there, but they never made enough of us to matter, as they shifted over to cyborgs like you instead. Lots of broken soldiers handy from all the various wars and insurrections we've been fighting in or causing for the last two hundred years."

Joie grunted. The profanity on the tip of her tongue wasn't pointed at him. Kehoe, maybe. Or his bosses. She wasn't entirely sure who was in charge of TRC these days, or Special Operations Command, though she could look the latter up.

The former didn't technically exist, except at security clearances well beyond what the average soldier ever saw. Even the average SOCOM trooper, like she'd been once.

"Why are you here, Carter?" Joie asked, circling all the way back around.

Somewhere, cops were strapping on the heavy armor and calling for help. Maybe airstrikes.

"Romana was investigating something on the side, Daring," he replied. "We don't know exactly what, but it had to do with that breakthrough that made it possible for the government to suddenly start churning out advanced warriors."

"Some secret government lab," she offered.

"That's what everyone says," he agreed. "Where is it? Who works there?"

Joie blinked.

He leaned back now, still looking like a grownup sitting in their kid's play furniture, given his immense size. He even smiled, however grimly.

"Shit," she muttered.

"Exactly," Carter said. "Everything leaks eventually. Human ego. Human nature. Something. Thirty or more years, maybe fifty, and nobody has ever even heard rumors about the place where all these fantastic new inventions come from."

"So what's your theory?" she asked.

"Got none, personally," he said. "Romana Pham was the one pursuing it, but she didn't have much to go on, the last time we talked."

Joie still couldn't get over this fugitive felon talking to her former partner. Like, sitting in a corporate coffee shop in Arlington and just *chatting.*

"And what do you think I can do, Carter?" she volleyed back at the man. "I have one eye, one ear, and one arm."

"You still have all that crazy shit locked up in your head, Daring," he smiled. "You were good enough to take me down, you know.

Granted, maybe you lack some of the tools today, but you knew her better than anybody."

That was possible. Except that Romana and Mitch had ended up together, once they both gave up on her getting her shit together. He might know something.

But no way in hell would Mitch want to deal with Kehoe or Carter. If they could even find the man.

Joie wasn't sure she could, but at least she had an idea where to look.

Joie wore a wristwatch because her phone was supposed to stay in her pocket with the ringer off when she was working. She glanced at it now and smiled at Carter.

"Assuming one of those two women who were here when you walked in called the cops, you have about twenty seconds to get off the grounds before they can fence you in," she smiled up at him innocently. "You should probably start running right now, just to be safe."

He scowled at her. Pulled out a business card just like Kehoe had and handed it to her.

"I'd like to talk more," he said, rising and putting his hand on her good shoulder as he went by.

Joie listened as the door opened behind her, then watched Carter Faulkener, the agent once known as *Mithras*, started running.

She'd have needed cybernetic legs to keep up with him, as he was already moving seventy kilometers per hour by the time he crossed the parking lot, arms pumping smoothly and moving like a Norse god as he fled.

In the distance, she heard sirens.

CHAPTER 4

In the end, Joie found herself in Amy's office, but only after Amy had thrown such a huge fit about the cops taking Joie anywhere. Her, Amy, Kehoe, and a female lawyer from their Head Office that must have abseiled from the back of a hovering assault chopper, like Joie used to do, in order to get here so quickly.

Someone *had* called the police. Probably the two moms in matching luxury sports-car vans.

Amy hadn't called the police. She had done something even scarier and called the Regional Manager. And apparently said one of those magical emergency keywords that only store managers knew. The one that got dangerous and high-powered corporate attorneys to drop everything and come into a parking lot skidding sideways like the first half of a bootlegger reverse.

At least all the cops standing around in the parking lot were ordering coffee to make up for the fact that no civilians were allowed on the property right now.

Joie found herself between Amy on her bad side and a Yale-educated rabid Chihuahua of a lawyer on her left named Clarke. Kehoe sat behind Amy's desk, not touching any of the paperwork and with the computer screen clamshelled closed.

"That's it?" Kehoe demanded, after Joie and Amy finished telling their bits. "That's all he talked about? Asked you about?"

"That's it," Amy spoke up before Joie could answer. "I can play you the security tapes if you'd like, but I presume from your badge that you already have an order in hand to make copies before you leave."

"And I will remind you that *I* will make those copies," the lawyer spoke up, her voice snotty and rude in ways that warmed Joie's soul. "That way there is no chance that some terrible accident befalls the originals, which I will also remain in possession of."

Rabid Chihuahua. Joie wondered if the woman knew Kehoe from somewhere else. They'd both gone to Yale Law, after all, which was what you did if you wanted to be President of the United States or an Ambassador.

Or a covert spymaster attached to a division of a department that didn't officially exist.

Joie just sat and watched, like a fan at a basketball game who had gotten court-side seats between the two benches.

Kehoe had a blue tie today under his gray power suit. White stripes diagonally aimed at his left shoulder.

Her own lawyer had a green tie with paisleys on it, under a maroon jacket and skirt that somehow looked like a serious version of Mrs. Claus. Or Santa Claus's lawyer niece, since the woman looked about Joie's age.

Joie hadn't said a word in four minutes. It was kind of awesome, however frightening it might be that Corporate would do something like this.

Or had someone told them who Josefina Dearing really was when she got hired, and they'd been quietly preparing for today?

That was even more scary. Unless they'd been expecting her to snap one day and hurt people. Then it made perfect sense.

Except for the fact that all the martial arts forms the Army had taught her assumed two hands.

Joie had studied all sort of forms before the Academy, during, and since. Mostly Cantonese Kung Fu and Okinawan Karate forms that had taken advantage of her great wingspan. Later, metal-laced bones meant that she could hammer with shins and forearms without hurting herself in the process.

She knew knives, but was trained to use bare hands at short range. And guns at anything over two meters if she had them. Like whenever she'd been outfitted with *Cyberarm, Mark II*. The one with the XM24E4 *Sunbolt* fusion pulse rifle built in and firing from her palm.

Everything the military had ever taught her had assumed two arms. These days, she was still learning how to do one-handed pushups. Pullups had been a pain in the ass even when she had both arms, considering how much she weighed, in spite of being long and slinky.

Argenite alloy was light stuff, compared to steel or aluminum. It was still heavy shit inside her.

Sifu Wěn had spent the last year teaching herself how to fight with only her left hand, just so Joie had something for her current limits, but nobody had ever created a proper martial arts form for someone like her. Everything was adapted from other forms.

Given the number of disabled veterans out there, she found that a bit absurd, really.

Kehoe had been staring at her the whole time, regardless of who was speaking. He finally spoke directly to her now.

"Would you consider a formal debriefing?" the man asked.

Amy bristled. She also had a pretty good idea that such a thing involved Joie volunteering to go to some private office or nearby military post to be interviewed without the benefit of her boss or legal counsel present.

How the hell had she gotten from West Point to here?

Joie shook her head.

"I don't know any more than I've already told you," she said. "Or what *Mithras* told me. You have the card he gave me, so I presume you're tracking down the phone number and email address and will be sending strike teams after him as soon as you can get through all the various proxy boxes that he's hiding behind."

"You think he's going to be impossible to find?" Kehoe challenged.

"I think he was impossible to hold, after I captured him for you last time," she replied, smiling sweetly and batting her eyelashes at the man just to frost the son of a bitch, reminding Kehoe that his people had let Carter Faulkener escape. "I can't imagine that he'll try to contact me again, knowing that you folks will all be on the evening news."

Kehoe grimaced, but Joie had seen the news vans and drones setting up shop just beyond the frontier edge of the parking lot. The one that an assault force sufficient enough to overthrow small nations was currently holding. Unless he put on a hat with a wide brim, or a mask of some sort, Taylor Kehoe was likely to be seen on camera by someone, assuming that they didn't park a blacked-out SUV right up on the sidewalk to make it harder for everyone else to have a clear line of sight.

Kehoe rose. Not defeated, but unwilling to invoke some of those secret authorities that Presidents and Secretaries of Defense signed off on quietly, right after they took office. The ones that let Kehoe run networks like her or Carter, back in the bad old days.

"You have my number, Daring," he said. "I still think it would be in your best interest to let us bring you in. If nothing else, to protect you from things you don't know about."

"I'm not interested, Kehoe," she rose with him, though kept the desk and Amy between them as he moved around towards the door. "You would have to order me back to active duty with an Act of Congress, which would be all sorts of fun to see on the cover of the Post and other news channels when it happened."

Sunlight. Like slime molds, spies were allergic to it. And secret agents.

Good thing she was a civilian these days.

Kehoe nodded, just enough to indicate that this conversation was far from over, and then departed.

The lawyer handed Joie a card.

"Any time, day or night, Ms. Dearing," Clarke said, then followed Kehoe out.

Probably chasing him and all his minions off the property, from the look on her face.

Amy surprised Joie with a hug. All one hundred and sixty centimeters of her.

"Any chance you have his real phone number?" Amy asked after a few seconds. "Is he single?"

Joie laughed. Something broke in her and she laughed and sobbed for nearly a minute as Amy held her upright, tears streaming down her face and snot threatening to run everywhere.

Finally, she got control of herself.

Carter was a handsome man. Not her type, but she could see Amy having the hots for him, in spite of locking hard on the man when he'd walked in. Tall, blond, muscular. Shoulders about a kilometer wide. Flat stomach. Ability to lift a motorcycle off the ground.

"He's older than your dad," Joie finally managed.

"Kids my age are boring in bed, Joie," Amy shrugged, which just set Joie to laughing again.

Stress, she supposed. Hoped. Something.

Not fear that she was about to be pulled back below the water, after it had taken her two years to make it to shore the last time.

"On the off chance that I see the man again, I will mention that," Joie said.

"Good," Amy said. "Now, you're about three hours long on the time sheet today, so you should probably clock out finally. And expect me to call you at home tomorrow to check on you, since this is your weekend coming up."

"Yes, mother," Joie said dutifully.

Amy was everyone's mother around here, regardless of how old you were.

She was *In Charge* and everyone who walked through that door understood that.

Joie found a computer and logged herself off duty. Overtime this week, but nothing she could do about that, and she wondered if Corporate minded the billable hours their legal killer had racked up today.

She hit the restroom, just to get all the coffee and adrenaline out of her system, then got a protein plate of meat, cheese, and an egg.

She didn't want to walk into any of the places around here, nor did she want to hang around the bus stop until all the cops left.

When she'd had two arms, an electric motorcycle had been her thing. Sleek, fast, and silent.

These days, she didn't even want to try to deal with all the crap that would come of retesting for a driver's license with all her new infirmities. Arlington County had a great transit system. It would get her home.

She had no idea what she would do at that point.

CHAPTER 5

oie had eventually given up and called Sifu—*Teacher*—Wěn after she got home. Explained her day. Asked the woman for advice.

Wěn Cōng Mǎ had come highly recommended from some people who didn't actually exist on paper and couldn't be traced. Her teacher didn't have any sort of security clearance, so all the woman knew about Joie was that she was a former soldier with a bum eye, a dead ear, and no right arm.

Her Sifu had figured all the other parts out as they went.

A knife would cut Joie's skin, but not penetrate, anywhere on her torso. Bullets might, depending on how fast they were going and what tip the shooter used. She weighed more than her Sifu did, in spite of the woman having a bulkier build and standing just enough taller than her in flat feet that you could tell.

She ordered Joie to the dojo. Not asked. Commanded.

Joie went.

The dojo was a small warehouse her Sifu had converted into various things. Mostly open volume with a long space on the right that was up a step. Sand, covered over with canvas and packed down hard.

Firm footing, but not a good grip in shoes. Just soft enough that you could fall and not break things.

Once you learned how to fall.

Joie entered the front door and bowed to the *bagua* mirror separating the waiting area where parents and friends could sit around or watch a class. The space had good *feng shui*. That had been why her Sifu had bought it, though Joie had never gotten the whole story.

Joie stepped up onto the wooden platform next to the training floor and automatically slipped her shoes off, then put her bag and jacket atop them. She had changed into baggy black pants in cotton and a white T-shirt, with a sports bra underneath almost exactly the same olive tone as her skin.

Sifu Wěn was sitting lotus in the middle of the mat, facing her, so Joie stepped to the edge of the mat, bowed deeply, and then approached the woman.

Her Sifu had already heard about both times Kehoe had shown up, plus Carter. Didn't know the whole story, but enough.

She nodded to Joie now while seated and patted a spot on the floor next to her. Joie knelt and waited.

"I had thought to call it Wounded Crane," Sifu said in a quiet, firm voice. "But that suggested that you are flawed in some way, so it would never do. I have not yet found the auspicious name for you, nor your fighting style, but we will get there."

She paused now and studied her for a long moment.

"Assuming you are allowed to stay," she continued, serious now.

Joie recoiled a bit. Blinked.

"Allowed?" Joie squeaked. "Have I insulted you, Sifu?"

"Oh, not me," she laughed, eyes crinkling. "All those other stupid fucks out there who think that missing an arm makes you weak."

Joie relaxed.

Sifu Wěn was in that strange fifty-something age among Chinese women that was almost impossible to judge accurately. Doubly so as her hair was salt and pepper. Ethnically, Joie knew that the woman was Cantonese. It was there in her vocabulary and her deep and abiding hatred of both Thai Kickboxers and Northern Shaolin fighters. Culturally, Sifu Wěn was thoroughly American though, back at least six generations, claiming to have had several ancestors who built the transcontinental railroad because white people were too stupid to get it right.

Things like that made Joie smile.

"Come," Sifu said now, rising and facing Joie. "You need mindlessness tonight, rather than mindfulness. Muscle memory, because I fear that you will be taken away from me soon, regardless of your preferences."

She placed one hand behind her back now, grabbing her belt to simulate Joie's movement. Joie actually had better flexibility and core strength than her teacher did, but only because she had decided that Joie needed to add Capoeira, Savate, and a little Jujitsu to all the other crazy shit either of them had picked up along the way.

Fast and agile when her teacher tended to be direct and brutal when she had to.

Quickly, they ran through a variety of drills adapted from various animal forms. Limbering everything and getting warm. Twisting, striking, blocking.

"Now," Sifu growled at her. "I am a mugger who got up this morning and made poor life decisions."

Joie laughed at that. The philosophy was simple.

Every morning, you decide who you are going to be. Every morning, you can choose a different path, but most people fall into ruts as teenagers and never challenge those walls as they get higher and higher every year.

Sifu Wĕn slouched now, like some punk on a street corner.

"Gimme yer money, bitch," she slurred at Joie with a drunk surfer accent.

Joie held up her hand shoulder high between them, palm facing outward.

The woman stepped forward and threw a punch.

The Army had been at great pains to make everything seem scientific.

Sifu Wĕn liked it simple.

Ninety percent of the time, someone is going to throw a right-hand punch at you, if they don't think you know any martial arts.

Most of the rest would involve a left hand coming in as a jab or a feint, just to set you up for that right.

The hand in the way distracted the enemy mind. It actually became the thing they focused on, causing them to punch it instead of your face.

Sifu flexed badly and threw a flat punch straight at her hand, rather than a cross at her jaw. She knocked it inward, caught the wrist as the fist missed hitting anything, and turned it over, forcing Sifu to collapse forward and rotate away from her.

Joie stepped up with the same motion and thrust her by that rigid arm, pushing directly away from her as she lifted that arm, then let go. A normal mugger would sprawl painfully and maybe crack her face on the pavement. Sifu Wěn tumbled forward, popped up, and turned around.

"Good," she said. "Again."

This time, she opened with a left jab. Hard enough to sting if Joie let it. Joie slapped it down, rotated in with a shuffle step, then caught Sifu's forearm between her wrist and the artificial tits they'd gone ahead and given her when they sliced everything open on the sides to get all that kevlar and stuff inside her.

Something about distracting people from the scars and damage.

Sifu Wěn tried to punch her with her right hand now, so Joie snapped her hand back like a woman with a fan to block it. Then she turned the hand palm out and booped her softly on the nose.

Her teacher laughed and stepped back as Joie let go. She could have given her a knife hand to the throat, a palm strike under the chin, or gouged eyes out, depending on how desperate the situation was.

Running away was also always an option, she liked to remind Joie.

They worked through several more iterations. Armed with a rubber knife. Or with a sap. Or with a baseball bat.

In every instance, she was getting Joie to move inside quickly. Get right up against them, where she was used to fighting and could counter with her one good arm in several different ways. Hand, wrist, forearm, elbow, upper arm, shoulder.

Kicks were rare. The French art, Savate, had trained Joie to strike generally below the waist with her feet, because high kicks, while impressive as hell, telegraphed and required an opponent to stand perfectly still to be hit.

Finally, Sifu just reached out and grabbed Joie's wrist without saying anything, twisting her thumb under in a painful way that turned her body badly.

Automatically, Joie skipped sideways to keep her teacher from breaking her arm, moving to her right with the twist.

Sifu Wĕn reminded her frequently that fighting should always be the third choice, after talking and running away. She ran, but sidled her left foot as she did, kicking her left foot softly as she did.

Because Sifu was holding her, their sudden, combined movement had the heavier woman off balance and trying to brace on a foot that was no longer there, so she ended up face planting.

Joie got about three meters away and came to rest, turned back defensively.

"I didn't teach you that," Sifu announced, a big aggrieved.

Joie shrugged and grinned at her.

Sifu Wĕn got slowly to her feet, twisting everything to make sure it all still worked.

"Let's do that again, but slowly," she announced. "I want to make sure what you did, so I add it to your form as I invent it."

Joie walked closer and let Sifu grab her again. She telegraphed slowly and they moved like dancers now, up and through the kick and the step.

"Gotcha," she said, nodding to herself. "Don't try that against someone like you or that Carter fellow."

"Why not?"

"Most of the time, they won't be as off-balance," she replied. "Plus, most of you weigh so much that a quick kick like that doesn't move the foot far enough to do any good. Maybe they stumble. Maybe not. Don't trust it."

Joie nodded now. Anyone with cyberware and bone inserts like hers would also be a multi-art black belt. However, most of her forms and katas didn't work nearly as well in her current incarnation, though she frequently did them in her mind when meditating.

Joie was unwilling to admit that she'd never have a cyberarm again.

More than once, she had considered hooking up with a local college cybernetics program and letting them experiment on her. Or one of those high-end private schools with exceptionally wealthy and connected high school kids whose parents were in the government, or one of the associated think tanks around here.

She'd always held back, though, unwilling to open herself up that much emotionally. Too many scars, and not just the ones you could see if she was naked.

"What's next?" Joie asked.

"Weapons training," Sifu grinned.

"I thought you said never to trust weapons, because they can be taken away, or not handy when you need them," she sassed her teacher now.

Throwing her words back in her face. That felt good, too.

Sifu Wĕn grinned some more.

"Indeed, deadly lady," she nodded. "Come."

She followed the woman to a door into a storage room that had been left over from the old space. Except that she'd cleared it entirely out, leaving two strike dummies at the far end of the room.

Nearby, a table was stacked with glass and plastic bottles like you might grab out of the refrigerator at the 7/11 down on the corner.

"What's this?" she asked.

"Been dumpster diving," Sifu Wĕn said with an innocent look on her face.

The door was closed, leaving them in a space about three meters wide and twelve long.

Sifu Wĕn grabbed an empty, cold coffee drink bottle, took two quick steps, and overhanded it by the neck at the dummy on the right like she might throw a knife. It hit hard enough to knock the dummy down, bounced off, and shattered on the floor next to him.

"Now you," she said, looking expectantly at Joie.

Joie had thrown knives along the way. Even killed a guy that way once. She inverted her hand to get a neck and hefted. Heavy. About as aerodynamic as her old ka-bar. Two steps and throw, the muscles suddenly remembering what they were supposed to do. Even left handed.

The other dummy was female. Joie's throw was high and nailed her square in the face, instead of between the tits like she'd been intending. Still knocked her over. As with teacher's bottle, hers shattered on impact.

"Understand that this is a double attack," Sifu Wěn said to her next. "Impact blow will bruise and stun. Possibly take them down, but not if they see it coming, so from behind."

"And the double?" she asked.

"On the ground, fucker has to stand up," Sifu Wěn smiled cruelly. "Most humans do that by rolling onto their hands and knees, then levering upright. They are rolling in broken glass when they do."

"Ouch," she commiserated with some nameless punk someday.

"A knife can be seen and understood," she continued. "Expected, even. And many of you know how to fight with them. A glass bottle is not a weapon. Until it is. Plastic water or soda bottles have the thump, but not the secondary collateral damage effect. I suggest you pick a flavor of tea or coffee that you like and learn to drink it at room temperature, just so you always have an excuse to have one with you. Similarly, a belt is just a fashion statement, until you unhook it and pull it free as a whip or chain. Get yourself something made of braided leather or real chain that can be used to beat someone to death with, rather than the crap at the mall."

"You're expecting that I will become a target for muggers?" Joie asked.

"I expect that they will pretend to be muggers," Sifu Wěn corrected her. "They will be something else, at least to innocent eyes watching from a distance."

"What do you know?" she pressed.

"Nothing, Joie," Sifu shook her head. "I am listening to your subconscious speak, even if you do not. You expect trouble to hound you mercilessly, so I am showing you some things that I think you will need to stay safe."

Joie stepped back, a little shocked. Then reconsidered what the woman had said.

Sifu Wěn was right.

Joie had already reached deep inside herself and flipped switches that had been off for nearly two years, even as she had continued what martial arts training she could do, while also working at the store.

The last two years had been her in hiding, and now she expected something.

Trouble.

Taylor Kehoe practically guaranteed that by himself.

Then Carter Faulkener showed up to chat?

What secrets had Romana been close to uncovering?

"Now, we will work on knife and chain techniques for a bit, then put on shoes and break bottles in here," Sifu Wĕn announced.

"For how long?" Joie asked.

"Until you are ready to go home," she said.

She'd been afraid the woman was going to say that.

CHAPTER 6

Joie approached her building with a new sort of trepidation and maybe a little anger. Carter had been nonchalant that nobody at the store was being paid to watch her. In fact, Amy had called in the big guns to protect her from Kehoe with the only weapon that would stop a punk like him.

Publicity.

But this was her home. Or was it? Certainly the place she slept these days, close enough to various veterans hospitals where she could get treated when she had needed anything as her broken parts settled. And this was the city she knew the best, outside of Fort Bragg or Joint Base Lewis–McChord out in the other Washington.

It had been what she needed for the last couple of years, once they forced her into involuntary retirement with nothing more than a pension and an honorable discharge rounded up to twenty years of service.

It had been enough, at least when she'd been barely hanging on.

Had she moved beyond that in the last few days?

Joie looked both ways as she crossed the last intersection, but it was late. Not night-owl hours, but close to midnight. She'd swung by and grabbed some takeout, just because she'd skipped a serious dinner and worked her ass off at the dojo.

From her bag, the smell of half-smoke and mambo sauce seemed to speak to her of warm, comfortable places, but those were DC kinds of food, almost unknown once you got beyond the immediate metro area. Other towns might call it barbecue sauce. Or maybe tangy hot sauce.

Mambo was a DC thing.

She crossed and entered her building. It was one of the newer places, as Arlington County went through another bout of gentrification and rebuilding, this time centered on the area known as Columbia Forest, south of 244.

Once upon a time, this side of the river had been all white, with DC itself being almost all black. These days, a Hispanic *chica* like her barely stood out at all, and then only because there were folks from literally everywhere, maybe just in her complex, but certainly within three blocks.

International district in an international city.

She got to her floor using the stairs and started down her hallway.

Joie stopped cold, midway.

She had left her lights off when she went to work this morning. There was a line of light visible under her door now.

Kehoe? That son of a bitch come back to quietly escort her to a facility where folks behind a two-way mirror would listen as she cussed up a storm?

She had left Clarke's card inside, but she had memorized the woman's number. Just like she had Kehoe's. Occupational hazard, to see a number once and commit it to deep memory to the point that it might surface ten years later out of the blue, leaving you to wonder if the guy had gotten out of jail yet, or just been deported home.

Joie considered turning right back around. Calling Sifu Wěn and asking if she could crash at the dojo tonight after all. The woman had offered, but that had felt like running away. Felt like it now, too.

She'd been running for two years, at least inside her head. Hiding from the big, bad world and hoping it would leave her alone.

Then Kehoe had knocked on her door.

On top of that, she was stinky, hungry, and tired.

That left a woman a little cranky.

Because she only had one hand, half the pockets in her life were useless. That was why she carried that messenger bag everywhere she went, instead of a purse. Less stylish, but able to hold things. Didn't have a gun or a knife in it right now, because getting the right kinds of permits required explaining to skeptical authority figures why she thought she needed them.

Which was just the first of a whole series of cans of worms Joie never felt like opening.

Plus, they only took away one of her hands. She could still kill with the other one if she had to.

Still, the bag was as close as her subconscious had been willing to let her get to carrying a go-bag everywhere she went. Joie had one of those tucked back in the closet, but it was two years old at this point and still assumed two arms and two eyes.

For now, Joie got out her keys and braced her feet to strike someone opening her own door.

Each lock went. Quickly. She put her keys away and considered the handle, flashing back to the look on Kehoe's face as he'd wondered about claymore mines and other surprises.

She put her fingers on the handle and turned it finally, the lag being hardly long enough for anyone to notice unless they were as primed for violence as she was.

She pushed it open and let it hit the doorstop without taking a step inward.

There was a guest, sitting at her tiny dining room table where she'd sat before.

Carter.

Joie kept from screaming profanities at the man.

Barely.

She stepped in far enough to close the door behind her, confirming that nobody had been out of sight in her living room. The bedroom could wait, because she would put someone through the freaking glass right now if they were in there.

Joie drew a breath and released it noisily.

Carter had stopped for fried chicken somewhere. And all the fixings. The apartment smelled lovely with grease and meat and spices. Fucker had also nearly overwhelmed her table with all his shit.

Joie walked around to the other side of the table. Took the chair Kehoe had been the last person to sit in.

"Make space," she growled as she sat.

Carter had killed most of his spread already, so he started shoveling empty containers and boxes into a big, brown paper bag.

Joie pulled her half-smoke out, along with fries and the little plastic cup of mambo sauce.

And a bottle of room temperature iced decaf mocha she'd gotten out of Sifu Wěn's refrigerator before she left. Carter's skull had been enhanced by both implants and virus transformations, but the normal soft spots on the front retained all their vulnerability.

Joie considered screaming at him now, but the walls weren't that thick around here.

And someone around here was on the government payroll.

So she just ignored the intruder and started to eat. Messy as hell, which was why food was first, then a shower.

The table was laminate over particle board, reinforced with a glue polymer and pressed into shape. Lighter than real wood. Cheaper. Most likely tougher. She was pretty certain she was the fourth or fifth person to own it.

She flinched as Carter reached into an inside pocket of his blue denim jacket, like he was going for a gun, but he moved slowly and pulled out a small paper envelope instead.

Then he really surprised her. Except that she figured that she shouldn't be surprised at this point.

Opening it, he placed four hunks of broken electronics on his side of the table, each about the size of a one-euro coin.

Joie recognized them. She'd hidden bugs like these in various buildings and houses over the years, when she was stalking a target.

Four? Kitchen/dining room. Living room. Bedroom. Bath. Standard configuration for a space like this. Who the hell was paranoid enough to put four down?

She knew, however.

Taylor Kehoe, or people working for him.

Idly, she wondered how long they had been there. Her work schedule was pretty stable. Days, with Sunday and Monday off. Easy enough to pick her locks and break in.

Joie put her fork down and ran her hands under the edge of her table.

"Already looked here," Carter said quietly.

Joie went back to her bratwurst.

"Can anybody catch you?" she finally asked between bites, aware that the man had walked into a coffee shop in Arlington, Virginia in the middle of the day, and still made it out.

"You did," he shrugged. "Still haven't figured that one out."

Joie chuckled around her food.

That might make her unique, then. Nobody else had ever beaten Carter, head to head.

Good thing she'd cheated.

"Safe to talk here?" she asked, assuming that he'd spent time this evening making sure of that, if he'd gone to the effort to break in with takeout while she'd been with Sifu Wěn.

"Should be," he replied.

Helped that he was out of food at this point.

"Kehoe really wants your ass dead," Joie offered. "Or buried over in Arlington National."

"I'd say he's welcome to try, but he's been trying that for nearly a decade now," Carter chuckled.

"So why are you here, *Mithras?*" she pressed.

In her head, this had suddenly turned into an *operation. Captain Daring* and *Mithras,* against the world? Or was she facing off with him?

Without her arm, her eye, and a week of prep, she stood no chance whatsoever. Carter was three or four times stronger than she was. Twice as heavy.

Almost as mean.

"We were talking about Pham," he said. "She disappeared. If that makes Kehoe nervous, then I should be involved, because that means something. Except that nobody knows what."

"Talking to the wrong person," Joie replied. "Haven't seen her in nearly a year. No messages. Not even a pornographic card on my birthday."

Which had been the point when Joie realized that she'd lost her best friend. Maybe forever. Or at least until she decided to pull her head out of her own ass and started living again.

Mitch had been the same way.

Still, they'd been right and that wasn't a thing she was willing to argue about. Not today.

Mithras just studied her face, as if he could see the truth etched into things. Along with the scars.

"Yeah, I see that," he said. "No hints, no ideas?"

Joie shrugged.

"The only reason they ever let me into the Veterans' Hospital is that my discharge was eventually rated honorable," she said. "Apparently, that argument could have gone either way, from what some rumors have said. I am officially an un-person now, at least at the Pentagon and TRC."

She watched him settle his weight back carefully. The chairs looked like wood, but even his mass would be enough to snap off posts if he got reckless.

"Do you want to be rescued from this life, Daring?" he finally asked as she finished her smoke and went for the last few fries before they got cold and yucky.

"What the hell would I do, *Mithras*?" she growled up at the man, not forgetting that he'd broken into her apartment with takeout. "All the missing parts make me a liability and nobody can replace them except with others that will be terminally flawed in design and execution. Booby traps, you know?"

"You still got the brains," he offered.

Joie couldn't help but laugh in his face. Felt like more stress, like with Amy.

"I can call you coordinates instinctively," she said. "But don't ask me to count too high without taking off my shoes. Middle of my class for academics."

"Top for physical," he reminded her. "Volleyball babe. I've seen old footage of you playing. Ruthless and better than anybody else on the court."

Joie couldn't argue that one, other than to say that it had been fourteen years since she'd graduated and been commissioned. That girl was long-since gone.

Hell, pretty soon she'd start getting invitations to her twenty-year high school reunion. Well, her parents would. No chance in hell someone could just type her name into a computer and find her without paying an expert. The Technology Research Command had that covered, even for a *soiled dove* like her.

"Retired and washed up, Faulkener," she countered with a sigh. "I got nothing left to prove at this point. You're barking up the wrong tree."

The food was gone. She shoveled all the trash back into the bag and handed it to him across the table.

"Put this in the recycling dumpster when you get downstairs," she said, politely telling the man to get the hell out of her home.

She rose and towered over the man for a minute, until he sighed and stood up.

Freaking huge. Amy thought he was hot, but Joie would have needed him to grow in a well-trimmed beard first. Less pretty and more rugged, maybe.

Something. Assuming she ever had any interest in the man except through a high-powered scope.

"Kehoe's not going to leave you alone, you know," the man rumbled at her as he got all the bags into one.

"Tough," Joie snapped. "I'll sic my corporate lawyer on him. Or worse, call in a few favors with senators that don't hate me. If he really wants to play hardball, I'll call the Post and offer to give them an interview. I'm not fucking around with you people, *Mithras*. I have been completely burned and nobody from the organization has so much as called to check up on me in more than a year, so they don't get to suddenly care now. And you still probably deserve to be spending time in a concrete box in Colorado, Faulkener. Whatever you're up to on the outside, take your fucking marbles and get the hell out of my life. Am I clear?"

She could tell that he wanted to growl at her. Snarl. Snap. Something.

Anything to get the last word.

Except that she saw something in the back of his eyes. A memory, perhaps, of the only person to ever take him down. Worse, she'd taken him alive and brought him to justice.

Wasn't Joie's fault that Kehoe's people couldn't hold Carter Faulkener after that. They'd trained *Mithras*, so they should have known better.

He nodded instead.

Joie stepped around him into the living room space as he moved to the door, opened it, and stepped out into the hallway. The man stopped, turned back, and stared at her for a long moment, until he nodded again at some internal conversation, and started walking away.

She closed the door, then turned and fell against it with her butt, blowing a heavy breath out. She turned again and set all the locks and the chain, then considered that he'd been in here.

Joie grabbed her chair and wedged it under the handle. Wouldn't stop him from coming back in, but he couldn't without making a lot of noise in the process.

She considered her living room. It was almost as impersonal as the dining set. Big television on a shelf that the last resident had left behind. Older model, but it still worked for the few times she actually sat down and found something to watch.

Third-hand couch with an open frame in white pine and hard padding like a futon, inside faded blue canvas. Ancient torchier-style lamp painted black next to it. Coffee table for setting her feet on after a long day, or putting her drink on.

She wanted a shower, but wasn't sure she felt safe stripping naked with enough noise from the running water around her that someone could break the door down and get in.

And Carter had been in here deep enough to find and remove Kehoe's bugs. Had he left his own set?

She needed to find out.

Right now.

CHAPTER 7

Joie didn't usually do much on her days off. That would require people to do things with. Or hobbies. Something.

She was two years into a new life, and less than a year into actually trying to do something with it. Hobbies felt like one thing too many.

So she had gotten up this morning and walked. Hadn't found any bugs last night when she tore her apartment apart, but that didn't mean anything. Early morning around her, because zero dark thirty was a thing her soul knew, even when her body insisted that she could be utterly decadent and sleep until seven in the morning without anybody complaining.

She had showered last night, but a second one this morning had released some knot in her back that had snuck in while she'd been sleeping. Her hair had been short when she'd been military. Not buzzed, because she needed to go undercover frequently, but boyshort and occasionally a fauxhawk done rockabilly style.

The last person to cut it had been at Bragg. Two years ago.

It wasn't much past her shoulder blades now, but putting it in a braid or a hair tie required more hands than she had and she didn't feel like paying someone to do it very often. Occasionally. Just to keep people honest.

Spring day. Normally, that meant hot, but a front had come down from the northwest, bringing a sort of cold drizzle that wanted to be snow, even in April. Might turn into sleet a few times as it rotated through. Miserable enough that almost nobody else was out with her as she crossed a parking lot.

Her bag was waterproof, as was the long peacoat she had found at a second-hand shop. Collar up. Knit cap down tight. Glove.

Walk.

Restless. That was what this was.

Joie found a spring in her step that had been gone so long she'd almost forgotten what it felt like.

Maybe like being alive, but she didn't want to go there, at least not without that one Navy shrink along for the ride.

She was just about at the far end of the loop her brain had apparently picked out this morning. Trees and neighborhood, rather than generica and shops, but there was a place to get coffee nearby. Three stores up from hers, on the corporate map.

Like it would make any difference, except that nobody here would know her.

The rain had relented some, leaving only that chill knife of wind that wanted to slice you to ribbons if you hadn't picked up the heavy coat this morning. Or not paid any attention to the forecast.

Joie locked onto them as the vehicle came around a corner in front of her. Why her combat senses triggered now wasn't a thing she had conscious control of. One moment, she was happily sauntering in search of warm calories. The next, she had shifted into lethal mode like someone had flipped a switch.

Dark box van, rather than an SUV or people carrier. Maybe black. Maybe just dirty as hell.

Running heavy on the axles, like it had a full load in back, except that when it hit the driveway, it bounced pretty good.

Armored, Class Four, a little pixie in the back of her mind whispered.

Unmarked. Smoked windows. Coming right towards her at high speed.

Joie didn't have time to get her mocha bottle out of the messenger bag as the machine suddenly turned sharply to show her the passenger side as a door sprang open and three figures jumped out.

Two men. One woman. All roughly the same size and shape. Comparable to her in both, save that they had six arms and she only had one.

Like her, dressed in black, but each of them was in pants and a jacket, rather than a warm coat. Gloves and stocking caps, though.

US Army issue, all of it. She used to own several pairs, including the boots. Hers were far more stylish these days, done in brown leather with snap buckles because tying laces was for the birds.

The taller guy was in charge, it seemed. He centered on her, as the other man went to her left and the woman to her right.

Joie kept all three of them in front of her, letting her ears track behind her for boots on wet pavement for a fourth. She might have expected a sniper, but nobody here had weapons drawn.

This felt like a kidnapping, rather than an assassination.

Had all the signatures. If she wanted, Joie could have cited the correct Army manual and page for doing this.

She had been that other guy, more than once.

Boss smiled at her like a predator. Like maybe he saw her as a wounded crane and thought she'd be easy meat for three of them.

"You gonna come quietly?" he asked with a hard growl in his voice.

Joie had shifted her feet as soon as people got out of the van. Left foot forward. Right diagonally back. That put her arm forward, where it would do the most good.

She didn't wait for the order from the guy.

Instead, she exploded to her left. The guy over there had been primed for her to run, so he was stepping forward to give chase. Joie caught him off-guard and off-balance with a backhand fist across the side of the skull. And then a knee to the stomach that let her pin him in place long enough to rotate and drive her elbow into the back of his skull, rather than trying to break his neck.

It was a delicate balance, but Sifu Wĕn had been careful about the difference between using brutality as an art form and lethality as a necessity.

First guy still went down like a sack of potatoes as she pivoted back, Capoeira-style, by rotating on her left foot and skittering a few steps away from the other two as they started to rush her.

"We're not here to hurt you," boss-man said.

Joie didn't bother laughing in his face. Almost felt like nobody had told these fools who she was.

Or at least who she used to be. Joie still wasn't sure she was anybody these days.

She did need to learn some new things, though. Sifu Wĕn was one woman, and tended to teach her solo, rather than as part of a class.

It had been forever since she'd sparred with multiple opponents at once. That was an oversight she needed to correct, she realized as her two foes moved to box her in.

Joie didn't figure they'd fall for that kind of feint again, and if both could grab her, she'd be in trouble.

Third guy wasn't going to be helping with anything until the concussion wore off.

She kept spinning and stepping. The driver got out now and started to come around the front of the van, which was his mistake. Boss guy looked back over his shoulder to say something and Joie charged.

Sifu Wĕn had studied her long legs and arm and suggested that someone had trained her in Crane forms and similar things at some point. Correctly, as those made the best use of reach.

Then the woman had started breaking her of that habit and demanding that she always get close enough to kiss her opponent on the nose when they sparred.

Nobody ever expected that. Most forms focused on keeping someone at a range of about one meter to fight.

Boss guy was all set for some stupid-ass high kick from the way his weight had shifted just before that. He did get an arm up to block as she blooped a feint at his face. That just gave her something to grab and use her inertia on.

And he was already moving wrong.

Sifu Wĕn called the move a Tasmanian Devil, after the old cartoon character. Grab, hold, start to spin then suddenly stop and throw an elbow up.

Sounded brutal when she caught the guy right on the point of the chin. Lots of nerves cluster right there, which was why it was occasionally called the glass jaw.

You had to hit it just right.

Or really, freaking hard.

Either one.

Boss guy was going to be seeing stars. Not for long.

Joie didn't need long.

She planted and thrust herself at the driver, not bothering to do anything but let him grab her with both hands as she got a running start.

Fool had forgotten the wall behind him in the form of an armored van. All the air rushed out of his lungs when she tried to flatten him against it as hard as her long, powerful legs could drive.

Hell of a way to try to breathe, when someone is attempting to collapse your lungs.

Joie grimaced and grabbed a handful of the driver's neck. She took a step and threw him into the legs of the woman kidnapper, only now catching up from being farthest out of position when it all happened.

Woman didn't see it coming. Driver couldn't do anything to help. They went down in a tangle of bodies.

Joie moved to the side door, looking in back to make sure no other kidnappers had been hiding out of sight with a medical kit that could knock her unconscious once they had her controlled and out of sight.

Nobody.

She jumped in and crossed to the driver's seat, letting the automated seat belt register her weight and start to move.

Joie reached across her body and threw the van into gear with the ancient style-stick on the console, then jammed the accelerator to the floor, both doors open, except that the driver's door immediately shut and the side door helpfully beeped and started slowly shutting as well.

She could drive this beast with only one arm. Nobody was in her line of flight so that they had to throw themselves to one side lest she run them over, either.

Still, it would be necessary to dump the van and do it quickly. It should have tracking beacons somewhere, just because that came standard with Army issue these days. And the kidnappers would be calling for help as soon as they got their shit together.

Did somebody have such a low opinion of her that nobody had told the kidnappers she might be dangerous?

Or did they think she was the same broken person she'd become after she'd stopped being *Captain Daring*?

Or was she more dangerous than anybody had realized? Sifu Wĕn had assured her that she was, but Joie had never listened to the woman's compliments.

Hadn't been ready.

Was she now?

Didn't matter. She needed to vanish.

Immediately.

CHAPTER 8

Carter looked up as Kehoe walked into the lounge, a mug of coffee in each hand. The man set one down on the coffee table in front of Carter, then took a nearby chair.

"It's done," Kehoe said quietly, sipping his coffee.

"Anybody killed?" Carter asked as he grabbed the other mug.

"One injured and headed to a post hospital, but nothing bad," Kehoe said. "I wish we'd been able to follow what that Chinese bitch was teaching her. Daring almost made it look too easy, from the preliminary reports."

"The teacher is Cantonese," Carter corrected him automatically. "They pretty much consider the northerners invaders. And I did warn you that the woman was likely to see training Daring as a challenge. She's damned good at what she does. Just too much of a wild card for you to have ever recruited her to train your own people."

"Is that teacher of hers better than Romana Pham?" Kehoe asked.

Carter shrugged.

"I've never sparred with her," Carter offered. "And not with Daring or Pham either, though I've seen tapes of both on the training floor as well as in the field. Only time I actually fought Daring, she kicked my ass."

"Daring's crippled," Kehoe kvetched. "She shouldn't be this good."

Carter laughed.

"She's not," he glowered at man. "She's half the warrior she was before."

"Really?"

"Yeah," Carter reminded him. "Now imagine what Joie Daring used to be like."

CHAPTER 9

Joie hadn't stopped to ask for ID from the team she'd just beat up. All she knew was that she was under constant observation these days, and hadn't noticed anything.

To be fair, she hadn't been paying attention, but all those old instincts suddenly came awake as though from a nightmare that had her heart pounding and her eye wanting to bug out of her head. She needed to get away from the scene, then ditch the van in such a way that she could vanish.

Fortunately, there was a metro subway stop nearby.

Arlington had finally gotten its head out of their asses in the mid twenty-first century and started digging more tunnels to connect everything to the DC side of the river. She could get underground before anyone else could lock drones on her, at which point they would have to either hack the CCTV feed from the trains or put bodies down there with her.

Didn't help that it was Sunday morning, so traffic would be pretty light. Folks going to church or museums for the most part, rather than the mad crush of workers, unless CIA or others suddenly had to scramble people because they considered her to be a national security threat.

Those idiots might.

She got to a lot and grabbed the little parking permit she would have to pay when she departed again, then parked the van.

Just to be a shit, she stuffed the ticket into her pocket. Might as well make somebody pay full price to get their van back. That or invoke national security privilege, which would be its own mess. Even in this town.

She sprinted across the parking lot now, pulling out her phone and happily getting into line with a group of Chinese students on a tour of the American capital.

High school kids, to listen to them rattle away in Mandarin, unaware that the tall *chica* could understand everything, including the casual racism about her nose and how was she supposed to clean up with only one arm that they flung at her from behind the wall of a supposedly foreign language.

Apparently they had mistaken her for a menial. A servant. Because she was Texican.

Amy never tolerated that shit from anyone, customers or staff.

Joie let them insult her however they liked. Calling attention to herself now by replying would just make it easier for someone to remember her later, and none of it really rose to the level that she wanted to ruin their day by having them all get swept up by Kehoe and his people to be interrogated.

She did consider it, though.

Through the turnstile and down the escalator. Joie paused just long enough to buy herself a sandwich and a bottle of cold brew from the corporate coffee shop, after checking that these had been delivered this morning. Always useful to know the patterns of her own company, since they had tentacles into every facet of American culture these days. Every city. Two on every corner, as the joke went.

Even when it wasn't a joke.

They were probably watching her credit accounts now, but hadn't moved to shut any off.

Yet, she amended herself. Might not, since they could use those to zero her geographically in seconds.

Hopefully, nobody had decided to arm a drone and take her out like she'd done with a few folks in places she wasn't legally allowed to talk about.

You could always blame that sort of thing on terrorists. Those had been the bogeymen going back more than a century. The only thing that changed was which country was pissed at the US for invading them or overthrowing their government today.

Joie had a pretty good idea of the count, having been there for a few of them.

Fortunately, this particular station crossed three subway lines, so anyone trying to chase her had six choices right now. Seven, if she didn't go anywhere and instead just hung out in a coffee shop restroom for a while before doubling back. She doubted that they had the necessary resources at hand to flood the system and find her.

Instead, her face and extremely obvious description would go out to every cop and agent. How many tall Latinas with one arm and an eyepatch was a cop likely to spot today?

And the note would be *Extremely dangerous, do not approach. Call for assistance at this number.*

Joie might not even know that she'd been made, except that the little voice in the back of her head that had been asleep for two years wasn't being quiet anymore.

She had seen that van and immediately understood what it was. What it meant.

Joie got down underground and turned her phone to airplane mode to block Wi-Fi and cell signal lock-in. Wouldn't stop a short-range ping from finding it, but would keep them from tracing her easily.

Then she pulled the patch and the cap off and stuffed both in her bag. Someone looking at her face would see the dead, gray orb that didn't track with her other eye. But they'd have to be staring at her to really see it.

Most folks absorbed the fact that she had an eyepatch before they even looked, so that would make her a little more invisible.

She stayed close to the Chinese tourists now. Black hair was black hair, and hers was long and down, like many of theirs, so from behind you might attach her to the tour group and ignore her.

Anything so that she didn't leave memories around here.

Joie did a quick mental inventory as she followed everyone onto the train. No weapons. Nothing even to take away from the goons and keep, so they really had been planning to take her alive.

Just way out of their league trying.

She hoped that someone was properly pissed at Kehoe for not warning them.

Or had it been someone watching Carter and wanting to know what she knew? Romana's disappearance had started all this.

Had she been taken? Or had she found something?

Was the woman still pissed enough at Joie that she might send goons to grab her off the street, instead of just calling?

Joie knew the answer to that. Kehoe was probably listening in real time to any phone call she might make, like when Amy tried to reach her later today and wouldn't be able to get through.

Would she immediately call Corporate Lawyer Clarke, or would she come by Joie's flat first?

Was Amy at risk?

Shit. Best boss she'd ever had. Amy Watanabe didn't deserve the trouble that her favorite gimp was going to bring, but Joie also didn't think that the woman cared. Or would change a single thing.

That was what made her a great boss. She was already a great person.

Burn that bridge later.

Maybe burn the whole city down, like she was Canadian or something.

Tour group was headed into DC, across the river, to see the sights, so Joie followed, sitting in the same car with a large group and looking at her phone like she was reading a book.

Away from the scene of the crime, where every stop, every minute, expanded the zone that someone would have to chase to find her.

Kehoe's folks would cap that pretty quickly and just ask Metro PD to find her for them. That and cybernauts watching her credit accounts or siccing AIs on every camera they could hack and telling them to find her.

Needle in a haystack, but computers didn't get bored or demand overtime, so they'd find her there eventually. The key was making sure that it took forever to do it. Wading through females with long black hair, even on this train, would take them a while.

Now, she had to figure out where she was going to hide.

CHAPTER 10

Joie was back in sunlight. These days, you didn't have to log out of the Metro system once you logged in. They just wanted to know what stations people were entering at and when, rather than worry about how far you rode or how long it took you to get there.

She'd traveled with the tour group, eventually taking the orange to the vicinity of the Monument and the White House. High security areas, but exactly opposite where a fugitive would run to, so hopefully that would keep someone off-balance chasing her.

By now, they'd found the van and knew where she had gone. Probably watching exits on cameras somewhere. She didn't have long, whatever she did.

Joie had trailed the group like a lost puppy, but now she turned at a corner and immediately started to stretch her legs, generating as much distance between them as she could without actually jogging.

She was dressed all wrong to be a health nut this morning. Worse, it looked like the sun was actually going to break out soon and maybe get warm.

Walking around in a peacoat, even unbuttoning it, might get

warm. Worse, others might drop down to rain shells, and she would stand out.

Joie liked this coat, even second-hand, too much to just dump it in a trash can as she walked by one.

At least yet.

She walked.

Someone wanted her under their control. Kehoe, *Mithras*, or some nameless, formless third entity that might be related to the disappearance of Romana Pham.

Or worse, somebody completely unrelated might have finally found her after looking for a number of years, and she was facing some old nemesis from her active duty days, chasing her around DMV intent on revenge.

Not Nemesis, though. Widow or younger sibling maybe. She hadn't left many survivors around when sent after people. That was a big part of the reason Kehoe had assumed she'd cut a deal with *Mithras*. She'd beaten the man, then brought him in.

Nobody else had ever done that.

That punk showing up twice in as many days just meant that Kehoe would be all *waxed and vaxxed* to come after her, like a boyfriend stalker she didn't need.

She needed to get out of the vicinity. DC and DMV were among the most heavily policed regions in the world these days. Lots of cops. And *other* folk.

Joie needed to be gone. Someplace where every fifth person she ran into didn't work for the federal government in some capacity.

She could call *Mithras* and ask him to take her in. He'd offered.

Something felt skeevy and off about the man, in ways that her backbrain didn't want to explain yet.

Kehoe would love to crawl over her ass with a microscope, so she might never get free again if that happened. Worse, he might offer to fix everything. Give her back her eye and her hearing. Give her two hands to do things.

Josefina Dearing wasn't sure she'd be able to say no to that kind of offer.

At least requiring Congress to pass a bill reactivating her would cause a lot of people heartburn. Especially the ones on the right committees to know some shard of the actual truth, instead of the blacked-out pages that most people got to read.

If she wanted to stay free, she had to stay ahead of the hounds. Mislead them. Drop red herrings in their path to cause folks to go astray and maybe even lose the scent.

She needed a burner phone if she was going to talk to anyone, because Joie wasn't even sure how long she could keep this one on her without it causing more trouble than it was worth, but that wasn't today's problem.

Next week, once she had successfully escaped the cordon around the city that Kehoe or someone was going to throw up when they decided she had escaped.

And she needed answers. Or at least information.

There was one place she knew where she might get them, assuming the man didn't punch her in the face when she knocked on his door.

CHAPTER 11

Joie had fallen back on the weirdest way she could think of to get somewhere, short of buying a car for cash and driving there.

It had been a close call, only because she was on the run and the last thing she needed was to break down in the middle of North Dakota and be stranded by the side of the road for a State Trooper to stop to help and end up arresting her.

Trying to arrest, anyway. At which point it would become a high-speed chase likely ending in an international incident if she went straight north in a stolen police car and tried to claim asylum at the Canadian border.

Once she told enough of the truth, they might even let her stay.

Kehoe might get serious about the folks he sent after her next time, though.

So she had dug into the stash of euros she kept in her messenger bag against emergencies and bought herself an Amtrak ticket.

She needed out of DC. Out of the DMV. Out of sight. She had questions, and right now the only place to get answers was in Seattle, Washington, all of a continent away.

At least they were upgraded to serious trains these days, though that had only been completed when she was a kid. Joie could only imagine trying to get to Seattle on the old trains, taking several days if she was lucky and nothing broke down.

She'd even managed to score herself a private room, so she didn't have to deal with people looking at her dead eye and wondering. Or remembering her.

From DC, they'd raced to Pittsburgh, Cleveland, and Toledo at three hundred kph average, with the new high-speed run stopping for only twenty minutes in each of three cities. It was similar to how the airlines did their hub and spoke system, getting people to central spots quickly, then letting them fan out.

They'd sat in Chicago for nearly ninety minutes, with Joie spending all of it in her private space with the shades drawn enough that she was just a rough outline to someone on the platform looking in.

Then they'd gotten into motion again. Thirty minutes at Minneapolis, with the next stop being Billings, Montana, a silver and white bullet ripping across the top of the country.

It had taken a little under five hours from DC to Chicago. The rest of the afternoon, as it were. The next leg was the sleeper, overnighting to Seattle before returning, roughly eleven hours each direction since they only stopped twice.

Joie stirred from her comfortable seat with the butt warmer and moved to the front of her car, rapping politely on the door frame of her conductor/concierge, a stumpy black woman with a smile bright enough to drive at night by.

The woman looked up, saw her, and bounced to her feet.

"Problems?" she asked solicitously.

"Kinda," Joie hemmed.

She'd considered trying to hide her eye, but the arm was a dead giveaway. All she could hope was that the woman was civilian enough that nobody thought to ask.

If Joie could get to Seattle without being spotted, she could disappear.

The conductor was out in the hallway now. Like Joie, she'd been enjoying the butt warmer, probably, and reading on a tablet computer.

"My phone is nearly dead and I didn't realize it before I left, to grab the charger," Joie told the woman. "Do you have tablet readers like this I might rent for the trip?"

"Certainly," she said, motioning Joie to back up two steps.

Joie watched her unlock a cabinet and pull out a device.

"I'll need your card," she said.

Joie froze.

The conductor studied her closely. Fortunately, a one-armed woman didn't look like a threat. Or a notorious criminal fugitive from justice.

Regardless of the likely truth.

"Is everything okay, miss?" the short woman asked, her voice careful now.

Joie had to make her lies convincing.

She swallowed nervously. That part was honest.

"I'm running away," she said. "It was sudden and I couldn't pack anything or he'd have guessed…"

"He?" the woman suddenly growled and seemed three meters tall.

Angry, too.

Joie assumed the woman had a violent ex-boyfriend somewhere in her past.

"Just what money I had on me," she said. "And I'm afraid if I use one of my accounts, he'll be able to track me. Watching everything and when he sees this charge, he'll jump on a plane immediately and be waiting on the platform for me. I can pay you cash."

"We aren't set up for cash, dear," the woman replied, pushing the reader into Joie's hands. "You just remember to get this back to me when we arrive, or leave it in your room. And let me know if I need to have a few gentlemen meet you at the station so they can make sure you are safe against anything."

"He's dangerous…" Joie started to say, thinking about who Kehoe or *Mithras* might send.

The next group might not technically be human, considering the upgrades.

"So am I, young lady," her conductor said in a stern voice like a school teacher. "I'll have some friends around. Pullman takes the safety and comfort of their people quite seriously. That goes back two centuries."

"Thank you?" Joie offered, a bit nervously.

She wasn't used to people helping her. Almost didn't know what to do with it. In the Army, everything was provided for you, including order. You protected your team, your platoon, and your people.

Joie was on her own.

Except that this woman wasn't about to let her just be alone. The fire Joie saw in her eyes was sufficient to understand that.

"Do you have enough cash to eat?" the woman asked next.

"I do," Joie nodded, still a little off-center. "I was able to stash money quietly away. It was only using my accounts for little things like this that threw me off."

"Well, the dining hall is also card only," she replied. "Let me have a quick chat with them and we'll get you taken care of."

"Thank you?" Joie repeated, still off balance.

Somehow, the woman got Joie shuffled unresistingly back to her room and the door closed.

Why had the woman done that for a complete stranger? Just another traveler? Wouldn't she get into trouble?

Except that she'd seen something in Joie. A sisterhood?

Joie was alone. Her against Kehoe and the entire TRC. Maybe *Mithras* and whatever organization he was fronting for.

Except, she suddenly didn't feel alone. She felt like a warm blanket had been draped over her by an auntie so she could sleep.

She powered up the reader and tried to concentrate on the words, but tears kept interrupting.

CHAPTER 12

Joie was a bit surprised when they arrived at Seattle and the woman conductor rapped on her door. She'd opened it to see two burly, black men standing there that were at least as big physically as Carter. Neither of them gave off the subtle signs of the augmentations that he had. The bone inserts of Argenite like hers. The muscles built up by genetic viruses. All those little things they'd done to that first volunteer to make him unstoppable.

At the same time, both of them looked like ex-jocks, towering over her and massive. They gave her a warm, fuzzy feeling just standing there.

"This is Josh and Chester," the conductor said. Her name was Teresa, Joie had discovered. "They will escort you to get your baggage. Do you have baggage?"

"Just this," Joie patted her messenger bag.

"Of course," Teresa said. "Josh, get her to the taxi stand and make sure she remains safe."

"Yes, ma'am," Josh said.

They ended up bracketing her like a team clearing a house. Josh led and she trailed. Chester had faded back some to look inconspicuous. As much as you could when you were that size.

The man walked almost silently, so she presumed an ex-linebacker or something who had remained in shape afterwards. Amtrak was probably a better paying gig than being a bouncer in a bar. And safer.

She followed Josh into the old Union Station building, through all the ancient white marble and around to the front. They were at the south end of downtown Seattle on a gray, drizzly, spring day where her peacoat only stood out a little.

Josh escorted her right up to the taxi stand and towered above the woman running it.

"Problems?" the dispatcher asked.

"If so, they chose not to appear," Josh rumbled with humor. "This lady needs to get off property without being tracked in your computer."

The dispatcher studied her. Joie let herself look vulnerable. It was a strange feeling.

Missing an arm, with her peacoat sleeve tucked in and tack stitched into place. Missing an eye with a burned-out gray orb replacing it.

The other scars weren't obvious. TRC had hired exceptional plastic surgeons for her.

Her not wanting to wear a bikini was mostly psychological. Joie knew she had the bod to pull it off, even with the mostly faded scars.

The stump made her self-conscious. Still.

The dispatcher nodded and looked around. She pointed at a driver third back and gestured them closer.

Turned out to be a woman driver when the car got near. The first two had been male.

Was there a whole sisterhood of women with stories about ex-boyfriends that she had missed along the way, too tall, too tough, and too dangerous for men to mess with? Nobody had laid a hand on her without permission that she could remember, though she'd been quietly warned about some senior boys in high school when she'd been a freshman. A few teachers you supposedly weren't supposed to be alone with. In the Academy, sexual harassment of any kind was supposed to be a one-way ticket home. Helped that more than half the faculty at West Point had been female. If the Army hadn't been quite as good, she'd been interested in programs where any demerits of that type meant you were bounced out and transferred to the infantry. She'd heard horror stories of the old days, when rapists were protected within the system instead of torched by it. How much had she missed?

The dispatcher nodded for Joie to follow her. She walked to the rear and opened the door, sticking her head in the open passenger window.

"Cash ride, unmarked, turn your computers off," the woman said simply in a clinical voice.

The driver looked up at the rear-view mirror at Joie now sitting in the back seat. Studied her, like the other women had.

Joie studied her back. Hispanic, like her. Darker, though. Harder features suggesting Incan ancestry, rather than Puerto Rican mixed with a variety of Anglos and other things along the way. Small, with cheekbones you might shave your legs on.

Ancient eyes in a young face.

"Yes," she said simply, nodding to both of them.

The dispatcher closed the door and looked around before sticking her head in the window.

"You get there safe," she said. "Nobody else will leave for five minutes to give you a head start."

Joie shivered at the tone. Deadly earnest, for a complete stranger. Except that both Josh and Chester were standing outside in such a way that Joie knew they were on overwatch for her.

She felt like she had stepped through a mirror into wonderland, or something.

The driver put the car in gear and drove out onto First Avenue without asking for directions. Turned right and headed towards Pioneer Square before she looked up in the mirror.

"Where do you need to get to?" she asked.

Joie blinked rapidly as she tried to assimilate a world the Army had never prepared her for.

She gave the woman a location up on Capitol Hill, east of and above downtown.

"Do you take euros?" she asked.

Dollars weren't worthless, but the constant inflation meant that they lost appreciable value almost monthly, because the government was never willing to raise taxes enough to balance the budget. Or, heaven forbid, actually cut back military spending from forty percent of the budget.

All those lovely toys. And, having them, one President after another felt the need to use them.

When nobody could stand against you, did that make you the bully?

Joie had a different perspective these days. Two years as a civilian after most of her life around military people or wearing green would do that.

"No charge," the driver said. "You keep your money and we'll get you to safety."

Joie hadn't even told any of these women why she was fleeing.

Was it enough that a woman was running away and in need?

What the hell did that say about the state of the world?

She had the money. Lots of it, stashed because she'd apparently been expecting some sort of long run at some point, however unconsciously.

Now, it felt like she had an entire, underground network of friends she'd never imagined.

She feared that she would need them before she was done.

CHAPTER 13

Joie had asked the woman to drop her on Madison and Fifteenth, at the south end of what Seattle traditionally called Capitol Hill, with what used to be the Central District below her turning into the International District as it continued creeping around and over Lake Washington.

If whoever it was managed to trace her to Seattle—*when,* she amended herself—they would need to dead end somewhere. A driver dropping her off and immediately leaving ought to cut that cord, because she wouldn't be able to tell them any more than that.

Whoever *they* ended up being.

The walk was pleasant. Seattle was having a gray day. She'd enjoyed those when she'd been stationed out of JBLM — Joint Base Lewis–McChord — south of Tacoma. Drizzle and enough chill that she didn't stand out, hair tucked under her coat and hat pulled down low.

Monday morning, lots of people were heading down the hill, or coming over from Madison Park. She was too early to be part of those rich, kept wives who hung out in coffee shops, but the neighborhood had gentrified hard and weird a few times.

Houses nearly two hundred years old, dating to the early 1900s, side by side with every architectural movement since, with pods and apartments tucked in. About the only thing that was missing was the Japanese-style coffin hotels you found down by the airport for travelers.

She headed north. Fifteenth was one of the business district streets, like Broadway to her left and Nineteenth to her right. Ground floor commercial with residential above them, making little neighborhoods out of the bigger one. Bodegas, coffee shops, antiques and second-hand stores.

The restaurants at this end opened for lunch, but she remembered a few on the north end, beyond the grocery store, that ought to be serving breakfast.

Joie had skipped eating a second meal on the train, mostly out of guilt that they wouldn't let her pay for it. That was still too weird to process.

If she could have, Joie would have called her Army shrink to ask, but figured that question could wait for six months. Until she got safely somewhere.

Wherever *there* ended up being.

The farther north you went from Madison, the closer you got to the Arboretum, and the wealthier the neighborhood got. An island of old, old money that had built the original mansions downtown. The Tech billionaires of the early twenty-first century had mostly built across the lakes, headed out towards the Pass by filling in Mercer Island, then Redmond, then Issaquah, then everywhere surrounding that.

If they spotted her, someone might be able to dig deep enough into her personnel file to understand what she was up to, but Joie didn't think that they would move that quickly. After all, she'd been stationed an hour south more than once, so she had other connections in the Pacific Northwest.

Still, it was a chore to stop at the diner, rather than walk up tp someone's doorstep and knock. They might not be awake, as it was barely seven in the morning.

So she loaded up on food. SOS. Shit on a shingle, even though the place was far too upscale for Army chow. Still, the waiter had asked the chef and that woman had given them the thumbs-up that she could make it.

Four halves of drop biscuit, with over-easy eggs draped lovingly across them. Cheese, gravy, and a couple of green onion tops chopped finely. Four sausage links on the side.

Enough food for all day.

Because Joie wasn't sure when it might be safe to eat again.

Joie dug into the mess when it got delivered and returned the thumbs-up to the chef. Not quite as messy and awesome as that one nautical-themed dive down in Georgetown, south of the city, where her and several mates from the post had staggered in one morning still a little drunk, to eat in the 1950s more or less, but really, *really* close.

Greasy spoon mess, at a place where some of the other customers were looking a little askance at her as they ate their egg-white omelets with chicken sausages and drank strange, green things.

Fatless, tasteless, and probably worthless, from a nutritional standpoint.

Joie was in heaven.

She burped loudly when it was done, to the consternation of the old hens and quiet applause from the chef and her sidekick behind the counter, bistro style.

Joie considered asking if the corporate folks could transfer her out to a local store, just so she could be in Seattle and eat at some of the places she remembered from the old days.

This place had certainly been upgraded to *dive* in her mind. The best kind, too.

Of course, she had to survive whoever was chasing her in DMV. And whatever they wanted.

Maybe start living again, too.

Joie wondered if Sifu Wĕn had any advanced students out here that she might train with, or if she'd need to find a way to convince her teacher that she'd lived in Arlington for too long. Wasn't like Sifu stayed put anywhere. Joie was aware of at least fourteen countries the woman had lived in long enough to mention over the last year and change.

Still, uprooting. Something she'd never been good at. Big part of the reason she was still single.

That and secret missions to places she wasn't allowed to mention except in secured rooms, to Senators and Generals with the correct security clearances.

Joie wiped her plate clean. Considered licking it, but that might be one step too many.

Then she realized that she was avoiding getting up. Trying to find any reason not to walk out the door.

For a long moment, she was utterly terrified at the next step, so much so that she nearly started cursing out loud when she finally processed it. These old hens, or the young ones, didn't need to learn new profanities today, however much she felt like screaming them at herself.

Because she was afraid.

Not of Kehoe. Fuck no, not that shit.

Of walking three blocks up and a couple over, and knocking on a door. Of the reception she might get.

She growled at herself finally and left a good tip for an exceptional breakfast. Forced herself to walk out into the drizzle that wanted to turn into either a wet fog or a cold mist.

Visibility this morning was under fifty meters, but that was her training speaking, not her rational mind.

Joie squared her shoulders and started walking.

She'd come all this distance, too far to chicken out at the last minute.

CHAPTER 14

"What do you mean: GONE?" Taylor practically screamed at the soldier. "How the fuck do you lose a woman with one arm in a city with this many cops and agents running around, you idiot?"

He was in his office. The door had been closed until now, as he'd been reviewing budget documents for next year's ask. Faulkener was in the building somewhere, probably down in the gym showing off, knowing him.

For a long moment, Taylor studied the Staff Sergeant who had apparently drawn the short straw when it came to telling him that they'd lost Daring. The man wasn't cringing as if expecting a blow, but stoic and scowling, like he'd let you have one free poke at him before he kicked your ass.

Airborne. Not SOCOM anymore, but affiliated still. Had the patch. Former expert who'd suffered enough low-grade damage over the years that he rated a desk these days. Hair coming in gray in the bristle cut.

Cold, hard eyes.

Yeah, he'd probably volunteered to walk in here, in order to protect whatever corporal had delivered the original message from the Pentagon.

"At present, all of the systems from which we can currently draw are not reporting any images that humans following up have identified as Captain Daring," the man said in a tight voice, falling into parade rest automatically as he spoke technical words precisely.

Probably controlling his temper so he didn't beat up the man at the top of his command chain. Active duty punks hardly ever reacted well to taking orders from a civilian.

"None of them?" Taylor asked, a bit surprised. "Even Daring isn't supposed to be that good. Is she getting help from somewhere? Someone we don't know about?"

"Unknown, sir," Staff Sergeant Stone growled back at him. "We have all the city security cameras in play, but nothing has come up clear enough to confirm. Local police have been BOLOed, but not reporting any sightings. Your orders?"

Taylor slammed his mouth shut rather than take exception at Stone's voice, verging on insubordination. Or just being a prick.

"Close the door when you leave," Taylor instructed the man. "I'll make a few calls and see what other systems we can access."

Stone nodded and stepped back, pulling the door silently shut with him. Taylor considered his options. Throwing an unprepared grab team at Daring had been Faulkener's idea.

Get her primed and into motion. Separate her from any support network she might want to rely on. Close all doors except calling one of the two of them for help.

Getting her back into the game, so that she might track down Pham for them. Clean hands. Clean blade.

Nobody knew that Faulkener was working for him these days, having had his *Road to Damascus* moment inside a supermax cell in Colorado and deciding that maybe he didn't want to be a pirate after all. Or live in a box for the rest of his life.

But even Faulkener's contacts had gone cold. Whatever Pham had heard or seen, it had been enough to make the woman vanish off the face of the Earth.

His agents weren't supposed to go rogue. Even Daring hadn't, though he and everyone else had thought she had at the time. Hindsight was an exact science, after all. Everyone had assumed she'd changed sides, too. Because Faulkener had never explained fully how the woman had managed to take him down.

She wasn't supposed to be that good.

And since she had been well and truly burned, he was pretty sure she'd never trust him or the government again. Didn't matter, since they had chosen to force her into motion, regardless of what she thought.

She was not, however, supposed to be able to vanish. Not from him. Not for this long.

Taylor wondered if that might turn into an issue.

He pulled out his phone and speed-dialed.

Bouchard answered on the third ring.

"Does this need to be secured?" he asked immediately.

"Yes," Taylor said.

He lowered the phone and pressed the red button that encrypted the signal. Heard a beep from the other end.

"Clear?" he asked the man.

"Clear enough," General Bouchard replied. "Are you calling with good news?"

"Just the opposite," Taylor admitted, no more emotion in his voice than talking about the Nats upcoming season. "She's vanished off the radar."

"How is that possible?" Bouchard asked.

"When I find her again, I'll let you know, sir," Taylor replied. "At present, I need you to raise the threat level at least one rating, so that we can insert some of our AIs into civilian systems normally outside our reach and jurisdiction."

"Just one?" Bouchard asked.

"Two would be better, but you'd get a call from a few Senators on the Intelligence Committee for an emergency briefing at that point, so I'm not certain we're ready for that escalation," Taylor said. "It's Joie Daring here, so they might demand that they be *read into* the file. Or at least order the Secretary to brief them daily until she's caught. That's only a problem if they want to talk to the woman directly after that."

Long silence. Pregnant pause.

Taylor had been afraid that it would come to this when they hadn't been able to corner her yesterday. Twenty-four hours vanished meant she could be almost anywhere now.

It had been a risk, but they'd gamed it out and found the odds acceptable. At least at the time.

More the fool him, Taylor supposed.

"We'll take it up one," Bouchard decided aloud. "There are other things going on that you aren't privy to, that would make the second step enough to make the President nervous."

"Central Asia getting restless?" Taylor asked, suddenly keenly listening to the man's pitch and intonation.

"I can neither confirm nor deny, Kehoe," General Bouchard replied.

"She shouldn't have any connections in that region, as far as we've been able to ascertain," Taylor said.

"It's still Captain Daring, Kehoe," Bouchard said. "Even washed up with an *RDR*, she knows too much for certain folks to sleep well at night. Not me. Probably not you. But there are those folks who ordered you to take her down. They have not admitted to fault or error in doing so. You'll get your authorization in about an hour."

He hung up before Taylor could ask the obvious follow-up question. Someone above General Bouchard had ordered the man to retire Daring two years ago? And *still* didn't think they'd been wrong to do so?

Nothing he'd read in her personnel file or the reports from agents watching the woman suggested that she was any threat of being a traitor.

Except that she'd stepped into the DC subway system twenty-four hours ago and vanished off the face of the earth, disappearing from the most sophisticated surveillance network on the planet.

Was there another conspiracy running in the background, with him as the stalking horse?

Was Bouchard setting him up to be a sacrificial goat here?

Maybe he needed to look into activating some of his own contingency plans.

He could burn them all down if he had to.

CHAPTER 15

Joie had walked up the sidewalk and onto the porch. Stared at the white paint behind the screen door.

Panic overwhelmed her for a moment, but the Army had taught her how to deal with those things.

Grinding her teeth, she pushed the doorbell, wondering if she'd been this afraid of anything since her first jump out of the back of an airplane.

The door opened and Joie found herself staring at Celeste Graydon. Mitch's mom. Who had come close to being her own mother-in-law at one point.

Before circumstances.

Celeste stared at her for a long moment, then her entire face broke into a smile.

"Joie!" she cried with excitement. "You didn't call!"

Celeste opened the door and suddenly Joie found herself engulfed in a hug by the much shorter woman before she could react.

Joie managed to get her arm up and around the woman.

Celeste was short and a little rotund. Gray haired. Anglo. Old, white money in Seattle, which had long been an old, white money kind of town, but Celeste hadn't minded possibly having a Hispanic daughter-in-law.

"Come in, come in," Celeste said now, dragging her by the one good hand into the building. "Donovan went to run some errands and have coffee with the boys. Can I get you anything, dear?"

Whirlwind. Like always.

Joie found herself in the front-room of an old mansion dating back to the beginning of electricity in this town. Semi-formal, only because this was where Celeste had meetings with whatever little group or club was over that day.

Joie tried to find words.

"You look a little ragged, Joie," Celeste continued, as if Joie had spoken. "Have you eaten?"

"I just came here from that one spot you introduced me to on Fifteenth, Celeste," Joie managed. "I might have eaten too much."

"Well, you should have called and I'd have walked over and joined you," the woman beamed. "What brings you to Seattle?"

There. Raw panic. That moment of terror that she'd made a terrible mistake, and was now about to compound it by bringing in the parents of her ex.

Joie found herself stuttering.

"Joie, look at me," Celeste said firmly. "What's wrong?"

She'd always liked Celeste. Donovan Graydon was a mostly retired architect. Celeste had made a career as a volunteer, busybody, and general den mother who had never run for political office, or she might have ended up running Seattle, too.

And but for the Army, Joie might be her daughter-in-law today.

"I'm in trouble, Celeste," Joie said.

"That much is obvious," the woman said. "Come with me into the kitchen. I'm going to need more coffee."

Joie let herself be dragged deeper into the house. It didn't help her state of mind when tactical brain pointed out that she wouldn't be visible through the big picture window in the front room if she was perched on a barstool across from the arm that separated the kitchen itself from the dining room.

In back.

Coffee would help. She watched Celeste fuss about making it, nattering to herself as she worked.

Finally, two mugs. Celeste leaned on the counter across from her. Joie sat on the stool.

Warmth seemed to melt that last dam of reserve that had been holding her back from talking as she took her first sip.

"A few days ago, my old Army commander showed up on my doorstop, offering me my job back," Joie began.

It ended up requiring two cups of coffee and a bio-break for Joie to finish telling Celeste everything that had happened since Kehoe had shown up. She'd left out anything classified, but most of it was straightforward.

"Well, shoot," Celeste said after Joie ran out of words and just sat there, staring at the woman. "I was hoping that you were here because you and Mitch were going to get back together."

Joie lost it. She laughed so hard she almost fell off her chair. Those turned into sobs before she realized it, wondering at all the might-have-been moments.

Somehow, she ended up crying on Celeste, unsure how she'd gotten there, but all the stress slowly washed out.

Joie, who had always—ALWAYS—prided herself on being harder, tougher, *meaner* than anybody else in the Army. The loner who got sent in because even a team might make too much noise.

One-woman wrecking crew, like all the old comic books she'd read as a kid.

Joie wondered if this was what growing up was supposed to be like. The Army took you in, broke you down, and turned you into a killer.

In her case, they had also skipped all the bits about introspection. Useful, when creating a cybernetic assassin. You didn't want them stopping to consider the ethics of blowing up a building full of innocents just to get someone.

"I haven't spoken to Mitch in more than a year," Joie finally admitted. "He gave up on me. Romana did, too. And I know they were an item for a time, but then I lost track of both of them."

Celeste leaned back and studied her.

"I know other men we can introduce you to, Joie," she said with a wry smile, "if my son is too hard-headed to forgive you. He and Romana only dated for a few months before they went their separate ways."

Joie felt her jaw drop open.

She wasn't all that close with her own parents after so many years of not being able to talk about her job. Celeste felt like she'd just stepped in.

"However, I'm willing to presume that such blind dates can wait until later," Celeste continued with a twinkle in her eyes. "You think that Mitch can help you find Romana? Or at least might know where she's gone off to?"

"It was a long-shot, Celeste," Joie admitted. "At the time, I needed to get gone from DC as fast as I could, and Seattle was about as far as I could go without crossing into Canada or Mexico first, to say nothing of getting on a plane."

"Where they would no doubt locate you immediately and order the plane held in place until federal air marshals could come and arrest you, yes," Celeste nodded sagely. "Well, I have good news and bad news on that score."

"Oh?" Joie asked, feeling her stomach want to collapse.

"Mitch is about as out of touch as one can get right this moment," Celeste informed her. "He was restless around here, and overpaid as a computer consultant with nothing to spend it on, so he decided to take a year off and just wander some."

Shit, had he left the country? Was he in some youth hostel in India or Uganda, where she'd never track him down?

Had she come all this way for nothing?

No, not nothing. She had Celeste, which she would have never imagined. And a chain of unknown women who had helped her merely because she was in need, trying to get away from a bad man.

She had never thought something like that existed, but the Army had been her life.

Until it wasn't.

Amy Watanabe had taken her in and at least provided something.

Now, she was alone.

Except she wasn't.

"Where is he?" Joie forced herself to ask. "Do you know?"

Celeste laughed.

"Working as a volunteer fire spotter, up in the North Cascades," she replied. "One of those old places where they have to use radios because the government is too cheap to employ satellite phones like everyone else. And even then, he turns off his phone most of the time, just calling me weekly to check in."

"What in the world is he doing up there, then?" Joie asked, utterly confused.

Mitch Graydon had always been in motion. He'd interned in college for one of those megacorp consultancies that you brought in to tell you which departments and people to fire or sell off, in order to be more profitable. And to be able to blame outsiders instead of the C-Suite afterwards.

Mitch had described himself as a corporate executioner more than once when they'd dated. She'd been at JBLM, down south, but come up to Seattle with some girls to dance, the first night she'd met him.

That had turned into…a whirlwind, but Joie wasn't sure it was a romance. Or maybe it was, like what you saw on that one cable channel. Except that they'd only made it to the point where the boy and the girl go their separate ways.

She'd gone face first into depression and been too stubborn to let anyone help her. He and Romana had ended up…something. Hadn't been an item long, to hear Celeste say it. Now he was up in the mountains?

Celeste was laughing at something. She finally got hold of herself.

"He's painting," she said, before bursting out into laughter again. "Sits on that overwatch with oils and commits art. I think he's pretty good at it, but I'm his mother."

Joie felt her jaw drop open again.

Painting? Sitting there for hours, putting oil on canvas? Mitch?

"Mitch?" Joie managed to ask.

"I know!" Celeste finally managed to get all the laughter under control again. "It's like aliens came down and transmogrified his brain one day."

Joie wanted to laugh. Wanted to share the joke. But at the same time she knew a few government programs that could do exactly that.

Not aliens. Nobody had ever proven aliens were out there, even after centuries of listening.

But getting inside someone's head and flipping a few switches? Child's play.

She had wondered more than once if the Army had done something like that to her. Or Carter. Him suddenly flipping those switches back might explain a lot of his supposed behavior over the last twenty years.

She kept that image off her face. Celeste didn't need to deal with that gnawing fear that occasionally woke Joie in the dead of night.

"So you talk to him weekly?" Joie asked instead.

"He usually calls on Saturday," Celeste nodded. "Sometimes Sundays if he has hikers coming through and it's busy, but it is still too early in the season for much. They just have to have people up there all the time and apparently have an entire program to do it with artists looking to get away from the city for six months or a year."

Joie paused, trying to figure out how she would get up there from here. There was no way that any transit system would get her there, and renting a car was just begging for some system to lock onto her accounts, then activate the beacon on the vehicle itself.

Kehoe would probably wait until she was in the middle of nowhere to hit her. Drop a team out of a helicopter on ropes, and maybe damn the cost of totaling the car if she refused to stop.

Would he be trying to kill her at this point?

At what point would he?

Too much unknown, and Mitch was the slenderest thread she had. Without that as a reason to keep moving, she either needed to give up to Carter or Kehoe, or leave the country and hope they couldn't find her.

Staying stateside was a guarantee that someone would track her down eventually. Even elsewhere was risky, but she could vanish into the populace if she got south of the border.

Still, that was only temporary. Joie had tracked people like that, more than once.

"You look distressed again, Joie," Celeste said.

"Too many bad choices," Joie admitted. "Not sure the best way to handle it."

"That's simple, dear," Celeste smiled. "You'll take my car and drive up there to talk to him. I know which trailhead and station he's at, but Donovan and I are far too old to be traipsing around in the spring snow and storms. Do you have any gear?"

"I have my peacoat," Joie said, tapping it where she'd laid it across a chair while talking earlier. "Not much more. I was out for a walk yesterday and haven't stopped running since."

Celeste rose and grabbed Joie's hand, dragging her to a door and down into the basement.

"Let's see what we have lying around," the woman said.

Joie held her tongue and let the woman help.

There was still a lot of trouble in front of her.

CHAPTER 16

Joie stood in the driveway and hugged Celeste again. And Donovan, since he'd gotten home from coffee with the boys while the girls had worked.

Joie was close enough to Mitch in size that she'd been able to raid some of his cold weather gear. Celeste had run Joie's clothes through the wash while they sat in the kitchen and caught up on the last several years.

She had a backpack filled with various outdoor and camping things that her Army mind had *insisted* she needed to bring into the mountains in spring, plus food and a credit card Celeste had practically demanded that Joie take with her.

Untraceable, at least until someone figured out that she'd been here to see Celeste and Donovan.

"I can't thank you enough, Celeste," Joie said as she finally hugged the woman one more time.

"Find yourself, Joie," the woman instructed her. "Like Mitch is doing. And remember that he has lots of handsome, single friends I can introduce you to if necessary."

Joie laughed and climbed into the front seat of Celeste's Subaru, turning everything on and getting the seat back and down far enough that she was comfortable. And turning the butt warmer to max.

Getting out of Seattle from Capitol Hill wasn't that difficult. Down the hill and onto I-5 northbound.

It was the emotional journey she wasn't prepared for.

What man wants an ex-girlfriend to show up on his doorstep with questions about another ex? Worse, what if he had company up there? Celeste hadn't said anything, but that wasn't necessarily the sort of thing you told your mother about.

She'd never really been close enough to her mother to talk about such things. Still wasn't. The distance was twice as far emotionally as physically.

And this was about as longshot a chance as she could find, hoping that Romana had somehow told Mitch anything that would mean something.

It might all be a fool's errand.

At least she wasn't going to miss work yet. She could always find a way to send Amy a message that she wouldn't be in to work tomorrow.

Any tomorrow.

Maybe she'd leave a message at the store in the middle of the night. There were still payphones occasionally, even in the twenty-second century.

She'd figure something out.

Monday afternoon. Not a lot of people on the road, so she was comfortable enough driving. She still missed her motorcycle. Getting her other arm back would let her ride on two wheels and too many horses.

That was the thing that might change her mind with Kehoe.

Assuming he hadn't been the one who tried to grab her off the street yesterday.

Yesterday?

It had been less than thirty-six hours ago.

Felt like weeks that she'd been running.

Joie supposed that it had. Years, even. Two of them. Hiding from herself and her past.

She wouldn't say she felt more alive than ever right now, but something had awakened in her.

All those years of Army life. Years spent in the shadows, hunting and killing bad guys. Making the world safe.

At least that was what she'd always told herself.

Joie wasn't so sure these days. Maybe she'd finally *civilianed* long enough to entertain doubts that all the death and destruction she was responsible for had actually done any good.

Probably made it worse, she was willing to admit.

Not bailing while in a sinking boat. Or spiking holes in the hull.

Seattle traffic hadn't gotten any nicer, so Joie stayed in the second lane and let the other slow-pokes set the pace as cars passed her on both sides, frequently honking and flipping her off.

Nothing she could do about it, except stay out of their way.

It was kind of how she'd lived for the last year. Head down. Work, dojo, sleep.

Try to put her life back together after it had come completely apart.

What did she want to be, now that she had to grow up?

Whole, but she didn't think that was an option. Not with what it was likely to cost her.

Hopefully, Mitch would have some answers.

Joie just needed to figure out what the questions were.

CHAPTER 17

"Seattle?" Taylor asked, making sure he'd heard Stone right the first time. "Why the hell would she be in Seattle?"

"Unknown, sir," the man replied. "We got a hit on a security camera at Union Station, downtown, showing her about to get into a taxi. Still trying to access that company's records to see where she went, but that will take some time."

"Get Faulkener up here," Taylor decided. "And leave the file."

The Staff Sergeant set the documents on Taylor's desk, then closed the door with a nod as he withdrew.

Taylor opened it and there was Joie Daring, staring back at him. Sure as shit, no doubt in his mind. Must have paid cash for a ticket, then kept a low profile, getting gone before he'd been able to get his AIs into the right systems to stop her.

Seattle?

Taylor knew she'd spent time at Lewis–McChord. That was their West Coast base these days, operating when facing East Asian threats. China, and the Russian Far East, which might have turned into the next war if Central Asia hadn't decided to get stupid right now instead, drawing all eyes that way.

Shitty timing, as it got Bouchard and others wound up when

Taylor had been trying to quietly get Daring to come in from the cold. Months of negotiations and meetings might be tossed into the trash can because of some egomaniac on Almaty who had to keep promoting his children like some sort of royal family.

Still, nothing to be done about it. Taylor closed the file and opened the main Daring file that had basically lived on his desk for a week.

Seattle? Mitch Graydon had lived in Seattle. Current whereabouts unknown, but the man had also been intimate with Pham, right?

Taylor swapped for the Pham file and confirmed it.

Yes, the man had been dumped by Daring and then started sleeping with Pham for a time when she'd been operational out of JBLM. And here in DC, when both of them had rotated to the East Coast.

What did that man know?

Taylor keyed the intercom.

"Sir?" Stone asked.

"Locate the Mitchell Graydon file," he ordered the man. "Civilian, associated with both Daring and Pham."

"I know the man, sir," Stone said. "Stand by."

Taylor supposed that a civilian involved with two of his top agents might have drawn some scrutiny. Stone was old enough to be the woman's father, though he'd never spoken with her on anything except nods and greetings in the hallway as far as Taylor knew.

Daring had always kept to herself.

A knock at the door interrupted his train of thought. Faulkener entered a moment later and tossed a file on his desk as he closed it behind him.

"Stone said you needed this," Faulkener offered as he sat uninvited and stretched out.

The chair creaked a little under his weight, but Taylor had specifically installed office furniture strong enough to handle the man's mass and strength.

Taylor studied the file long enough to confirm Graydon and then looked at the man sitting across from him.

"Mitchell Graydon," Taylor said. "What do you know?"

"Pham was fucking him at one point, according to her file," Faulkener replied.

"So was Daring, before that," Taylor filled in. "She was definitively spotted in Seattle six hours ago. Short of somehow using that as a starting point to run for Canada, he's the only thing I have connecting either women in Seattle."

"I need to run him down?" Faulkener asked with a hard leer.

As if violence was the only solution the man knew. Not far from the truth, but violence was not always the *best* solution. It would solve any problem, but sometimes that made it worse in the long run.

"No," Taylor decided abruptly. "We're both going. I'll have Stone route us to JBLM on a small jet. Then we'll grab a team from Lewis. By that time, we'll have narrowed down her location enough to box her in."

"If you use folks she knows, I can't be with them," Faulkener reminded him. "I'm not supposed to be working for you."

"I'll drop you somewhere with a rental car," Taylor sneered. "Hopefully, you still know how to get around in a strange city. That way, if we spook her, she might call you and you can be handy."

"How do we explain me being close?" the giant asked.

"Leaks in my office," Taylor smiled. "Like you've been doing. Although if you do know any underworld types out there, this might be the time for you to reach out to them and see if you can burrow your way in like a tick. Pham could be anywhere, but someone has seen her. We just need to convince them to talk to us."

"Right, then." Faulkener rose. "In that case, I need to update my go-bag for those sorts of plans. Gimme an hour down in the armory to grab a few things. You taking her arm with you, in case you can reel her in?"

"I am," Taylor said. "Doubt she'll go for it, if she's running this hard from us, but anything is possible. I am not, however, taking the other two."

Faulkener laughed uproariously and departed. Taylor waited for Stone to stick his head in and gestured the man inside.

"I need the first jet to Tacoma," Taylor said to the man.

"Communications team with me so I can stay in touch from there. Alert Lewis that I need a combat team on standby when I get there."

"Am I going?" Stone asked.

"No, I need you here running the office," Taylor told the man flatly. "The officers just push paper around and have meetings. They don't actually do anything useful, most of the time."

That got an honest smile out of the man, but Taylor knew Stone's generally low opinion of officers, folks like Daring and Pham notwithstanding.

Stone did not particularly respect Faulkener. Mostly because the man had gone rogue more than once, and might yet do it again. Taylor had contingencies in place, though, same as had eventually burned Daring.

When you are going to live for maybe another one hundred and fifty years because of the treatments, you take a longer eye towards things.

Stone departed to start things in motion and Taylor dug out his phone.

Bouchard needed to know that the game was heating up.

CHAPTER 18

Joie had gotten to her exit, dropped down into town long enough to pick up two bottles of flavored coffee that were heavy and glass, along with hitting a drive-thru for a burger and fries. A quick pit stop and some supplies and she'd headed into the mountains.

By early afternoon she was at the trailhead. Later than most hikers, but she was prepared and trained for this sort of weather. Drizzle now and it would get cold tonight, but she had a bag rated to ten degrees and an old, nylon tent that would deploy in about five minutes into a half-dome cozy for two.

All she was missing was a big dog companion, looking at some of the folks headed downhill as she parked, put up a sign indicating she planned to overnight for two days, and headed out and up.

Trees. Old growth and thick. Joie had been living on posts or in big cities for too many years, but about five steps in and suddenly it all came rushing back. She kept tapping her thigh for a holster that wasn't there. The backpack was light and commercial, so it fit her better than what the Army had always issued her.

She wasn't military anymore, but the quiet parts in the back of her mind refused to stop whispering firing lanes, cover, and everything else that had been pounded into her over the years.

The trail switched back and forth several times, leaving her blind a lot of the time. At the same time, she was running into couples coming down, so she could hear them talk to each other.

At one point, a boisterous German Shepherd came bounding up, tail wagging ninety klicks an hour as he got close.

"Ruger," a woman's voice called loudly.

The dog froze, everything except his tail, then he looked over his shoulder and woofed happily.

A short blond came around the curve ahead of her.

"Ruger!" she called.

This time, the big puppy raced over and took up station next to the woman.

"Sorry about that," she said as the two of them approached again.

Ruger strayed enough to sniff.

"Is it okay to pet him?" Joie asked.

Always ask. Especially big dogs. They were trained like soldiers where she came from, just like she had been.

"Normally, he's not this playful," the woman admitted. "Not sure what got into him."

"It's okay," Joie said, holding out a hand to be dutifully sniffed and then licked before someone rotated in place so she could scritch him down the spine and to that magical spot just above his tail.

The leg started stuttering as she did.

"You've had dogs," the woman said.

"Been around them forever," Joie admitted. "They usually like me."

"He never likes anybody," the hiker laughed. "That's why he's safe to hike with. Nobody wants to bother me up here. Just you?"

Joie felt a moment of paranoia bite her in the ass.

"I'm coming up late behind some friends," she lied easily. "They already should have the camp set up and the soup on, but I had to do some things in town this morning at the last minute."

"Well don't let me keep you then," she said. "Weather promises to get ugly tonight."

Joie nodded. She'd seen the same forecast, but refused Celeste's offer to stay overnight and come up tomorrow.

She needed to stay in motion. Too easy to just settle down somewhere, which would let Kehoe or *Mithras* find her.

Joie realized more and more today that she didn't want to be found.

"You be good, Ruger," she told the big slobbering beast as she stopped petting and stepped to one side.

He woofed happily at her and then chased off after the woman in great bounds.

Joie supposed that most single women might not be entirely safe, this far from civilization. No easy way to call for help, though you generally had a signal off some satellite, except in the worst weather.

It was the people you might encounter that would be the issue. Predators who might think a woman alone was a victim. Especially a one-armed crane.

She smiled as she started uphill again.

Maybe she'd get lucky and some moron would want to mug her. She had a lot of angry energy built up that she could take out on them.

CHAPTER 19

Carter watched the black SUV drive away and turn the corner before he took a step. Wanted to be alone. Entirely alone.

At least as much as he could get with Kehoe still holding his leash.

Carter wondered if now was the time he should consider stretching it. At least a bit.

Or maybe more.

He had a backpack on that was obviously military issue, but that didn't mean much around Tacoma, Washington. Lots of soldiers around here. Lots of ex-soldiers and gear floating around.

He had specifically gone for jeans and a purple sweatshirt with the UW Huskies logo on the front, with a rain shell over that. He had also packed some serious cold weather gear quietly, just in case he needed to get crazy around here.

Hard to vanish off the radar in a city. Piece of cake in the mountains. Just open your phone and pull the battery so it can't be pinged. Maybe drop both in a faraday cage bag, US Army issue as well, and nobody can find you.

Carter didn't assume that Daring was looking for an ex-boyfriend like Kehoe did. She might do that as well, but the teams had also done a lot of wilderness training around here and over on the Olympic Peninsula, just to stay in shape. Like you went to Louisiana for swamp training.

He pulled out that faraday cage bag now and pulled out a second phone, powering it up and letting it connect to the universe for the first time in a few months. It would want to update the software, but he could deal with that later.

For now, he dialed a number from memory. It got answered on the third ring.

"Yeah?" a gruff voice growled at him.

"*Mithras*," he answered. "In town and need to borrow a truck or something."

He would have liked a bike, but he wouldn't have been able to pack his leathers without a long and involved explanation to Kehoe, and finding stuff to fit his frame on the fly was impossible. Most men his height had beer bellies going.

Plus, he expected the need to off-road, if he was right and Daring was going native.

Worse come to worst, pickup trucks were a dime a dozen around here. Farm country, this far south, especially inland on the other side of the base.

"Got one," the man said. "Where are you?"

Carter looked around and placed himself.

"I can be out the front gate and over by that one burger joint in about thirty minutes," he said. "Buy you dinner?"

"Already ate," the man said. "You need a flop?"

"Maybe," Carter said. "Undercover at the moment and going into the backwoods for a while."

"Nobody staying over the garage this month," the man said. "Need it?"

Carter did the math. He had funds, but like Daring, using them would put him on a map in seconds, if anybody was looking.

And right now, a lot of eyeballs were focused on the Puget Sound.

Staying off the grid. Seeing if Daring would call him for help. Or if she gave in and let Kehoe *rescue* her. Whatever.

Maybe he did need to stretch his leash a little.

"Yeah," Carter decided.

"See you in thirty," the man said, then the line went dead.

Carter slung his pack over his shoulder and started double-timing it toward the front gates.

CHAPTER 20

Joie had moved quickly, even walking uphill. The weather had started to turn about an hour after she'd met Ruger, raining now hard enough that she had a borrowed hat with a brim over her knit cap that was keeping her ears warm. The peacoat was knee-length, and would keep her dry and warm as long as she kept moving.

More and more folks had gone by her in the other direction, some of them moving quickly to get home.

For now, she was alone. Up over the first big ridgeline and down towards a valley that ran north-south from when the ancient glaciers had furrowed the ground to create Puget Sound and the various lakes.

She was alone. Really alone for the first time in days.

Amy had been there for her. Then the conductor on the train and the women who got her to safety without ever asking any questions. Just recognizing need. Even Celeste had only kissed her on the cheek and sent her out with the car and directions and a credit card.

Joie was on her own now, walking into a stormy wilderness and hoping that the man at the other end didn't slam the door in her face.

She didn't think Mitch would. That wasn't the same thing as knowing. And Celeste had been pretty certain that he'd been alone up there.

But not sure.

Fool's errand, maybe, but it felt good to be in motion, however uncertain her path or her future was.

Joie emerged from under the trees now and studied the terrain. She was back at that first orientation training nearly two decades ago, listening in her mind as the drill sergeant laboriously turned cadets into officers. Usually with a great deal of profanity involved.

She had memorized the map that Celeste had on her wall, showing the vicinity. Joie looked to her left now, down and across and then up.

There.

It wasn't dark yet, but it was getting close. She had a flashlight if she needed, and could assemble the tent quickly enough. Still, it was a little more than a kilometer from where she stood, perched on the next ridge where the person there could see both valleys by just walking around the catwalk on the outside of the tower, or standing inside and looking out windows.

Below it was the cabin where Mitch was staying, solar panels glinting with late afternoon sun and smoke coming from the chimney. Joie let that be her polestar and started walking.

The temperature was dropping quickly, and she wondered if there would be snow soon.

CHAPTER 21

Joie knocked loudly on the wooden panel, then stepped back. She stayed on the porch, but only just barely, as far back as she could get without stepping out into the rain that was starting to get chewy.

The boards in the cabin creaked. She heard Mitch moving around, coming from the side opposite the fireplace and approaching. He moved to the door and peeked at her through the hole.

She wondered if he would recognize her, hat on, coat buttoned, and late afternoon wet dimness limning her.

The lock clacked and he opened the door.

Stared at her for several seconds, face unreadable.

"Joie?" he asked, disbelief evident.

"Hi," she offered back. "Are you free to talk?"

His face fell the rest of the way slack at her words. Joie hoped that there wasn't a girlfriend in there to ask questions. She had no claim on the man. Wasn't even sure he wouldn't just slam the door right now.

This wasn't about her, though.

"Yeah," he replied, staggering back a bit. "I was just finishing dinner. Can I get you anything?"

"I brought a half kilo of coffee and some frozen buritos," she said, stepping forward, but not before tactical brain demanded that she stop, pivot three-sixty and study all the terrain for approaches and firing lanes.

She hated that it was still so automatic, but the Army had burned that into her soul and reinforced it every chance.

Finished, she stepped into Mitch's world.

Warm and cozy. That was her first impression as she slipped by the man and started unbuttoning her jacket. He closed the door and stood nearby, watching her.

Art. Mitch had mentioned a few things he'd done as a teenager, before focusing his intellect on business and money. Turning himself into a mercenary with a power tie.

The space was a hollow box, studio style, with a bed towards the back. A walk-in closet that was large and a bathroom that was small had been chopped out of one side, with a fireplace across from the kitchen area. A dining room table was strewn with maps and painting supplies.

Mitch had hung pictures everywhere. Oils, vibrant or dark. Large or small.

Joie slipped the backpack off and rested it next to the door, then hung her jacket on a peg.

"Sit," he said, gesturing to the other chair across from where he generally worked. There was a couch facing the fireplace, but that felt like where he relaxed in the evening to read or something.

Joie planted her butt, then popped right back up and dug the coffee and food out. He had a fridge next to a stove, so she stuffed the coffee in the freezer and left the buritos on the counter. She could skip eating tonight, because she'd had a big lunch, but he grabbed them and put them on a plate.

She sat again and watched him work. Mitch had never been domestic, even as a bachelor. More of the take-out and recycle than cooking meals from scratch. There was no take-out up here, unless you made a deal with a place down in town to fly a drone up.

She could see pizzas coming that way. Maybe when you wanted to splurge.

"Coffee?" he asked over a shoulder. "I also have decaf."

"Decaf would be better," she answered. "Would like to be able to sleep at some point. And you should just go ahead and put the buritos in the freezer for now, on second thought."

He turned and studied her for a second.

"I brought a sleeping bag and a small tent I borrowed from your mom," she hastily added, in case he thought she was here to seduce him.

Was she?

Didn't feel like it. Joie felt that familiar pang of loss, but not a follow-up urge to walk over and kiss him.

Instead, she watched him make coffee. He'd been the one that taught her the AeroPress. Hand-grind the beans with a burr. Dump them into a columnar container and add hot water. Stir as it slowly seeps through into the mug below. Press with a manual piston and dump the grounds into a composting bin nearby for roses and blueberries.

She still did it, minus the hand grinder that required two limbs.

He even added the right dash of cream before setting it down in front of her. His was half gone.

They sat, facing each other across the table. Nobody had spoken in minutes. Not even small talk.

"Mom sent you up?" he began quietly, possibly recognizing the hat she'd hung with the coat.

"I stopped by there this morning," Joie replied. "She gave me directions, gear, and sent me out with her Subaru."

That got a reaction from her ex. A lot of it shock.

Joie studied him closer now. Brown hair going thin and likely to recede to the top of his skull by the time he was forty-five in another decade. Dark eyes staring out from a square face with a solid jaw. Pale skin with freckles.

Mitch was a little shorter than she was, but had been in as good a shape when they'd met, a runner who did CrossFit and other things almost as demanding as the US Army.

Mitch sucked on his lips for a long second.

"You could never tell me the truth," he said simply. "Or at least the interesting bits. Why are you all the way up here tonight, Joie?"

She flinched under the tone. Mostly because he was entirely correct. She'd never been able to tell him where she'd gone, or what she'd been doing. Most of the US military didn't have a high enough clearance to know those things.

And yet, he'd never minded, once he understood that she *did things* for people and could never talk about it.

She owed him the truth. Wouldn't change what she'd done to him. Or pushing him away.

Joie wasn't here to get him back. She was trying to find Romana.

Maybe so her former partner could have him back instead.

"I used to be an assassin for the US government," Joie began simply. "You always suspected the truth, and you were right."

"Arms like you had are not common," he agreed.

"Mine was so experimental that I couldn't even be fitted for a replacement without them first changing my hardware," Joie said.

"And someone was so pissed at you that they wouldn't approve it?" Mitch asked with a nod.

"Something like that," Joie nodded back. "That's not why I'm here."

"Why are you here, Joie?" he pressed.

So she told him.

CHAPTER 22

Joie sat at the far end of the couch from Mitch as he digested everything. He was blinking too much, but that would revert to normal soon. Shock and adrenaline. She was familiar with it.

He got up silently and stirred the fire, adding another log. Then he turned and stared at her.

The whole story had taken nearly an hour to get out, as his analytical mind kept rewinding her to cover certain spots in greater detail.

Deep-diving, to use his vocabulary.

Finally, he sighed.

"I haven't seen Romy in about six months," he said.

Romy?

Joie had called her partner many things. Some were even repeatable in mixed company. Mixed meaning civilian rather than gender. She'd never been a *Romy*.

"Last time was in Boston," he continued after the briefest pause. "After we'd decided that it wouldn't work after all."

Joie hoped that it wasn't her fault. She'd refused both of them when they tried to help. They had spent enough time together trying to fix her that they had finally looked at each other.

She'd still been in bed most of the time, trying to figure out how her whole life had gone wrong.

"Kehoe is certain that she found something out," Joie said. "Something she wasn't supposed to know, though I have no idea what it might be."

"Kehoe," Mitch said, putting the fire iron away and returning to the far end of the couch, a whole middle pillow away from her. "He's the guy in charge of Technology Research Command?"

"Top civilian," Joie corrected. "Spymaster, I suppose would be as good a term as anything. There's a whole military chain of command as well. Not sure who is Commanding General these days. Kehoe was usually my controller, beyond whatever project or program manager I was working with at the time."

"And he gave you no clues to go on?" Mitch asked sharply.

"None," Joie shrugged. "Both he and *Mithras* think I know something, but I've been out since he blew me up the second time."

Something changed in his face. It wasn't obvious what, but she'd been intimate with the man long enough to read his moods.

"What?" she asked.

He'd had a thought, but wasn't sure he should share it with her.

"Tell me more about this *Mithras* punk," he commanded her quietly.

"Carter?" Joie asked, a bit surprised.

"No," he replied. "The program that created him."

"Project Herakles," she said, leaning back now to dig up her old briefing memories from when Kehoe had set her on the task of taking the man down.

"Herakles?" he asked, a bit of disbelief in his voice.

"They were aiming to create soldiers so amazing that they were functionally demigods," Joie nodded. "Someone had a sense of humor and a degree in English Lit along the way."

"Tell me about them," he ordered.

Joie let her eyes unfocus as she leaned back and stared at a spot on the rough-hewn log walls.

"They originally invented the Argenite alloy by mixing titanium, platinum, and a bunch of other things, so that you have something stronger than steel while still much lighter," she said. "My arms and leg bones are laced with the stuff, same as theirs. That's why I weigh more than you do. We all also have that advanced ballistic cloth under our skin and over the ribs that will stop a bullet and turn most knives."

"You're still ticklish, though," he said with a grin.

Joie felt herself blush as she continued, glancing over at the man.

He was still seated way over there. Emotionally as well as physically.

"Instead of cybernetics like I have, they were treated with a series of engineered viruses that rewrote parts of their DNA," she said. "Like a lot of our medicine can do today, except that it made them grow taller and develop incredibly dense muscles. Carter is far stronger than I am, even when I had my other arm. All of them were. Are."

"What about the demigod part?" Mitch pivoted now.

"So the great fear, going back centuries, was that the scientists would accidentally create a *homo superior* that would eventually either wipe out the rest of humanity, or see themselves as a new ruling class," she replied. "They made sure that the treatment left someone permanently sterile, man or woman. It did slow down their aging process significantly, though. Carter was one of the first, nearly thirty years ago, but supposedly he's only the physical equivalent of his mid-thirties, even in his fifties."

"Did they make these superm soldiers smarter?" Mitch asked.

"No," Joie shook her head. "That was a bridge too far, as I understand it. Same brains as before, so they tended to pick highly patriotic soldiers for the program. Mostly enlisted men who had been identified as exceptional troopers in basic and then watched as they progressed. I remember Kehoe mentioning once that the sergeant who originally recruited Carter Faulkener as a skinny kid had marked him down for something special. He would have never imagined, but nobody knew what the future was bringing in those days."

"So what happened to Herakles?" Mitch questioned. "Are they still making them?"

"I'm not sure," Joie said. "I was their first experiment with significant cyberware upgrades to wounded warriors, and that seemed to be where they turned to a decade ago. At the time, *Mithras* had also gone rogue and become a mercenary terrorist for hire, working for all sorts of bad guys out there for money."

"Are you finally willing to talk about what happened to you?" Mitch asked her next.

Joie felt everything go cold. Clench up. Withdraw.

But she had invaded his home. Come all the way up here and disturbed his peace of mind by bringing her problems with her.

She sucked a heavy breath down.

"It's hard," she admitted.

Mitch nodded, waiting patiently.

He'd waited patiently then, too, but she'd out-stubborned him, hard as that was to believe.

Except that her grandmother had called her *hard-headed distilled*, more than once.

"Kehoe sent me after *Mithras*," she finally said, able to talk about it with someone else for the first time.

Even her shrink hadn't gotten more than the bare bones. Army babe. Tough *chica*. Badass, solo warrior.

Who might have finally discovered that she needed friends.

Mitch just watched.

"Nobody had ever beaten the man. Carter," Joie continued, flashing back to all those briefings when Kehoe had finally gotten pissed enough to escalate Carter Faulkener to the top five list. "Nobody. When he'd been with us, he'd been unstoppable. That went to his head, like most men."

Joie grinned at Mitch. He was kind of a unicorn that way. His ego was wrapped up in doing the job, which had involved coming in, identifying who to keep and who to cut, and then leaving without letting any of the ugliness accumulate on his soul.

Just doing a job. That he'd been promoted so far and so fast was a testament to how good he'd been. She hoped that she'd get his story eventually, but she'd shown up on his doorstep with her needs. And he'd always been willing to take care of her needs first.

"Carter was available, but you had to pay him a lot of money, in gold or something else untraceable," Joie spoke. "And it was always short-term gigs, rather than a senior henchman for your organization.

Shooter, bomber, something. No retirement plans and health insurance things.”

Mitch smiled at her. She’d always assumed that one of her missions would finish off what that bomb in Egypt had done the first time. That much, they had talked about, when it came to her job.

“You took him down,” Mitch said simply. “How?”

“Fucker’d started reading his own press releases,” she growled with a smile now. “Thought he was all that and a bag of chips.”

“Pride before the fall,” Mitch nodded somberly.

“Something like that,” she replied, wondering how much that described her as well.

She stopped and chewed on that thought for a moment. This sort of introspection was a new thing.

Joie wasn’t entirely sure she liked it, but she understood what it was and why it would help, long term. And why the Army had made it a point not to teach her these tools when she killed people for a living.

“They’d made him bigger, stronger, faster,” she said. “Bulletproof in a lot of ways. Tougher than everyone else. Kehoe sent me because I was still *meaner*.”

“Meaner?” Mitch asked, like he’d never seen those sides of her.

He might not have, thinking back. She’d always tried to just be a woman around him. Mostly had succeeded, too.

“His skull will turn a knife or a baseball bat,” Joie said. “But he still has a few holes in his armor, though by now he might have figured out how to protect himself.”

“What did you do?”

“Hit him in the face with a blast of enhanced capsaicin,” she laughed. “Nasty form of experimental pepper spray. You can take a few things ahead of time to largely immunize yourself down to just the sort of hard burn you get from good Cantonese food. I had.”

“Cantonese isn’t hot,” Mitch replied, a little confused.

“Americanized Cantonese is bland,” Joie agreed. “They did that for white people when they came over in the eighteen and nineteen hundreds. Their stuff back home was just as hot as Thai, with a lot of the same ingredients.”

“So you surprised him with pepper spray?” Mitch asked.

"Blind and gasping for air makes it really hard to fight someone pounding on you with a cyberarm," she grinned. "Beat his silly ass unconscious, shackled him with shit designed for those punks, and stripped him naked so he didn't have anything hidden in his gear. Didn't figure there'd be anything stuffed up his ass, but scanned him anyway. From there, called in a chopper, winched that fucker out the window, and disappeared with him into the La Plata sunset."

"But Kehoe assumed you'd been turned?" Mitch asked, circling back to what happened when she'd gotten back to post.

"Nobody was supposed to be good enough to take the man down," she said, proud.

"Was Kehoe setting you up to be killed?" Mitch stared at her. "Getting rid of you and blaming *Mithras* or his organization for it?"

Joie felt the world fall out from under her feet. She found herself gasping, hyperventilating, doubled over and wondering if she was going to be sick.

Mitch sat perfectly still and studied her.

Set her up? Had they decided she was too dangerous?

Two birds, one stone? Maybe get both of them killed, or at least damage *Mithras* so badly that he was lame or needed a hospital?

She'd had the Mark II arm on that one. The one that had the M31A2 *Starbolt* Squad Energy Weapon built into the forearm. Load four ammunition disks around the elbow. Fire out the palm. Hammer the living shit out of someone in heavy armor. She'd bounced Carter off a few walls until she'd softened him up enough to surprise the son of a bitch.

Was she supposed to have been lost in action that day? Then she'd screwed it all up by not just surviving, but winning?

Kehoe had accused her of being turned. Of making a deal with Carter to take him in alive because supposedly no prison could hold the man. Captured, instead of the dead that everyone had expected.

Because nobody could take *Mithras* down.

Until she did.

Joie finally caught her breath. Why would her own people want to kill her?

Until this moment, that thought had never crossed her mind, even in the weirdest scenarios she had envisioned along the way.

It made absolutely no sense at all.

Except that Romana Pham, her former partner in crime, dancing, and bad karaoke, had simply disappeared from the middle of one of the most secure Army posts in the world.

Gone, without a trace.

And both Kehoe and Faulkener thought she might know where Romana had gone.

She was blinking too rapidly, racing madly down various logic trees that didn't lead her anywhere except back to her own tail.

Why had she never seen it?

"Because there were too many trees in the way," Mitch said quietly.

Joie realized she'd been so wrapped up she'd been muttering to herself. And she wasn't alone. She reset everything as well as she could and turned to the man.

To the corporate efficiency expert that you hired to chop your organization up and make it better.

To understand how things *worked*.

"Trees?" she repeated.

"You can't see the forest," he said. "For all the trees."

"I've been missing something, all this time, because I was looking at it all wrong?" Joie asked.

Mitch nodded.

"What, though?" she pressed.

He shrugged.

"Something you saw or heard," he replied. "Or at least they thought you did. Something associated with *Mithras*, perhaps. Then Romy saw or heard it, or discovered something and needed to vanish as well because it would make her a target."

"Do you have any ideas?" Joie asked.

"None, but I wasn't there," he said. "And I haven't seen her in a while, either, so she might not have found whatever it was until after me. Anything special about…where did you capture the man?"

"La Plata, Argentina," Joie said. "Regional capital near Buenos Aires."

"Anything interesting about Argentina, besides a culture of borrowing money they later default on, time and again?" he grinned.

"I have no idea," Joie replied. "But now maybe I have someplace to look."

"If you're on the run, how in the hell would you get to Argentina?"

It was her turn to smile.

"They teach us all sorts of things in this line of work," she said. "Evasion is an extremely vanilla term for the real guts underneath, but folks like *Mithras* and myself have to be somewhat connected to various folks who are not entirely on the up and up. That's how we find other people."

"I see," he replied flatly. "So tomorrow, you finagle your way south?"

"Something like that," she agreed.

He was nervous. She finally understood why. Studio cabin. One big room. One bed.

"Is it okay if I sleep on your couch tonight?" Joie asked carefully. "Or should I set up the tent in the back yard? Coming up here, neither Celeste nor I were sure if you were actually going to be alone, so I was prepared to rough it."

He relaxed, exactly one degree.

"The couch is fine," he said. "Knowing you, you'll be up before dawn anyway. Going to stay for breakfast?"

"Only if you get up early enough," she said with a warmer smile. "Got a lot of ground I need to cover tomorrow."

He rose now, so she did as well. He was barefoot and she had boots on, so she had about five centimeters on Mitch. He didn't step close for a hug and a kiss, so she kept her distance.

She'd driven him away with her stubbornness. She didn't have the right to just waltz back into his life and expect anything.

Or demand it.

He dug out a spare blanket and puttered around a bit as she stripped down to panties and a T-shirt. Mitch had seen her in less. Much less. Still, it was awkward, and not in a good way. She was nervous around the man. About being seen even half-dressed.

Who the hell had she turned into?

Still, Joie let him tuck her in on the couch, then turn the lights off and withdraw to the bedroom all of about five meters away.

Joie didn't think that she'd be able sleep quickly, considering how her last few days had gone.

She was out like a light.

<h1 style="text-align:center">CHAPTER 23</h1>

Carter liked his two phones. Completely individual hunks of silicon, rather than just letting one handle multiple accounts and inbound numbers. Smart man did that, because folks like Kehoe could hack the one to know everything it did. But only if the government knew about it.

One let him talk to Kehoe and all those punks. The other one they didn't know about. At least he didn't think so. Certainly, they'd have tossed his ass back into a supermax prison if they'd caught him doing some of the things he had with it.

Carter always made sure to set it to airplane mode, then power it down, then pop the battery itself out. Made it a pain in the ass when you put it all back together, because it took the thing ten minutes from power-on to actually being ready to talk.

It also made it damned near impossible to track him when he turned it off.

It was on today. Both of them.

Kehoe had had his people track Mitch Graydon to a Forestry Service cabin out in north bumfuck, where the man had apparently spent a good chunk of the winter. Why the fuck anyone would do that was beyond him.

Carter was down in Everett. He'd spent enough time around here to know the naval base and various stations. And the people who serviced them.

Not all of it was all that legal, regardless of NCIS folks and other cops trying to keep a lid on things. Too much money involved, when you had entire carrier battle groups that needed stuff. Shit ton of money changing hands. Easy enough for some of it to stick to something and then cross back under the table.

Carter was in a dive. Best way to describe it. Not a biker bar, because even those folks were smart enough not to start trouble this close to that many sailors who might decide to get even. No, it danced on the line between sailors and locals who worked on the wharves and docks themselves.

Hard people. Quiet for the most part. You came in, ate, left, and didn't bother anyone.

The cook was one of those diamonds in the rough. Carter had almost sent letters to the folks in France, telling them to drag their silly asses over here, just because Carter had eaten in a few joints with a star. Wally's Diner was at least as good. Maybe doubly so, considering it was American diner food.

And it was that amazing.

Demigods burned a lot of calories in a day. Not quite double what he used to, but dieting involved only consuming as much as most hungry soldiers.

Today was a splurge. How often did he make it all the way out here, anyway?

Shit on a Shingle. That was what the menu called it.

They had the shingle part right. That was about it. Big, freaking plate.

Two drop biscuits split open and laid out. Four eggs over easy like a benedict atop them. Bacon and sausage gravy everywhere. Cheddar cheese over that. Four slices of bacon and two patties on the side of the plate, also covered over with everything.

About the only complaint Carter had was the coffee. It was Seattle. Those poxy shits started at a dark and always tried to roast it all the way down to coal or something.

He'd eaten asphalt that was tastier.

But Wally's was an experience, and you had to do it all. Including the surly, just-past-middle-aged waitress who had started to flirt with him when he sat down, then thought better of it and left him alone in his corner booth.

Oldies tunes from the mid-twenty-first century echoed quietly off the bare, brick walls. Old soda and neon signs from God-only-knows how many other bars back. Not enough noise to smother conversations, but maybe enough that the cook wouldn't hear every word said. Assuming he was quiet back there.

Carter was about halfway through his trough of food when the woman walked in.

Short, almost squat. Take a one-hundred-eighty-centimeter-tall model and squish her down to one hundred and fifty centimeters. Broad shoulders. Expansive hips. Wide, planar face. Thai eyes and golden-brown skin just accentuated it.

She made eye contact at the door. Scanned the rest of the joint with hard eyes. Nailed the waitress like a spike as she started walking his way.

"Some coffee?" the woman asked as the waitress got close. "More cream, because he's used it all up."

That wasn't fair. Carter had known she was coming, so he'd left her two of the little thimbles. Or yeah, he'd have used it all to soften the coffee down.

The waitress nodded mutely and went to work.

He called the woman Irene. That had been the name she'd been using when he first met her a decade ago. She might be forty now, but Asian women had this weird tendency not to show any aging until they turned sixty and then it all arrived over the weekend. She fell into that mold.

Irene sat. Smiled at him in a knowing way.

"Surprised to see you in civilian clothing," she said offhandedly.

Carter shrugged.

What she meant was that she'd heard he'd been caught. Thrown in a prison he wasn't getting out of because he'd finally run into someone who knew what he could do and how to hold him.

The only way out had involved returning home and becoming a good little soldier again.

"Leashed," he offered, just so she didn't think he was back in the terrorist business. "Longer than they'd like it. Shorter than I would."

"So it's true?" Irene asked with a smirk. "Captain Daring kicked your ass in Argentina?"

Carter grimaced. Scowled at her. Went back to his food before it got cold.

No man liked admitting that a woman beat him up. At least it was Joie who had done it. He could live with that.

Irene smiled.

The waitress arrived with a fresh mug, a refill, and a new bowl of cream things.

"What brings you my way?" she asked after the woman departed.

Carter had considered all the things he might tell Irene. And her organization. They weren't remotely friends, but had done a lot of business in the old days.

"There have been new developments," Carter said around a mouthful of biscuity goodness. He added some coffee to wash it all down, even as bad as the coffee was. "Captain Daring is back in play. So am I. Neither of us are what we appear to be."

He watched Irene digest that tidbit. He'd just suggested that Captain Daring—the paragon of American values—had gone rogue. And that Carter Faulkener had turned into the good guys.

How weird and stupid had the world gotten when that turned into the truth?

Irene's eyes got big as she worked on her coffee. Two cream. Two sugar. Almost Canadian that way. Wally's might deserve a second star if they would just do something about the coffee around here.

"What are you looking for, *Mithras*?" she finally asked.

"Information," Carter replied. "She's vanished completely, somewhere in the vicinity. Confirmed in Seattle two days ago. I flew in yesterday with some old friends from DC. She doesn't want to talk to any of us, because she has several phone numbers she could call if she wanted to. Instead, she's on the run."

"Who fucked up?" Irene asked.

Carter let that one slide. Irene was technically the enemy these days, though she'd been a friendly middleman back when he'd been on the wrong side of the law. He certainly couldn't tell her anything remotely related to the truth.

Carter Faulkener might want to go back into business again, one of these days. Deep cover for the US government, as it were, since he was always afraid that Kehoe could somehow destroy him this time if the man wanted. How, he had no idea, but that didn't stop his paranoia.

It was better this way. Official cover. Retirement benefits, one of these days. He'd already put in twenty-six years active duty, if you only counted the time he'd been actually taking orders from folks like Kehoe. The years in the middle wouldn't count, unless he did something so amazing here that he had some leverage to negotiate with.

"I'm not sure it was a fuckup, Irene," he replied. "Misunderstandings have abounded."

Shit, wasn't *that* an understatement?

"Captain Daring on the run?" she grinned. "You chasing her for your old masters?"

"They would like to ask her some questions," he said. "She has chosen to go dark rather than participate. The bosses brought me in because they don't know anybody in the shadows that they might ask. I'm on a long leash, but I haven't given up anybody north of the Canal."

He'd had to burn more than one South American organization, in order to convince Kehoe he was willing to play ball. There were an awful lot of other folks out there who didn't appreciate American soldiers interfering with their culture.

Not that anything could convince the Department of Defense or any number of presidents to stop being assholes to the rest of the world. Otherwise, he might have simply retired someplace like Bermuda with all that cash stashed in various places. Bought his own island and hired two pretty women to serve him rum drinks and dim sum all day.

Irene studied his face. Carter finished his food and burped.

Gods, that was amazing.

He studied her. They both sipped coffee.

"So what's the ask?" Irene finally said.

You either traded money or information. She'd gotten several useful tidbits, even this far. Enough that she would listen to him with an open mind. At least he hoped so.

"My bosses want Daring brought in and controlled," Carter said. "Having been there myself, I wouldn't wish that on anybody. Especially not Captain Daring. They also have no idea how to track her, since she's rather expert at staying low to the ground. Could have taught the next generation, but for some unfortunate misunderstandings along the way."

"Like blowing her arm off and burning her cover?" Irene asked in a sweet voice that still concealed a rusty razor blade underneath.

Carter nodded.

"Like that," he agreed. "I personally want to know how far she can run. It might be in my best interest to do the same thing, one of these days. I'd like to know if one could actually get away."

"So we should help her?" Irene's eyes got deadly serious.

"Not hinder her, at least," Carter replied. "Not mistake her for Captain Daring attempting to infiltrate one of the organizations around here as a prelude to destroying them. She's on the run. Why, I'm not sure. It must be something big, except that my bosses have chosen not to bring me fully into their confidence, or I would be able to share tidbits with you. Daring's probably willing to deal, if someone approached her cautiously. Not suggesting you attempt to track her down, because we've been failing, even with the resources we have at hand."

"But not *hinder* her," Irene completed the thought.

"Consider it a training exercise," Carter offered. "Someone who doesn't know your organization at all, attempting to utilize it to make a clean break from my bosses. Or maybe you vector in a semi-competitor and see if they have the operational security to survive when they get tossed into a meat grinder. Or not, if you want them removed from play. The options are rather broad here."

"I see," Irene nodded in turn. "And you think you might be back on the market, one of these days?"

"That is my fervent goal," he said. "That they kiss me on both cheeks and bid me *adieu*. I might retire at that point, either entirely or at least from field work. I'd like to have options that don't involve me buying a bar or getting a job as a bouncer, as it were."

"I will see what I can do," Irene said. "Leave you voice mail at that number?"

"Indeed," he agreed. "The usual operations cutouts and delays are to be expected. You won't be able to call me on the other phone and chat, without someone at Langley or Bragg listening in and asking questions, so make it a ticking bomb emergency if you have to."

"Agreed," Irene said.

She slid from the booth and smiled at him.

"It is good to see you again, *Mithras*," she said. "Even in spite of the circumstances. Hopefully, we'll be able to do it again sometime."

"I would like that," he replied.

Irene turned and sashayed out. That was the only verb he could come up with that covered that walk.

Carter studied the empty plate and considered what he should do next.

Kehoe was still hunting Joie, after all. He only needed to get lucky once.

CHAPTER 24

Taylor hated helicopters, but there was no alternative he was willing to entertain here. This deep in the wilderness and this high up would have required hours of driving and more hours of hiking. So he had ordered the folks at Lewis to assemble him a small force and put it on two rotorcraft.

He was up north with them, because he needed to be present. Taylor had doubted that Daring would go see an ex-boyfriend, except that they had both been intimate with the man, her and Pham. He might know something. Something he'd been unwilling to share with investigators who Taylor might have sent, had he considered it.

Daring might have come to Seattle for other reasons, but this was the nail that stuck up above the others when Taylor examined all his explanations.

Taylor had brought a force with him in case Daring had decided to come up here and hide.

"Sir, we're coming up on our target now," the call came over the headset.

Taylor was aft with the doors closed, the lone civilian here. One of the soldiers slid the door open and pointed at the ridge nearby. On his orders, they had come out of the east. Not that he expected to fool anyone, but any little bit might help. If Daring was here, he'd rather drive her back towards civilization than force the woman to go into this kind of wilderness.

She was good enough to survive up here alone.

The other helicopter was leading them in. Watch tower on the ridge, with a small cabin next to it. Clearing below with a short hike, left over from some clear cut or burn in the semi-recent past.

Chopper number one landed and disgorged troops. At least they hadn't decide to jump out of the side in lines, like they did in training or to impress visiting generals.

Taylor watched the tower as his craft circled. It was midday. A figure emerged from a door and walked around the catwalk, binoculars in hand studying them.

Wasn't Daring. Two hands holding up the lenses told him that. Male. Probably Graydon, as there weren't really supposed to be strangers up here, though he understood that to be a guideline, and not even a rule.

First rotor pulled out and his craft inserted. The team piled out and joined the others, setting up a perimeter with more than a dozen trained killers, all heavily armed and ready to go into the brush after Daring had he ordered it.

Taylor got out and got clear. The two helicopters went into orbit at that point, as nothing had happened. They could evac the team, spot a runner, or do whatever else he needed.

The male had descended from the tower during all this and was walking Taylor's way, with several troopers covering him. Nobody should be hot right now, but they were all locked and loaded. Easier to let them be paranoid than to try to explain that they probably didn't need to.

Still, if everything was casual, why did he need them in the first place?

Taylor didn't bother explaining. He could pull rank when he needed to, and this had been one of those rare circumstances when it had been appropriate.

Taylor moved to meet the man halfway.

Mitchell Graydon. He had a bit of stubble going and his hair was longer than the personnel pictures Taylor had seen. Same man.

Calm. Unsurprised, which suggested things to Taylor.

The clearing had fallen largely silent, with only the whomp of blades in the distance.

Graydon walked right up to the point that a heavily armed male sergeant stood up like a bodyguard, then the guy stopped.

"She's already gone," he said without introduction. "You could have just called."

Well, fuck. Faulkener had been right, after all.

"Let's talk inside," Taylor offered.

Graydon looked at the force surrounding them.

"Cabin will be a bit crowded," he replied blithely.

"Captain, go ahead and set up a perimeter," Taylor said to the man in charge. "Sergeant, you're with me."

Everyone leapt into action as Taylor watched. Graydon had a bemused smile on his face, then turned and walked to the cabin without looking back. Taylor and his attack dog followed.

The inside of the cabin was about what Taylor had expected from his inquiries with the Forestry Service people yesterday. Spartan, but lived in. Warm, in ways Taylor couldn't really explain.

Maybe it was the art on the walls. Graydon was a painter, from the supplies left around and the number of canvases. Not all that bad, either, though Taylor wasn't really a fan of oils. Nor any kind of expert.

The sergeant came to parade rest just inside the door and more or less vanished, which was why Taylor had selected the man. Graydon moved to the freezer and opened it, pulling out a jar that he set on the counter.

Taylor recognized the AeroPress setup as nearly identical to what Daring had used, save that Graydon had a hand grinder he could still hold with both hands. The jar held beans that got reduced. A tea pot was slowly boiling.

"If I ever see her again, she'll get a laugh out of this," the man said as he worked.

"Why is that?" Taylor asked, willing to play the straight man here if Graydon wasn't going to be hostile.

"She brought me these beans when she came up," he said with a grin over his shoulder.

"When was that?" Taylor asked.

"Day before yesterday," Graydon replied as he started grinding. "Stayed the night. Slept on the couch. Left first thing yesterday after an early breakfast."

Shit. Faulkener really had nailed that one dead to rights.

How did the man know Joie Daring so well? Or was it a factor of the training they both went through, that they knew how they would have reacted, and could anticipate things?

Two years ago, he'd followed through on his orders to burn Daring because of suspicions that she and Faulkener had worked out a deal.

Now he wasn't so sure that he hadn't fucked up.

Or maybe *he* was the one being set up? Taylor let that niggling thought grind quietly away in the back of his mind, just as Graydon was grinding beans in front.

The beans got immersed, soaked, pressed. Silence otherwise, as Taylor ruminated and Graydon worked.

Finally, the man put a mug in front of him and settled across the table.

"Just like that?" Taylor asked, a bit surprised.

He'd come up here with enough force to intimidate the man. Maybe threats if Graydon didn't play ball. All of it wasted.

"Just like that," the man agreed. "She warned me that I'd probably have guests soon, but I wasn't expecting assault teams in helicopters, to be honest. Figured you'd park five-ton trucks at the trailhead and make it a picnic weekend or something."

Taylor couldn't help but wonder if Daring was playing him now. Distracting him while she did whatever it was had brought her to Seattle.

Couldn't be as simple as an ex-boyfriend, could it?

Except that Pham had dated the man as well. And more recently.

"When was the last time you saw Romana Pham?" he asked as he sipped.

This was pretty good coffee.

"Six months ago in Boston," the man replied. "Almost seven now, I guess. I was there at the end of a project and trying to decide what I wanted to do next. She was *passing through* on her way somewhere else like she did so you could probably look up the actual date. I didn't ask. Didn't figure I had the necessary security clearances for something like that, then or now."

Taylor didn't scowl, but he considered it. The man's file and corporate background had suggested an extreme intelligence, coupled with incisive drive. In *any* other circumstances, just the kind of person Taylor would have considered approaching about a civilian analyst position with TRC. The pay wouldn't be as good as he'd been making in the private sector, but the benefits blew right by, when you were considered a federal government employee. Especially these days.

"So what did you and Daring talk about?" Taylor asked, mostly just to see what Graydon's limits were. And how much she had briefed him.

"Might-have-beens," Graydon replied. "Choices you make on the road of your life, when you arrive at forks. Or have them thrust upon you."

That last bit was said with just enough sneer that Taylor understood what he was referring to. Turning Captain Daring into a broken civilian under circumstances that might not hold as much water as they had two years ago.

Taylor nodded. He'd had a few of those. Hardly any choices he regretted.

At present.

Trading Daring for Faulkener might be one of them, at the end of the day. He wasn't sure yet.

"Did she mention Pham?" Taylor went ahead and asked.

"Only that you were looking for her," Graydon replied. "And likely to ask me all these questions when you showed up."

"She was expecting me?" Taylor asked, a bit surprised at that one.

"One of you," Graydon said, waving at arm at the quiet sergeant by the door. "Suit or combat gear wasn't clear. Or maybe that tall asshole."

Taylor had to snort at that. He'd heard Carter Faulkener described a lot of ways over the years, but never as *that tall asshole.*

Fit him, though. Taylor decided that he might have to steal that line and use it later.

That Tall Asshole.

"She leave a forwarding address?" Taylor asked.

"Nope," Graydon smiled. "Said she had her phone turned off and disabled so you couldn't track her, so she couldn't even get messages short of me emailing her and expecting a long delay in answers. Mind you, I hadn't actually spoken with her or emailed her other than on her birthday in nearly a year before this."

"Anything else you'd like to say, Mr. Graydon?" Taylor asked.

"Only that you and the tall asshole aren't all that different," the man replied. "If I thought it would do any good, I'd punch you in the mouth right now for what you did to Joie, then maybe chase you down the side of the mountain with a baseball bat. But you brought all your goons with you, and thus I need to behave. Still, you fucked up big time, so I'm not the least bit surprised that she won't trust you. I'm pissed because now she won't trust me either, because she knew —*KNEW*—that you'd come around. That means I can't help her when she really needs friends. You aren't her friend anymore. Maybe her enemy, though she didn't go that far with me, so I'm just going on what you did to the woman. You broke her, you son of a bitch. You know that, right?"

Taylor nodded but remained silent. Graydon wasn't a physical threat. Not with the sergeant handy. If the man needed to vent right now, maybe he would feel better later and relax. Brains like that were rare.

Never burn a bridge until you have to.

He'd had to with Daring. And every morning now when he got up, it felt more and more like a mistake, though Taylor had no idea *why* the order had come down.

Faulkener certainly hadn't woken up one morning and decided to cut a deal with her, regardless of what the reports said. That had come later, when the man got tired of getting his meals through a slot in the door in a concrete egg in Colorado. Toilet and en-suite shower included. All the books you wanted to read.

Absolutely fucking zero freedom to do anything more.

Taylor wondered how soon the rush of freedom would go to his head and *Mithras* would decide to go rogue again.

Boy, was he in for a surprise.

Taylor rose without trying to get the last word. Wouldn't do any good.

He pulled out a business card and placed it carefully on the table as he drank the last of Joie Daring's coffee. She'd really picked out a good roast, wherever she'd gotten it.

Taylor wondered if he might be able to put enough AI bots on security cameras down in the valley to see where she had found it, just so he could get some.

"If you hear from her, I would appreciate a call, Mr. Graydon," Taylor said. "Maybe she'll be in trouble and need friends who can help. All I ever wanted from the start of this was to ask her some questions about things that she might have seen before. That she ran doesn't necessarily indicate guilt on her part. As you said, I broke her and she won't trust me or my organization, probably ever again. We are not the bad guys. We are the United States government, though to some people that makes us bad. Thank you for the excellent coffee, and we'll get out of your hair."

He nodded to the man and turned to the sergeant, motioning at him to open the door. Coming up here had been a dead end only in that she'd already left. He had learned a few things about the rest of the game board that hadn't been clear before.

Things maybe General Bouchard didn't need to know at the moment.

Assuming that man wasn't already responsible for them.

CHAPTER 25

Joie had stuffed a rolled-up, spare shirt that Celeste had given her into the sleeve of the light jacket that she'd gotten with the shirt, just to make it look more like she had two arms. One wing stood out in people's memories. Anything she could do not to would be helpful.

She was inside a convenience store. One of those corporate franchise genericas you found everywhere. Quick stop for some chips and dried jerky and to stretch her legs. She stood quietly in line as she got rung up, everything bagged, and headed back out to the parking lot.

Celeste had also given her this rain shell, much lighter and done in that northwest blue and gray you got from that one outdoor company down in Portland. Almost college colors in this part of the country. Or neutral, when folks around here took their sports a little too serious at times. Still, better than wearing a NAVY sweatshirt.

She'd considered smuggling herself into Canada from here. Not all that hard to do. It had been a long time since the Canadians had been chummy with the US. Mexico was friendlier these days, but the last half of the twenty-first century had seen a lot of upheaval in the old alliances.

She even had connections that would gladly meet her at some middle-of-nowhere spot along the border and keep her safe.

Hopefully, that was exactly what Kehoe and maybe Carter were expecting. Without physical torture, Mitch wouldn't tell them that she was heading back to the scene of the crime, as it were. Hopefully, Kehoe wasn't that desperate.

Hell, she wondered if the man would try to recruit Mitch, one of these days. Good time to catch him, after twelve years had burned the man out to the point he'd needed a sabbatical. According to Mitch, almost nobody came back from such things. You took the time and realized that you were unhappy, and that the job had caused it, so you went and did something else.

Only a tiny percentage came back into the fold, refreshed and ready to rock. Mostly, they moved on, but maybe got a better gig and reached back to pull you over. Or let you in on some Next-Big-Thing before anybody else heard about it.

He'd worked for corporate vampires, so he had one hell of a good rolodex, if he wanted to dig into it. Joie shuddered to think what would happen if those sorts of folks started working for TRC. Even under the table.

New American Empire time?

Maybe she really did need to burn them all down, just to get even for what they had done to her?

Out in the parking lot, Joie automatically scanned everything for signs of trouble. Habit, cranked up to *need* at this point. She couldn't even turn it off, so she didn't try. Instead, she walked over to the Subaru and opened the passenger door. Got in. Smiled at Celeste as she closed it.

"I will remind you, yet again, that your actions may constitute aiding a fugitive to elude justice," Joie said to the woman.

"God, I hope so," Celeste laughed as she dropped the electric drive into reverse. "I haven't had this much fun in years."

"Is Donovan safe without adult supervision?" Joie asked as they got back out onto the little side road that would drop them onto I-5 southbound.

That got an even bigger laugh.

"He's completely house-broken at this point," Celeste said. "At worst, he has the gang over for a marathon Dungeons and Dragons game while we're gone, like he was in college again, and he has to go get a bunch of beer then clean up the pizza boxes before I get home."

Joie had never gotten the role-playing bug. Mostly because she'd done too much of that in her real job, back when she'd had one. Pretending to be someone else, and doing all these things in character while telling a story.

Her body count had never included dragons, but it had been pretty impressive, depending on the statistics you wanted to use.

"I still don't understand why you are doing this, Celeste," Joie said.

"You needed to get somewhere," Celeste replied. "And you are being hunted by folks who have too many computers looking. And they are looking for a young woman with one arm, so you'll stand out. If I drive, they have to have made the connection that you came to me, and I doubt Mitch would say anything to them. So they can't track you because I'm doing everything."

"But why?" Joie pressed. "Mitch and I broke up a while ago, and badly. I was a little shocked that he didn't slam the door in my face when I showed up."

"It's a girl thing, Joie," Celeste said, turning serious now as she set the machine to auto-drive and leaned back. "You are not particularly girlie, being a total jock, so maybe you missed it growing up. And you had the Army as your family after that. Men still like to think that they run the world without our help. We mostly let them labor under that delusion, because women work to help each other."

"Like the conductor on the train?" Joie asked.

She thought back to some of those whispers in high school that she'd never taken serious. Guys or teachers to stay away from, but she'd tuned them out.

"And the woman running the taxis," Celeste nodded. "Or the driver who didn't ask any questions about dropping you up on the hill nearly twenty blocks from my house, on a random intersection. Each of them tacitly acknowledged that you were running away from some man. Believe me, we've all been there."

"All?" Joie asked, wondering how much of life she'd missed, either preparing to go into West Point, excelling when she got there, and then surviving everything that had happened since.

"Joie, every woman I know has been sexually harassed at some point," Celeste scowled. "Many have been physically assaulted as well, though those numbers are nowhere near where they used to be. You probably have been and didn't know it. Or didn't recognize it as such. Historically, men letting hands stray, when women weren't always in a position to say no. Size matters, but only in that circumstance, when he might have fifteen centimeters and twenty kilograms on you. You sometimes have to go along for now so you can escape later. So yes, each of them were seeing themselves in a situation where some man was a danger. You needed to escape. You still do. If they arrest me, fuck 'em. Donovan has two numbers to call. One is a journalist with an axe to grind. The other happens to be the junior Senator from Washington state."

Joie fell back into her seat. Numb. Shocked. It was almost like she'd been blown up again, either time, and her body was pulling everything in to her core to keep her warm as a sudden ball of cold ice took root in her belly.

Celeste was right, though. She'd had the Army to take care of her. Until they'd turned on her and cast her out into the wilderness. Now, she had gotten the help of random strangers to make it this far. Even Celeste kind of qualified, as she'd jumped into the mud puddle with both feet.

Joie had never colored outside the lines. Wasn't sure she really knew how to, not counting all the highly-classified shit she'd done for the military.

However, she suspected that Celeste Graydon was about to provide her a world-class education.

Joie changed mental gears now.

"How long to Mexico?" she asked the older woman.

"We've got the sleeping bags and tent, plus gear," the woman replied with a twinkle in her eyes. "Technically, you can drive there in about two days if you just left things on autopilot, but I want to vanish off everyone's radar for a bit, so we'll camp tonight in a quaint spot in northern California that Donovan and I used to hit when the kids were young. If we spent a day with the car in the sun, it would have all the juice it needs to get us to San Diego without stopping at someone's rest stop station, but we should cut inland and hit either Fresno or Bishop. Did you have a need for Vegas as we go by?"

"I do not," Joie replied.

Why the hell would she want to show up in the place with some of the most extensive security camera systems in the world? Even those could be hacked by Kehoe's people. Joie had seen them do exactly that, when chasing after someone who thought he could hide in plain sight.

"So we'll just drive for a while tomorrow, and find a spot," Celeste nodded. "There are any number we can camp at. Eventually, the question is whether we try to cross at Tecate, Mexicali, or Yuma if we go far enough east."

"Mexicali would be best," Joie said. "I have friends on this side that we can contact. Not as much drug smuggling as the old days, but people still need to come and go. Once we're across, it becomes much harder for them to track me."

"Are you certain that you want to do that part of the run alone?" Celeste asked. "I'm happy to come all the way to Argentina."

Joie grinned at her new friend. Could she call the woman that? She thought so, since they were almost to Oregon now, in the process of outrunning a major manhunt for her.

"In the US, I don't stand out all that much for the color of my skin," Joie replied. "In Mexico, you would. However, if you really wanted to mess with people, you'd skim across the top of the border, maybe going all the way to El Paso and then crossing the bridge on foot. That might trigger Kehoe's systems, if they came out and talked to Mitch at some point."

"Anything to stick it to the man, dearie," Celeste chuckled. "As I said, most fun I've had in years. Even knocking off politicians by funding challengers in primaries pales by comparison."

That was when it finally hit Joie in the mouth, as it were. Celeste and Donovan were about as upper-upper-middle-class, white collar suburbia as you could get. White picket fence. Mitch had been raised in that world.

Joie had been born in Texas, outside one of the posts where her parents had been serving at the time. They'd busted their asses to make sure she got good grades and could get into West Point. In retirement, she hadn't talked to them as much.

Since Kehoe had ruined her life, she hadn't been able to deal with her extended family wanting to come take care of her. Too smothering.

Except that they'd been trying to be a support network for her, even before she understood what that meant.

Joie still wasn't sure that she did, but she'd gotten more over herself now. Maybe.

She'd gone to return Celeste's car and gotten talked into a girl's road trip.

Because helping each other was what girls did.

Even weirdos like her.

"Yes?" Celeste asked. "You muttered something."

"Sticking it to the man," Joie repeated louder. "He even has a name, this time."

CHAPTER 26

Taylor was back at the Fort Lewis part of the post. The old portions, back before they'd added an Air Force base, then merged it all back together again a century ago. Faulkener was with him as well, in the office that the base commander had assigned him. Two chairs across the desk, one of them already groaning under the man's mass.

"Nothing?" Taylor asked.

"So far," Faulkener replied. "Mind you, it's only been three days. These things take time to gel."

"With four days head start, she could be anywhere on the planet," Taylor snapped. "She's got to be getting help from somewhere. Someone. Who haven't we looked into?"

"Not sure I follow you," Faulkener replied.

"Daring knew we'd come to visit Graydon," Taylor started ticking things off on his fingers. "Warned him, in fact, so he was prepared for us. She wanted to know something. He either didn't know, or won't tell us, which amounts to the same thing. You went off and talked to folks who won't take my calls, but I presume they haven't gotten back to you with anything?"

"That is correct," Faulkener said. "Given the small number of folks around here who knew her on active duty, I think that official and unofficial channels would have been able to track the woman."

"Ergo, she left town," Taylor said. "Probably the same day she left Graydon. Drive down the mountain, stop for food, just keep going."

"What car is she driving?" Faulkener asked, sudden concern on his face. "Shit, we *have* missed someone. Who?"

Taylor snapped erect and alert. That trailhead was an hour from town up winding roads. That meant she was in a car, since she couldn't ride a motorcycle anymore. How the fuck had he glossed right over that for three days? Where the hell had she gotten a car???

He grabbed his phone and started dialing.

"Stone here," the Staff Sergeant answered on the third ring.

"Joie Daring," he said by way of introduction. As if there was any doubt. "We found her buying burritos and coffee at a convenience store, right?"

"Yes, sir," the man said in his usual grumpy voice.

"What was she driving?" Taylor asked. "Can we get a description of the vehicle itself?"

The long pause on the line told Taylor that everyone had overlooked that bit. In town just one day and she had a car. Either she'd bought it for cash, or someone had loaned it to her.

Who did she know in Seattle that well?

"Stand by, sir," Stone said. "I will call you shortly with information, and route whatever pictures I can find."

The man hung up and Taylor put the phone down. Faulkener was all ears.

"We fucked up," Faulkener said. "Too used to punk-ass terrorists on horses, or people who don't know that we're reading their mail as fast as they are. We've gotten lazy and sloppy."

"I am not necessarily arguing with you, Faulkener," Taylor said. "Also wondering if we need to add this as a regular training exercise for the team."

"Legally, we are not allowed to operate inside the United States," Faulkener said in a mechanical, sing-sing kind of tone. "*Posse Comitatus*, and all that."

"This is not a law enforcement action," Taylor snapped at the man.

"We have been attempting to conduct wellness inspections on a retired veteran whom we suspect might be in trouble. Doing this next year as a training gig is covered. We'd need to do it in Germany at some point for real, so we might as well see what we can find. If nothing else, she's showing us all sorts of holes in our procedures that I don't think anybody appreciated before today."

"Can I be the rabbit next year?" Faulkener asked in a too-eager voice.

"We'll talk about it around Christmas," Taylor deflected the man.

Faulkener would love to disappear completely off the gameboard at some point. Maybe not return afterwards. Depending on certain agreements they might come to in the meantime, Taylor Kehoe could even see letting him.

Might be useful to have someone like *Mithras* breaking the trail, though, if Taylor suddenly discovered that powers at higher pay grades were indeed setting *him* up for a fall.

Taylor knew too much. And too many Senators. If they wanted him taken down, he suspected it might take the form of a car bomb eliminating him and all nearby witnesses.

The phone rang.

Stone.

"Talk to me," Taylor said.

"She's in a late-model Subaru Hatchback," Stone said. "Wasn't able to get the plates, but it is green with that gray body panel thing they started doing a few years ago instead of the racing stripes. I've got folks trying to access other systems, but most stores don't transmit their data to corporate, being franchise owned. Plus, they have different retention rules on a case by case basis."

"That's enough for now," Taylor said. "Set that as a tier two thing to just run in the background. Find me any similar models that have been for sale in King, Pierce, and Snohomish Counties in the last month. Then see if you can hack the state DMV and get me a list of anyone who owns something similar. Cross-index that list to Daring and Pham's personnel files to see if they knew someone out here who could let them borrow it. Also, assume that maybe we have a soldier or sailor, so track everyone stationed in Washington state against similar vehicles that have base stickers and throw them into the bucket. I'm guessing you'll get a hit pretty quickly once you do that, so call me immediately."

"On it."

The phone went dead again. Stone never wanted to be an officer, or he would have gotten promoted. All Taylor had to do was aim the man and then step back to let him work.

"Now what?" Faulkener asked.

"There's a Cajun place outside of base, across the highway," Taylor said. "Let's go dark for a bit and get some food."

Faulkener rose with an inquiring eyebrow raised.

Going dark could simply mean getting outside of JBLM and not having mess hall food.

And it also might mean something else.

CHAPTER 27

Joie couldn't remember the last time she'd camped without having to worry about watch rotations or personnel issues, instead of just sitting and watching a small fire burn while making s'mores.

It had been a fantastic three days on the road. Northern California. Somewhere in the inland valleys south of Bishop. Now, they were close enough that she could see the fence that marked the Mexican border, an ugly black line cutting the valley in two and accomplishing absolutely nothing at all.

Celeste had kissed Joie on the cheek like a kid going off to her first day of school and kept driving, planning on having dinner in Yuma. Joie had her messenger bag, with a rain shell rolled up and added to her usual gear. Everything else was in the Subaru, leading the hounds off to the east when they finally caught up with Celeste, including that peacoat Joie would really miss.

Calexico, on the US side of the border, was just like any number of towns she'd known growing up. Poor and a little ramshackle, but extremely proud of their roots and still talking about the old days when the border was nothing more than a sign, however many generations ago that memory was.

Two official border crossings, with the canal to the east of town adding a layer of difficulty if you wanted to cross. Mexicali, just across the fence, was a much bigger town, with Calexico itself almost the equivalent of a rich, white suburb. Except that there were few white people around here, save for tourists from somewhere else.

Celeste would have stood out on this side. She would have been painfully obvious over there, however well meaning. But along the way the woman had taught Joie something she'd never really understood. Joie had been wanting to get away from the poorer parts of her family for most of her life, seeing the poverty rather than the extended families, loud and boisterous when she needed to study if she wanted to get ahead.

Where had it gotten her? Standing facing a border wall with one arm, one ear, and one eye.

And a lot of regrets she needed to sort out. That, however, could wait until later. She had a job today.

She turned and started walking. The day was lovely. Clear skies and warm without the heat that would come later in the season. Not a lot of folks around, as tourists tended to drive in from somewhere, cross immediately, and then keep going south.

Joie was okay with that. She didn't stick out, other than a missing arm.

Around a corner, past a bookshop, and into an alley she went. The place had been built originally with a storefront over a street and a small parking lot off the back, but the shop had long since expanded backwards, half-dead cars being repaired. Other ones being stripped to fix the first ones. A general mess as she stepped to the edge of the asphalt where the alley ended.

A man happened to be looking her direction. Young, maybe twenty. Big guy she didn't recognize. He was wearing coveralls that protected him from grease and dirt but didn't hide the muscles.

He smiled.

"Hey, mama," he catcalled her in Mexican Spanish. "Something I can help you with? You got needs?"

Joie started to scowl when another guy popped up from behind an old Ford pickup and took a look.

"Oh, shit," he said. "Juan-Pedro, be nice to her or she'll kick your ass."

"You shittin' me?" Juan-Pedro asked, turning to the older man.

Pedro *Dos*. Middle-aged. Mexican-American only because his family had been here for five hundred years and stayed when it stopped being Mexico and started being California. Hair salt and pepper now, a little long and scraggly. Mustache that was still a big, black caterpillar on his lip.

Joie smiled at Pedro *Dos*. The name went back to three kids in elementary school deciding they wanted to hotrod cars when they grew up. All of them happened to be named Pedro, so Pedro *Uno* ended up owning the joint, with Pedro *Dos* running most of the weird stuff.

She wondered if Pedro *Tres* had moved on, and been replaced by a kid. Made sense, if they called him Juan-Pedro. Everyone who worked here was Pedro. Everyone in town knew that.

"No, I ain't shitting you," Pedro *Dos* said, grabbing a rag and wiping his hands as he started walking this way. "Even with one hand she could take all of us. Hey, Joie. 'Sup?"

Joie relaxed. Juan-Pedro had looked like a predator. Pedro *Dos* knew better. And probably still remembered getting half-drunk and thinking that he could arm-wrestle a cyberarm.

Silly goose.

"*Uno* is inside," *Dos* said, nodding over his shoulder. "Come in and get a soda. Juan-Pedro, you take a break and join us."

The way *Dos* said that left no question that the kid was expected to shut up and follow.

But then, Pedro's was a chop shop. At least of sorts. Legitimate enough business, most of the time, fixing up old cars, some of them so ancient they still ran on gasoline or had maybe been converted to bio-diesel.

It was all the other things the Pedros had their hands in that she needed today.

She followed *Dos* into the building. No AC, but shade and doors open on both ends to let a little bit of a breeze flow through.

Uno was sitting in an office, yammering in Mandarin at someone about a parts shipment. *Dos* walked over to a refrigerator and pulled out a glass bottle of Coca-Cola, twisting the top off and handing it to her before grabbing himself one.

Like *Dos*, *Uno* was middle-aged. His hair, however, was entirely gray now, slicked back. He liked being clean-shaven. Unlike *Dos*, starting to get pudgy around the middle from not climbing over and under cars all the time.

Dos pointed Juan-Pedro into one chair and gestured for Joie to take the other one while he leaned against the doorframe.

Uno's eyes had gotten huge when she walked in. Bigger when he looked close at her face and missing arm. Never missed a beat, scrolling through an impressive display of Chinese profanities with a fluent accent.

Finally, he got whatever answer he wanted from the other end and hung up.

"Gimme," he snapped at *Dos*, so the other Pedro grabbed a bottle and handed it over.

Uno studied her for a long second as he opened the bottle, then took a drink.

"We fucked?" he asked in English.

Joie just snorted.

"They'd have dropped a strike team on your ass so hard you'd have woken up in a cell in Vermont in that case," she replied. "The kid speak English?"

"Some," *Uno* replied, shifting now to Mexican. "Juan-Pedro, this is *Yosefina*. Old friend. Dangerous lady so keep your hands to yourself. Hear me?"

"Yes, sir," Juan-Pedro replied glumly.

Like this wasn't their first time on this merry-go-round.

Uno turned his smile back to her. Like *Dos*, around fifty. Grandkids starting to run around town these days. She stopped and wondered if Juan-Pedro was somebody's. Maybe *Tres*'s son when dad had mostly retired?

"So what brings you to Calexico, beautiful?" he asked in a friendly voice. "Finally retired and here to seduce me away from this life of crime?"

Joie laughed and turned to *Dos*.

"I keep telling you," she grinned. "You'd have to have a tournament or something if you really wanted to impress me."

"Yeah, but there's nobody in town whose ass you couldn't kick, so it wouldn't be fair," *Dos* chimed in. "Even with only one arm this time."

Joie grinned, then let it slowly sober. She took another drink and let the men settle. Old friends. Old contacts. Old goofballs, because *Uno*'s wife Sarah could kick anybody's ass if she got angry enough to take off her apron.

Then you better just start running. Even cybernetic badasses from West Point.

"I need your help," Joie said seriously. She turned to show *Uno* and *Dos* the damaged side of her face and head. And the missing arm that was just a stump ten centimeters long where her arm would have latched on.

"Heard through the grapevine that you'd gotten burned," *Dos* said. "Bosses got mad at you and issued a permanent retirement. What happened now?"

"Romana apparently disappeared four months ago," Joie explained. "They think I might know something."

"They who?" *Uno* asked.

"The first person to show up on my doorstep was Taylor Kehoe," she said.

Both older men hissed and growled at that, but Kehoe hadn't made a particularly good impression on them. Something about being a rich, Yale, *Blanco* with an attitude problem and a superiority complex.

"Then who?" *Dos* queried.

Joie grinned and let the tension build.

"*Mithras* himself walked into the coffee shop where I work, ordered a cup, and wanted to chat," she said.

Both men turned white. Everybody knew Carter. And knew that he was supposed to be in prison.

She didn't imagine it would take long for that tidbit of news to flow up and down the line.

"*Madre de Dios*," *Uno* whispered, even crossing himself automatically. "Shit's way out into big trouble, isn't it?"

"I'm on the run," Joie said simply, turning to Juan-Pedro now. "I used to be a US government agent, Juan-Pedro. The other Pedros are old contacts and old friends, in spite of being on the other side of things most of the time. Everything you hear will remain strictly confidential. Am I clear?"

Uno and *Dos* both added comments to the back of that. The kid had turned a little pale, but nodded. If he worked here, he knew what went on. Just needed to know that it went beyond the simple criminality that was their usual stock in trade.

"Yes, ma'am," Juan-Pedro said. He turned to *Uno*. "Wow."

"Told you she could kick your ass," *Dos* chimed in. "I've seen her do it to bigger boys."

Juan-Pedro nodded and drank his Coke.

"So what do you need?" *Uno* asked.

"I need to get across the border without leaving fingerprints," Joie said. "I had a ride down here from Seattle. She's going to go stay in Yuma for a few days and then drive home, hopefully distracting everyone."

"Border's easy," *Uno* said. "But Sarah will kill me if you don't come to dinner and spend the night. *Dos* can get you across easy enough tomorrow. We have shipments coming and going all the time. What's your final destination, or should that remain secret?"

"Way south," she said, indicating that Mexico just happened to be the first stop.

And the easiest way of getting out of Kehoe's immediate sight and reach. Carter probably still had the contacts to follow her, but it would take him time to track her this far.

Eventually, he might figure out that she was headed to Argentina. Joie wondered what Kehoe would do at that point. Or Carter.

Uno nodded. He turned to Juan-Pedro and ratcheted the intensity up a notch.

"You never saw this woman," he said simply. "She doesn't exist when she is not in the room with us. That includes conversations with the family. Anyone in the family, including your dad. Clear?"

"*Si.*"

"Good," *Uno* said. "You have now been initiated another level, Juan-Pedro. I'll explain more of it next week, then tell you a lot of the interesting bits in a month or so, once we're sure the men hunting her have either come and gone, or missed tracking her here. Don't fuck it up, Juan-Pedro. I want to retire one of these days and sell you the shop, but if the Feds put us out of business you'll be selling used cars for your cousin."

Joie liked the way Juan-Pedro shivered at that. A cogent threat to ruin his life, as it were. Having met that particular cousin, Joie agreed.

Uno turned back to her now and smiled.

"So I'm taking the afternoon off," he announced to the two men. "Try to not burn the place down while I'm gone?"

"Down?" *Dos* asked in a helpful voice. "So just setting things on fire won't get us in trouble, as long as the building survives?"

"You get the fire department called on us and you can explain to Maria why they had you arrested," *Uno* snarked back at him. "I promise I won't get you out until tomorrow, so you'll miss dinner with Joie."

Another threat of a fate worse than death, but that got smiles all the way around.

Hopefully, she wouldn't bring down a lot of grief on her friends. Kehoe was still an asshole.

CHAPTER 28

Joie ended up riding in a pickup truck on the passenger side of the bench, rather than being ducked down in back of a sedan like she'd been expecting. It helped that *Uno* had a big hacienda outside of town, so they were quickly alone on the drive out. He'd left the windows down, so she had to be careful that the baseball cap he'd given her to wear didn't blow away.

Outside, the machine looked like one of those mid-rwentieth-century International Harvester pickups. Inside, she suspected that most police cars couldn't keep up. It was amazing what you could do when you had a bed of batteries across the bottom providing weight and the technology to print and crimp steel into any shape you wanted.

If the Pedros had wanted, they probably could have moved to Los Angeles and made a fortune in one-off car designs.

But that would have involved breaking up all the families, moving away from all their friends. Joie had only now begun to understand why he never had. She had a lot of catching up to do at this thing called living.

Outside, the afternoon was starting to wane.

"So are you back in the business now?" *Uno* asked as he drove.

Joie thought about it a bit before responding.

"I don't think so," she finally said. "At least I don't want to be. The only people who could fix me could just as easily implant bombs or something next time they wanted to turn me off. A little charge of plastic explosives contained inside my head and they could turn my brain to mush, whenever or wherever."

"Should I start looking for some other folks that might be able to build you replacement parts you could trust?" *Uno* asked.

She turned to stare at him, mouth open.

"That shit didn't come out of a lab in Virginia, Joie," he noted. "Enough folks have advanced arms like that now that someone is building them, at least at a workshop level, if not a factory somewhere. Or at least the parts. Maybe in Mexico. Maybe Vietnam or someplace in Asia. Sure, it wouldn't have all the polish, but you might know a guy who could help with that, too."

She remembered to close her mouth before she caught any flies.

What did it say that the people most wanting to help her had to break the law to do it? Granted, *The Pedros* were used to that. But even Celeste had opened herself up to all manner of criminal liability if Kehoe decided to be an ass. A bigger ass than normal.

"Maybe when I get back," she said.

He nodded, accepting that as an implicit promise that she would come and visit them when she was done with whatever it was at wherever she was going that might be the root of all her problems.

Assuming she wasn't in a prison somewhere.

They fell silent.

Not long after that, *Uno* turned into a long driveway that wrapped around a few hills and up into a small canyon where enough water accumulated to make things green. Not the lush American front yard, but fruit and nut trees with catch basins for dew and rain, plus a well that went pretty deep. It was almost another world in here, away from the harsh, dry desert outside.

A few youngsters looked up from what they were doing to see *Uno*'s truck roll into a spot, but like kids everywhere, they were hesitant to talk to the one-armed stranger that got out.

Until Sarah came out as Joie followed *Uno* up the driveway, and suddenly Joie found herself engulfed in a hug.

"JOIE!!!"

Sarah was tall, so it wasn't like Celeste, who only came up to her chin. Sarah was nearly her height, lean and rangy rather than turning into a Mexican grandma, even when she was. Long, white hair, with some black at her shoulder blades. All of her kids were younger than Joie, just starting families of their own. Some still lived here, while others had gone off for school or jobs.

"What are you doing here?" Sarah asked, as she let go, took Joie's hand, and dragged her into the house.

The air conditioning was on, so it went from a little too hot to so cold she was shivering in about four steps.

Joie got put on the couch, with Sarah still holding her hand next to her. Pedro *Uno* ended up in his chair across from them. A few nervous faces peeked around corners, but none of them looked more than five.

"I was in the neighborhood and stopped by to see the Pedros," Joie began.

An hour later, they had all ended up in the kitchen, with Sarah cooking more food and folks starting to wander in from work or other wings of the house. Joie had been careful not to mention anything that a nine-year-old might repeat to get anyone in trouble, but when they presented her as a friend from out of town, most of the kids went back to playing and ignored her.

The adults already knew most of the things they needed to keep quiet about.

"And at that point I rolled up here and got a hug," Joie finished up, sipping some of the coffee *Uno* had made for her.

"Staying tonight and then crossing?" Sarah confirmed.

Joie nodded. "Whenever *Dos* needs to head out."

"It is utterly despicable, what that man did to you," Sarah sputtered. "All those…"

She caught herself short of saying words that you didn't use in front of children, but Joie understood her. As did *Uno*.

To the older kids, the young adults, Joie was just a traveler their parents knew. Dinner proceeded that way, with *Dos* and Juan-Pedro showing up later. Juan-Pedro ended up being *Tres's* boy. His dad and mom Sylvia showed up and it turned into something of a parents' meal, with *Uno, Dos, Tres,* their wives, and Juan-Pedro at one end of the long table, while everyone else mostly ignored them at the other end.

Eventually, Sarah showed Joie to a guest room and closed the door as they sat on the bed.

"Why are you doing this, Joie?" Sarah asked. "You don't have to."

"Everyone thinks that Romana saw or learned something," Joie replied. "That she might be in trouble. If so, she's likely to trust my old bosses about as much as I do, so maybe I can help."

"Are you sure she needs it?" Sarah probed.

Joie stopped cold and stared at the older woman. Another one like Celeste who would have been happy to have her as a daughter-in-law or niece or something if she'd had any available men the right age around.

"I don't know," Joie admitted.

"Are they dogs chasing a fox?" Sarah asked. "They lost her, so they start baying after you, hoping you will lead them to her?"

"That's why I'm trying to sneak," Joie said. "I'll get a burner phone in Mexico. Maybe another one when I get where I'm going. I have no idea where Romana might be, but if nothing else, this has woken me up from the zombie fog I've been living in for two years, so some good has come of it."

Sarah leaned close and kissed her on the forehead like a mom would.

"You just stay safe," Sarah said. "Let the rest of those *pendejos* go to hell until they learn to treat people better. *Uno* told me that he offered to find you a new arm and eye. You should take him up on it."

"I'm afraid that I would want to go back to that life," Joie admitted. She could do that with Sarah. "Without my arm or my eye, I get up and have to move forward instead of looking back."

"You might change your mind if they painted racing stripes on it, instead of making it look like flesh," Sarah laughed.

Joie had to agree. She'd been trapped in a mental box where she assumed that only TRC could replace her arm and give her one as good as what she'd had. Other arms would be slow, awkward, and have hardly any strength, because that was what you could get these days over the counter in most department stores.

Still better than a peg leg or a claw hand, but she'd had two arms for the longest time. Touch sensitivity as good as the rest of her skin. The ability to see in the dark, and incredibly long distances.

At the same time, it had been more than ten years since her original arms had been designed. And Kehoe had brought a woman with him that first night that Joie had taunted as a Mark II or III, to her original Mark I.

What might be available, if she didn't have to deal with government paperwork to get it?

"We'll see," she temporized as Sarah studied her face.

The woman laughed and stood up.

"You sleep now," she ordered with a grin. "Huevos Rancheros and all the fixings for breakfast, because if I know those men, they will hide you all day and forget to feed you."

Joie laughed with her. *Dos* could be a little single-minded when he got focused.

She was still getting used to having friends.

CHAPTER 29

Taylor took the call as soon as he saw it was Stone.

"What have we got?" he asked immediately.

"Good news, bad news, and good news," Stone replied in that cryptic, technically correct way he did.

"Go," Taylor said.

Across the table, Faulkener was finishing up shoveling an impossible amount of food into his pie hole.

"So the cross-reference got us a hit pretty quickly," Stone said. "2102 Subaru, registered to Donovan and Celeste Graydon, parents of Mitchell Graydon. Given the connection, I presumed a few things and fed it into various law enforcement systems. Said vehicle was last spotted in Yuma, Arizona six hours ago at a fish taco stand."

"Shit," Taylor groused. "What resources do we have in the vicinity?"

"Almost none, sir," Stone replied. "Border Patrol and a few military units occasionally seconded for training and the like, but nobody in the know we could safely deputize."

"Yuma tells me she's crossing into Mexico to get somewhere we can't track her as easily," Taylor said, speaking so Faulkener could follow. "Stone, find me a flight to Pendleton or some other base in

Southern California. I'll figure out how we get the Mexican government to help while we're in flight."

"Very good, sir," Stone replied and hung up.

"Yuma?" Faulkener asked.

"Drove in Celeste Graydon's Subaru," Taylor replied. "First, she took Amtrak to stay off our radar. Then she drove cross-country."

"We won't catch her on this side," Faulkener said. "I would presume she'd makecontacts with coyotes we probably don't know to get her across. Then where?"

"Wherever it is, we're a day or more behind her, so I think we need to jump ahead and go straight to Mexico City. If they discover Captain Daring has gone rogue and is running around on their side of the border, I imagine we'll get a lot of help."

"Has she, though?" Faulkener asked. "Gone rogue? The *Federales* still have a reputation for shooting first and asking questions if anybody survives. Should we even tell them? She's doing what we want, running hard enough that folks might help her get to wherever Pham is. And doing it without help from us."

"That's the exact problem," Taylor said, flagging down their waitress to get the check. "How has she been able to stay this far ahead of us? DC to Seattle. Seattle to Arizona. We're losing ground on the woman, and she's supposed to be a broken-down ex-soldier. This was supposed to be easy, chasing her. Even Captain Daring isn't supposed to be that good. What I still haven't been able to figure out is who is that other player that's been helping her evade us. And it has to be somebody big."

He handed the waitress his credit card as he forced a smile. They were used to soldiers in here, but him getting a phone call that suddenly made him nervous might start rumors that something was happening that would require soldiers to be deployed. That would circle the entire base in minutes if he wasn't careful.

Taylor needed to make a call, but most assuredly couldn't talk here. That meant back to the base.

He felt like a kid who had to pee as they crossed the highway and got back through security into areas where he was surrounded by soldiers. Not that these folks gossiped any less than civilians, but it would be different ears hearing.

Faulkener accompanied him into his assigned office and sat as Taylor called General Bouchard.

It went to voice mail. Hopefully, that meant that the general was busy with a Senator or a mistress, rather than he had decided to start ignoring Taylor's calls. Now was about as bad a time as Taylor could imagine for the man to burn him.

At the same time, if Bouchard was setting him up, they might be moving to a weird kind of endgame that required Taylor to protect his own ass first.

"General, this is Taylor Kehoe," he said when the line beeped. "We've tracked our target to Yuma, Arizona, and are assuming that they will be in Mexico already or shortly, using methods other than the official crossing. I need to get your authorization to work with the Mexican authorities directly, and to fly down there. I'll be getting on a flight to LA as soon as my people can arrange one. Call me when you have a chance."

He hung up and scowled at Faulkener. That was fine, as the man was doing the same.

"Go pack," Taylor said. "We're southbound as soon as Stone can find something."

"You don't seem pleased," Faulkener noted as he stood up.

Taylor nodded.

"Who's helping her run now?"

CHAPTER 30

Carter smiled as he returned to his room. Not much to pack, as he'd assumed this was just a way station and hardly unpacked.

It was the change on Kehoe's face that delighted him. Carter had always wondered if there were layers of duplicity and double-dealing going on with TRC. Looked as though maybe some of the seams were becoming visible. If so, that opened him up more options.

Kehoe had suddenly started looking over his shoulder, at least metaphorically, which meant that maybe he was afraid his bosses were about to do to him what he'd done to Daring. Carter still thought that was about the dumbest thing he'd ever heard, but nobody had asked his opinion.

Still, it was worth the risk. He pulled out his spare phone and powered it up while he stuffed things into a bag. They were in officer transient housing, so the crypto-security should only be normal and an extra phone suddenly joining the cellular network wouldn't raise any suspicions.

He finished about the same time that it locked in, so Carter picked it up, logged in, and opened the text service.

Heading to Yuma AZ immediately. Developments on project. Contacts in NorMex?

He hit send and powered everything down promptly. Irene would understand and hopefully had friends south of the border. He doubted it, but it put information in her hands that she could parlay into favors from one of those groups when she reached out to them. If nothing else, it made her look good and hopefully she would smile at him when it came time.

He slung his bag and considered the sudden change in circumstances.

If someone was about to burn Kehoe, Carter needed to make sure he didn't end up collateral damage.

Even if he wanted to be close enough to watch the explosion.

CHAPTER 31

Joie stood in the late morning sun as Pedro *Dos* finished rearranging cars. They had crossed the border with him driving a semi that had a double-decker trailer full of cars, and her hidden in the front one on the lower level. And old beater Mallory sedan from the mid-century.

She had been under the back seat, where a smuggling compartment had been built in. Not much bigger than a coffin, but she could pop the seat up or open a panel to climb into the trunk, as needed.

Dos finished and climbed out, walking over with a huge grin on his face as he handed her the keys.

"I know it looks like a piece of shit," *Dos* began, pointing at a vehicle that was half bondo and half faded black. "However, this is one of *those* cars, so make sure you find a highway somewhere to open it up and get used to the feel. The air dams underneath are almost invisible, but will suck you right down hard to the road at over one sixty kph. That means bootlegger reverse and crazy shit like you used to do. Downside was that you lost a serious percentage of your battery life when we carved out the secret compartment, so you only have about four hundred kilometers range right now before you need to charge."

"Solar skin?" Joie asked.

"Only the parts with paint," *Dos* shrugged. "The whole point is that it must be a junker someone bought, got about halfway to rebuilding, then gave up and sold on."

"You don't mind me driving off with your personal baby?" Joie teased him.

"Makes me get off my ass and finish one of the other ones," he laughed. "Maria wants a pickup like *Uno*'s, but without all the horsepower. Worst thing that happens is that you get arrested somewhere and they sell it off. Not like anybody can trace it back to us."

"Thank you," Joie said, voice serious now.

"Anything you need," *Dos* said, engulfing her in a hug before steering her to the car and watching her get settled.

Joie wanted to automatically reach out with her right hand to drop it into gear, but that was the missing arm. She settled for awkwardly crossing and leaning as everything got adjusted. She was taller than *Dos*, and all of it was legs, so the seat had to go back and down. Mirrors were all wrong. Everything.

He climbed back up on the rig and started rolling. She fell in behind him. They were about an hour south of Mexicali, just a little beyond Puerto Peñasco on the eastern shore of the Gulf of California. The morning was brilliant and clear, climbing up towards hot later but the water nearby kept things moderated.

Joie flipped a coin in her head at this point. If she cut inland to Hermosillo, she could make better time on the highways south. Alternatively, if she stayed on the coast, she could hit places like Guaymas, Los Mochis, and Mazatlán on her way to Guadalajara. Sinaloa had once been a rough and dangerous place for anyone, let alone a one-armed woman traveling on her own. That had changed over the last half-century or so.

Still, *Dos* had left her with a revolver, tucked into the door itself, where her left hand just had to drop down and grab hold. Joie hoped that it wouldn't come to that, which wasn't the same as it not happening.

She cruised for now, deciding to stay on the coast. Eventually,

Kehoe would track Celeste to Yuma, and presumably they would cross over to chase her.

Mexico wasn't like the US. The poverty was even worse, but more importantly, the people didn't accept the level of constant surveillance. Cameras would be shot, crushed, or stolen pretty quickly, so eventually the various governments had given up trying.

She could be invisible here. At least as invisible as possible. More than once she wished that she'd had the time to find a replacement arm, except that all the commercial stuff worked with different sockets and software from her custom rig. It would require a mechanic with mad skills to adapt something, or a long stretch in the hospital getting the old stuff removed, and she had to assume that those sorts of folks up north were being watched. Or had already been contacted and warned.

Should she just go to ground here in Mexico for a while? Skip the trip to Argentina and hope that Romana was okay and didn't need her help?

That siren call was tempting. However, were the situation reversed, Joie would want to know that someone would come for her. A sisterhood of sorts, quiet and operating in the shadows.

Friends whom you might know for all of five minutes, but who could completely alter the trajectory of your life in that time.

Joie had already run into a dozen such women.

She needed to pay them back by making sure that the risks they took for her meant something. That was the conclusion as she listened to the hum of the tires and meditated her way around slower buses and various vehicles, weaving into and out of traffic.

She needed to be *alive*, and not just getting out of bed every morning and going in to the coffee shop.

Amy would forgive her for quitting unexpectedly. Had probably been raising enough of a stink that their corporate lawyer, Aysha Clarke, was bothering the pentagon about a missing employee.

Joie chuckled as she considered the ultra-secret Technology Research Command suddenly having to field calls from annoyed Congresscritters.

She considered the gun next to her. Considered the hotrod beater she was driving. Considered her destination, so far to the south that actually driving there might take months. And even then, she could only get as far as Panama before she needed a boat or an aircraft to get her over the Darién Gap.

Most importantly, she needed a plan. Still, she was finally in a place where she could look ahead, instead of forever over her shoulder.

CHAPTER 32

Taylor checked the incoming call and took a deep breath before he answered. He and Faulkener were aboard an Air Force transport headed south. One of the older model Cessna jets from thirty years ago that hauled mid-level officers around when they weren't important enough for the newer stuff.

Still, it had been available and Bouchard had quietly approved the flight.

The General was on the phone now.

"Sir?" Taylor asked as he answered.

"I've been briefed by Sergeant Stone," the man replied immediately. "Once you land in Los Angeles, you'll be refueled immediately for transit to Mexico City. I've been on the horn with General Perez down there and brought him in as much as necessary. Not all of it, but enough to make him an ally."

Taylor cursed in his mind, but didn't let any hint of it into his voice. Manuel Perez was a former General in the Mexican Army that had been lateral-transferred to the Ministry of the Interior. Nothing at all like the US Department of the Interior. The Ministry was more like the Department of Justice.

Perez was one of the bosses of the secret police down there. Taylor had worked with him, as had Faulkener and even Captain Daring, though she had expressed an extremely personal distaste for the man. Apparently he had propositioned her more than once.

Exactly the last man Taylor would have wanted chasing her.

Still, beggars and choosers.

"Excellent news," Taylor said, adding a smile on his face that hopefully got picked up by his voice. "Will they be allowing us access to their surveillance assets?"

"I'm not sure, Kehoe," Bouchard replied. "Perez was extremely interested in what she was up to, since she was no longer active duty."

"What did you tell him?" Taylor asked, feeling his stomach sink.

This had started as a way to get Daring to tell him what she knew about Romana Pham. Somewhere along the way, it had morphed into a manhunt, and Taylor wasn't sure that all the cowboys understood that they wanted Joie Daring alive.

He could have just killed her himself, had that been the need.

Was she likely to end up there anyway?

Just what had she done to piss off Bouchard and his superiors?

"General Perez knows that Daring is a fugitive that the Department of Defense wants apprehended," Bouchard said. "That the Mexican government is being asked to help, on the presumption that she secretly crossed the border. What else should I know, Kehoe? Especially the parts that don't get relayed?"

Taylor doubted that last bit. If Perez was involved, his gunslingers would be, as well.

"We don't know why she ran, sir," Taylor said. "Mitch Graydon might have known something, but I doubt we'd get him to tell us at this point without threats, and I'd rather have him as a potential recruit later than another one that mistrusts us as much as Daring. We know she came south. Right now, it looks like Celeste Graydon drove with her, so it is entirely possible that she never left the US, but I doubt it."

"Why is that?"

"Everything she has done has been to get off our radar, General," Taylor replied. "Amtrak. Cross-country road trip. Once she's in

Mexico, she stands out far less than most of our operatives, giving her an advantage. What we don't know is where she's going next."

"That's why I asked for General Perez, Kehoe," Bouchard said with a smile that was obvious in his voice. "He'll hound her pretty hard. Eventually, she'll make a mistake and we'll have her."

"Yes, sir."

Taylor tried to sound positive. Perez had a reputation for shooting first.

Joie Daring didn't do him any good dead. Worse, she might finally decide that if they were trying to kill her, she needed to change sides, as she had been accused of in the first place.

Everything up until now had been with her staying neutral.

Taylor listened as the general hung up and wondered what it would be like if Captain Daring decided to stop running and start hunting him instead.

CHAPTER 33

Joie had always loved Guadalajara. Jalisco State had always been one of her favorite places to visit when she had spare time. Here, she could disappear into the crowds, much like south Texas back home. The beautiful, cool afternoon was growing late and traffic was picking up on the streets around her.

She had parked the car in a nearby garage for now. If this worked, she would find a long-term spot for it and send *Dos* the information to retrieve it.

Actually, she would do that anyway. This would either work or not, and she would know in the next fifteen minutes. Joie pulled out her burner phone as she went ahead and paid for a week of storage at an eye-watering rate. Sarah had slipped her a wallet filled with both dollars and pesos before she left, so she could afford it.

And she would pay them back later for everything they had done for her.

She took a picture of the front, then texted it and the address to *Dos*. Someone would come for it. Or he would hire someone local to bring it north.

Joie turned her attention to the bar across the street as she approached. Mariachis and middle-class kind of place, to look at it, but the well-dressed man standing at the front looked more like a bouncer than a host.

She had the pistol tucked into a holster on her waistband for now, under the rain shell Celeste had given her. Joie had been afraid that being on the run would mean eating bad food and having problems with her pants. Only having one hand to button things meant that they always needed to be baggy.

The stress of the last two weeks had shaved off over four kilos. Not that she hadn't wanted to lose them, but not like this. She needed a belt to keep her pants up right now.

The gun fit just fine.

The goon at the front door, standing there in his nice suit, picked her up out of the group of pedestrians as she moved close. Joie couldn't do anything about the way she was dressed. At least not without spending more of Sarah's money when she didn't know how much she needed.

She presented herself in front of the man with a smile that matched his scowl. He was about her age, so mid to late thirties. Heavy in the way of muscles and iron, rather than the lean pretty boys that gym rats turned into.

Solid. Badly-tailored black suit that didn't conceal the pistol in a shoulder holster. Dark hair that had the look of dye.

"Do you have a reservation?" he sneered, eyeing her jeans, T-shirt, and light jacket.

"No," Joie smiled up at him. "Could you let Ernesta know that Captain Daring is here and would like to talk to her?"

"Who?"

"Just tell her and see what she says," Joie said. "I can stand here for five minutes before I decide that I'm done waiting and go elsewhere with my business."

She moved to one side and tucked her left hand into her back pocket. If she had two arms, now would be when she crossed them, and her mind still wanted to do that. Her scowl deepened.

Give the man credit, he turned and gestured someone inside closer. A waitress appeared. Joie heard him whisper her name in the woman's ear and then sent her off, matching her scowl for scowl across the doorway once they were alone.

Nobody else came along to get in, but this was not the sort of place where casual tourists were welcome. Private club, and all that.

It took the waitress four minutes to return. The woman had turned pale, in spite of her Nahua-looking heritage and normally darker skin.

"This way," she said carefully, heading deeper.

Joie smiled at the bouncer, then turned and ignored him.

The inside looked like a high-end restaurant. That was what it was. They just didn't open for business for another hour or so, and then only for reservations, usually private parties for locals with a lot of money and the right political connections.

She followed the smaller woman across the vast, cathedral-high space and up a small staircase tucked in the back. There was a mezzanine overhead across the back and right side, where smaller groups might be seated. All the tables up here were currently empty save one.

An older woman sat at the head of a long table with five other men attending her. A queen with her court. Two looked like gunslingers, while the other three looked more like lawyers or accountants. The gunslingers were twitchy.

Ernesta Hernandez had gray hair a little past her shoulders. Thick and rich. Medium height. Medium build.

"I have a pistol that I would like to put on the table for now," Joie said carefully to the woman as she got close. "Then get it back when I leave."

"Iggy," the woman said.

One of the bodyguards rose and moved carefully closer, staying out of the line of fire of the other one. Joie pulled back her jacket and let the man grab it out of the holster, stepping quickly back.

"Is that it?" Ernesta asked.

Joie turned to show her the empty sleeve where a cyberarm had once been.

"So, it really is you," Ernesta Hernandez said now, somewhat impressed. "Come, sit and tell me why the dangerous Captain Daring has come to visit."

The two gunslingers moved up and away to face inwards. There was a chair next to Ernesta. She slipped into it and nodded.

"Thank you for seeing me, Señora Hernandez," she said. "I have come to ask a strange favor and don't have many people I could contact."

That got a lot of interested looks from the lawyers and accountants that worked for the woman. They knew her at least by reputation, though last time Joie had been here, it had been to help the Mexican government utterly crush one of this woman's fiercest competitors in the local underworld. But those folks had moved on from narcotics and illegal booze and started dealing with munitions and revolution.

The sorts of things that got Captain Daring sent after you.

Ernesta Hernandez was fourth generation in the business, if the old reports had been accurate. Had been the child with the most business sense and the most ruthlessness, when her brothers had gone into law or medicine instead.

"I had heard rumors that you were no longer employed," Ernesta said, reaching out and pouring a glass of water from a pitcher on the table.

All the paperwork was face down right now. Plus there were several briefcases nearby that probably held more. None of which Joie cared one whit about. Even if someone else wanted Ernesta, she was a free agent these days.

Joie took the water as a peace offering and sipped with a grateful nod. This meeting could still go sideways, could have already gone bad, but she had a reputation that was going to hopefully save her life. At least in here.

"Two years ago, there was some sort of terrible misunderstanding with my superiors," she began. "As a result, I was revoked, as they might say. No longer an agent for the US government. Retired entirely and put out to pasture."

She shifted enough to show everyone the empty sleeve, then pointed the dead, gray cybereye at all of them. Not wearing her eyepatch no longer felt strange, but the reactions of the people around here confirmed why she'd put it on in the first place.

That little flinch they couldn't suppress when they saw her eye.

"And yet you are here, and introduce yourself as Captain Daring," Ernesta prompted.

The two bodyguards were still twitchy, but that was a professional thing. The lawyers were probably worse, because they might know who she was.

Or who she had been, once upon a time in America.

"The US government is hunting me," Joie explained baldly. "I lost them in Seattle, crossed into Mexico, and have been trying to stay off the radar since. However, I need more help than I can call on, because I need to get somewhere quickly. Thus I thought I might ask you."

"You mentioned a favor," Ernesta said soberly.

"I am no longer a soldier," she reminded the woman.

"True," she nodded. "But perhaps there is information in your head that might have value."

Joie nodded. At this point, she was almost past caring who she burned, except that there were certain lines where they would stop trying to arrest her and just send Mark III cyberbabes after her instead. Then she would be back where she'd been with Carter Faulkener.

Dead preferably, alive if necessary.

"The terrorist once known as *Mithras* is no longer in prison," Joie said, turning to include the lawyers in her statement. All of them perked up. One paled appreciably, so he knew what the man was really like.

"And you know this how?" Ernesta asked.

"After my old bosses showed up at my apartment, *Mithras* walked into the coffee shop where I worked the next day to try to recruit me. I have seen him more than once since."

"And you chose not to accept his offer?" Ernesta probed.

"Have your contacts heard about him breaking out of that supermax prison in Colorado?" Joie smiled innocently, glancing around. "Has anyone ever gotten out?"

Long shocked pause on their part. Eyes grown big. Skin a little pale.

"So you might forgive me if I suggest that it smells like three-day-old fish, ma'am?" Joie asked.

"You think he turned?" Ernesta asked.

"I might suspect he has *returned*, perhaps," Joie offered. "Remember, thirty years ago he was a US agent such as myself, before he went rogue the first time. Then other times. Until I find out who he is really working for, a little voice in the back of my head suggests that the timing of him showing up in Arlington, Virginia and being able to move around freely in the US leaves me…*concerned*, shall we say?"

She caught the meaningful glance from Ernesta to one of the lawyers. That story would get tracked down. Probably not worth much on the surface of things, but it might also save this organization from accidentally hiring a mole that was sent to destroy them.

The Mexican government had inherited corruption from the Spanish centuries ago and never really done anything about it in all that time. Too much money floating around that made it easy to *fix* things. As long as you paid your bribes on time, nobody bothered you.

And you didn't cross any top officials.

"And you need to get somewhere quickly?" Ernesta asked. "Faster than you can drive? Where?"

Brass tacks time. How big a favor did she want? How much was it going to cost?

She couldn't imagine them charging her money, even if she might have had enough. Hell, she could have boarded a plane, but her passport would trigger every alarm in the world right now.

And driving as much of it as she could would take weeks, if not months, as much fun as it might be to simply vanish off the face of the earth for that time.

"Argentina," she said simply, unwilling to be more specific.

It was a pretty big country, as far as geography went, but it was still mostly centered on Buenos Aires, and La Plata was functionally a suburb these days. Kind of like Los Angeles or Seattle, where city just went on forever.

Ernesta wasn't prepared for that answer. Most people running from the US would stay in Mexico. Large population, all her rough color and a language that let her hide. Central America was small in terms of people.

Argentina was still far more like the US than any other place. Lots of European immigration in the twentieth century, and a caste system that still equated value with skin color. Blond hair and blue eyes were a cultural thing they had inherited from the Nazis that fled there in the 1950s. It had only gotten worse as the twenty-first century had progressed and passed.

"Argentina?" Ernesta confirmed.

Probably had been expecting Vietnam or something. Maybe China. Joie could speak Mandarin, but not pass as a native by any stretch. And the ex-pat community there was too small to hide in.

Joie might also be done hiding. Not done running yet, but all of this was just building up a head start so she had time to start planning traps for the men and women coming after her.

"Argentina," Joie confirmed. "It is related to the apparent disappearance of my old partner, Romana Pham, four months ago from Fort Bragg in North Carolina."

She liked the blink of interest at that. TRC wouldn't appreciate that information getting out, but they'd made the mistake of making her a civilian, then leaving her in that state.

Had Kehoe been smarter, he might have just arrested her on suspicion of something that first night and hauled her off to Langley or someplace to sweat her.

Of course, that would have immediately made her his dire enemy. Even Kehoe might be smart enough not to burn those bridges without a damned good reason. He'd certainly walked a fine line at the time.

And Sarah might be right that they were just selling her more rope. A longer leash, as it were, to see where she dragged them. Joie was already playing a longshot here, based on Mitch's ability to see patterns within chaos.

If this didn't work, she might transfer herself to a corporate coffee shop in Mexico City or maybe come back here to Guadalajara.

Make Kehoe and Faulkener sweat a little if they wanted to bother her.

Assuming Amy would let her go. Never underestimate that woman.

"How soon were you wanting to get there?" Ernesta inquired.

Tantalized was the word Joie would use to describe her.

"I don't have the time to drive there," she replied. "Considered finding a cargo ship headed south that I could pay for passage on. But the sooner I can get there, the sooner I can answer a few questions and maybe get on with my life."

"Where are you staying?" he asked "Here in Guadalajara?"

"Yes, but I haven't gotten a room yet," Joie answered carefully.

If nothing else, she could sleep in the car. Or walk to one of the tourist places nearby.

"Let me make a few calls and see what I have handy," Ernesta said.

Joie gave one of the lawyers her burner phone's number and rose with a polite bow to the woman. The bodyguard even gave her back the revolver without much fuss. She'd been trained on a range of semi-automatics, but every one of those assumed two hands to do things. Six-shot revolver was easier.

It forced you to aim before firing, rather than hosing down an area.

Joie asked and was shown a way down the back and out the kitchen, into a delivery dock off an alley.

It wasn't that she didn't trust Ernesta Hernandez. She was a businesswoman, just like the rest of them.

Still, Joie'd felt eyes on her as she stood out front acting tough. Possibly a mistake on her part, as a surveillance team might have spotted her and even now be vectoring in trouble on her.

Joie needed to vanish for a while.

CHAPTER 34

Taylor saw the name on the phone as it rang, grimaced, swallowed, smiled, and answered with a polite tone.

"Hello, General Perez," he said carefully. "What can I do for you?"

"We've spotted Daring," he said with what Taylor could only qualify as something just short of a mad cackle.

"Where?" he demanded.

"Guadalajara," Perez replied. "About to walk into a meeting with Ernesta Hernandez herself."

Oh, shit. One of the biggest smugglers on the western side of the Americas? Not just narcotics, but all manner of things that should have faced excise taxes when they were imported?

Taylor gulped.

"What are your immediate plans, General?" Taylor asked. "And how quickly can we get into the air for Guadalajara?"

He was sitting in a hotel in Mexico City. Staying in one of the nicer rooms with a fantastic tourist view that did absolutely nothing for him. If he wanted to look out over a city from the thirtieth floor, he could have gone back to his office in DC.

Still, the food was good and he was getting excellent cooperation from the Interior Ministry.

At least as long as he didn't ask too many questions about how they really operated.

"I am sending a car around for you and *Mithras* now," Perez said. "And I have contacted the airport to make sure your jet is ready to fly. We can depart in under an hour, then it takes about an hour to fly direct. I'm making arrangements for a second team to meet us at the airport."

"Second team, General?" Taylor asked, his heart and stomach sinking in unison.

"Correct," Perez cackled again. "The first team will be moving to capture Captain Daring and bring her to a safe house we use in town for interrogations."

"Very good, sir," Taylor replied. "I'm heading downstairs now."

The man hung up without another word.

Shit shit shit shit shit.

Taylor grabbed his overnight bag, stuffed a few things into it, and walked across the hall to pound on Faulkener's door. The man answered quickly.

"Guadalajara," Taylor told him, shooing the man in deeper. "Get packed. We're gone in five minutes. Perez is sending a team to arrest her as we speak."

"Is he completely daft?" Faulkener asked as he quickly got packed. "Does he know who he is dealing with?"

"I suspect that we've got undercurrents here, Faulkener," Taylor said. "Unrequited lust and all that. Perez is probably thinking with his dick. Or expecting her to be a civilian who works in a coffee shop that he can just show up and terrorize."

"Moron," Faulkener grumbled. "Can we bring in professionals yet?"

"If Perez fucks this one up, I'm pretty sure Bouchard will call their President and demand that we be given *carte blanche* to work with, but we have to go through the motions first."

"So what, we find her, force her to disappear with an expectation that you've sent kill teams after her now? You think that will make it easier later? Worse, what happens if one of those fuckups manages to shoot her. She and I are only bullet-resistant, you know. What if someone kills her?"

"Then this mission is over, just like that," Taylor said. "But until she forces Bouchard to start overruling people, there is not a lot I can do. At some point, I hope to be able to turn you loose, but until anybody else realizes otherwise, you're currently in the States, listening to the police band for mentions of her you can exploit. This might be enough that you could catch a flight south, so you're two days behind her."

"Like I said, complete, fucking morons, the lot of you," Faulkener groused.

But he fell into line and they walked to the elevator in companionable silence. All the man's seething rage at the situation was inside for now. As it should be.

Taylor could have told Bouchard that Perez would go cowboy on this one.

Had that been somebody's plan, all along?

CHAPTER 35

Joie had spent a lot of years as Captain Daring, after Lieutenant Dearing got herself blown up in Egypt. Going into strange places, frequently without any help, other than a team parked nearby that could charge in if she needed them.

She was used to operating without a net.

Guadalajara spoke to her right now. Whispered in her ear.

If pressed, Joie would say that the pattern of the city had just shifted, but she couldn't point to any one thing as the cause. The sound was a little off. Or the light. Something.

Some subconscious thing that suddenly poked her in the back of her head and said *move*.

She'd gone out the back of Ernesta's place because of it. Into the alley, across and down a little bit, moving into the seedier spots that always tended to remind her of a Hollywood movie set. Pretty on the front. Empty and raw on the back.

Joie wouldn't say these were her people, but she'd spent far more time in the shadows, watching in preparation before a strike, even if she might actually saunter in the front door in a slinky dress if the mission called for it.

Most of them had involved kicking in the back and lobbing

grenades in. Stun or frag were almost always left undecided until the last moment.

The air whispered to her of stun grenades coming out of pockets. Joie broke into a jog.

She didn't draw the pistol, if only because that limited her options. It did call to her though as she began to speed up.

At the end of this alley, a big SUV suddenly turned off the main street and came rolling slowly towards her, windows blacked out and riding low on the axles, like that team back in Arlington had done.

Her pistol would be useless here, if they had already gone for heavy equipment. Hell, her old XM24E4 *Sunbolt* cyberarm fusion pulse rifle might not hurt that thing if it had sufficient armor. She'd have needed her XM29E1 *Supernova* Heavy Cyberarm cannon.

That one killed armored cars. And assholes in powered battlesuits.

A normal person in this situation would stop and back away right now, running in the other direction in hopes of getting away from pursuers. That would drive her, herd her right into the rest of their team.

Joie charged.

The big vehicle jammed on his brakes as she got close. She went for the passenger side, assuming that the driver wouldn't get out unless he had to.

The alley wasn't big enough to turn around, but there was barely space for them to open doors to engage. The smart move would have been to stay inside the vehicle with the doors locked.

Somebody hadn't briefed these boys and girls any better than the folks in Virginia. The two doors on the passenger side opened as she came even with the fender.

Joie swerved around the front door and then slammed all her weight into the back one, just as someone stuck his head out. Didn't crack the bullet-proof glass. Might have cracked his skull.

The front door passenger was male. Small and stocky. Dressed in black combat gear heavier than a uniform but not full armor. Just ballistic plates and helmet like you might wear to a riot.

Fucker had a pain stick in one hand. One meter of alloy, with the handle insulated and the rest attached to the nasty great-grandson of the commercial stunguns that civilians might buy for protection against a mugging.

One touch from that and she'd likely be on her knees seeing stars. They trained you to understand how such things worked and felt by using them on trainees. She hated riot control training.

He wasn't ready for her, as he was trying to get out of the vehicle to engage.

Joie punched him in the throat as he looked up at her in surprise. At least they were intending to take her alive.

She wasn't sure if that was a good thing or not.

She knelt, going down almost as quickly as her stunned target, mostly so nobody could change their mind and shoot at her. Plus, he'd dropped his stick. She grabbed it and rotated in place as the back door opened again.

They might be wearing plastic armor, but nobody had insulated them effectively. Joie touched her target with the hot end of her new toy as his boot hit pavement. He screamed like a wounded rabbit.

In her head, she was counting seconds until backup could be vectored this way. No other SUV had entered the alley, so they were probably spread a little thin trying to enforce a perimeter. That might have been what triggered her combat training.

It would not take them long to give her the bum's rush at this point.

Joie exploded into motion, standing again and reaching across the inside to stab the driver of the SUV as she climbed up and got into the passenger seat. Nobody was wearing seatbelts and the driver's side rear door was open because that soldier had exited and moved around back to find her.

The driver jolted hard and subsided.

Joie reached across and shut the vehicle down, ejecting the keyfob and tucking it into her pocket. She had to put the pain stick down to do it, but she hated them anyway, so it wasn't a great loss.

She listened as her last target moved around the rear of the beast, drawing her revolver and sliding out to center it on his face as he came even with the rear wheel. The asshole coming around the car was wearing a helmet that might stop a bullet, but not a facemask.

Not at this range.

.357 Magnum looked big enough to stick your dick into it without touching the sides, when someone had it pointed at you from this close.

"Drop it or I'll kill you," she said in cold, hard Spanish, an angry voice that summoned up everything that had happened since Kehoe first knocked on her door.

He didn't have any space to maneuver right now. No place to duck or evade. She's splatter his silly ass all over the alleyway if he gave her any reason at all.

The stick hit pavement. His hands hit sky.

"Turn around," Joie ordered him.

He complied.

She didn't have time for subtle, so she kicked his knee out from under him as she holstered the pistol, then grabbed the stick up as he went over backwards and cracked his helmet on pavement. Probably a mild concussion. Better than bleeding out.

Joie gigged him like a frog just to make sure he stayed down for a while, then dropped it.

She ran.

CHAPTER 36

Joie hadn't been entirely sure where she was until she suddenly emerged from an alley near the cathedral. Not the big one downtown that was the tourist-trap Hollywood set, but the one a bit more uptown, where the upper middle class locals went to pray.

She considered finding some priest, just so she had five minutes inside to sit and relax while disturbing his comfortable life so badly that *he* might need a priest.

The moment passed and she began to walk. The evening crowds were heavier as folks emerged from work and began to plan for dinner. Perhaps themselves taking a walk around to relax, as the day had simply turned out glorious.

In her back pocket, the phone vibrated with an incoming message. She'd turned off the ringer, assuming the need for stealth even before she'd walked into Ernesta's place. Now, she pulled it out and keyed it open.

Heard there was a commotion. Safe to call?

Unsigned. Not any number she had memorized, and there were none programmed into the burner phone.

Still, not many people knew this number. She pressed the button and put it to her ear as it rang, moving off to one side to get out of the pedestrian traffic around her. There was a shop nearby with a glass front. She studied her reflection in it and scanned her rear perimeter.

"Hello?" a man's voice answered tentatively.

"It's Daring," she said. "They missed."

"Hang on," he said.

There was a pause, then a laughing voice came on the line.

"Chickens missing heads," Ernesta said. "That would describe the scene outside my restaurant. I would probably have been taken in for questioning, but I had prudently moved elsewhere. Those marauders in black were Federal troops, and not all of those have been adequately bought."

Joie snorted. She wasn't sure she'd ever met an honest official down here. Beat cops, sure. Their honesty usually meant that they couldn't be trusted to be promoted by corrupt bosses.

And there was always so much money floating around, in an impoverished country, that people could be bent.

"At the same time, I suspect that this might be a lovely time to take an extended vacation," Ernesta continued. "Get out and see the sights. Let things settle themselves out around here before there are any misunderstandings. Are you still rated for Dassault jets?"

That last line jarred her a little. She'd never been fully rated to fly jets, mostly because of the training time, both the initial investment and the regular hours needed to maintain that certification. There was also the need for a medical certificate, which no honest doctor would ever have given her, given how many after-factory parts she had. Not just her breasts, but damned near everything it felt some days.

Then she remembered. When she'd destroyed those local rivals, that had been her cover identity to get close. It had helped, back when she could paste up a checklist on the heads-up display that had been her right eye, to remind her. TRC had been excellent at making their agents instant experts, but those sorts of things tended to fade in a few weeks afterwards.

"I am unfortunately rusty these days," she replied.

Safer not to pretend. That way she wouldn't get put on the spot to try to fly an aircraft she didn't know.

"That's fine," Ernesta reassured her. "I have a pilot, but it would be easy enough to list you as a copilot on the manifest. Almost nobody ever looks at the flight crew. You'd be amazed."

Joie supposed she would be. Nobody had ever mentioned that sort of thing to her, but she could see how easy it might be to swap out a crew member, when the local customs officials might be more centrally focused on the person owning a fantastically expensive jet.

"Okay," she offered.

She was prepared to hide for a few days and then perhaps go grab *Dos*'s car, assuming he didn't show up for it. But she'd come to Ernesta for help.

Even criminals were generally honorable people, and she'd never had a reason to tangle with that woman's mob. That she was aware of.

She had, unfortunately, brought Mexico City down on the woman, but that was probably a normal occurrence, given the kinds of cat and mouse games they played.

More importantly, Joie had learned something interesting, both about herself as well as the world around her.

She could have friends. It wasn't necessary to be the big, bad, lone wolf all the time. Celeste had been one in a line of women who had helped. Sarah as well. Given all the crime lords in Mexico that Joie might have asked for a favor from, Ernesta Hernandez's gender had played heavily into Joie's decision.

Men still ran the world for the most part, but Joie was starting to see that women allowed them that hubris, while doing their own things where nobody was looking.

"Here is an address," Ernesta said after a momentary gap. Reading it off a piece of paper maybe. "If you can get there in the next hour or so, we can be gone not long after that."

"Is it safe to fly right now?" Joie asked.

"Is anywhere in Guadalajara or Jalisco safe?" Ernesta countered. "All the more reason to slip out of town before they get serious and lock things down, Joie. Plus, we can get out of their reach quickly enough, perhaps landing to refuel in Panama or Ecuador as needed. I don't want to necessarily fly straight there, as they might be tracking us."

"Thank you," Joie said, surprised at this turn of events, but touched.

She didn't have to do it all alone.

Not anymore.

CHAPTER 37

Carter could have told them what a monumental fuckup it would be to bring in a man like General Perez. Nobody had bothered asking someone with knowledge of the other side of Mexican law and order, though.

The fool general had ordered a team in to arrest Daring even before picking up the Americans and heading to the airport. Dumb. This was Captain Daring they were dealing with.

Carter assumed bad blood somewhere. Probably the old goat had propositioned Joie at some point and been sent packing about as rude as that woman felt like being.

The last thing Carter needed in a situation like this was all those undercurrents added. Still, maybe this was the mistake that would convince Kehoe and Bouchard to turn him loose and let him try to work Mexico.

Daring had made incredible time getting this far south. Must have a vehicle around somewhere that she'd been driving. Why Guadalajara, Carter had no idea, but just getting her into motion again meant that he had an impact zone from which he could work.

Puerto Vallarta wasn't far away, and was still one of the top tourist spots in all of Mexico, at least for Americans going more than a day trip across the border. Mexico City was the other direction, and would be all wound up now to stop her from heading through.

It helped that just about all of the highways in central Mexico passed near or through the capital. Wouldn't require many troops to bottle her up, and those orders had already gone out, assuming that she might try to run under them even as they flew to get her.

Except that the stupid general sitting across the jet's aisle and forward, a drink in one hand and a celebratory cigar in the other, had ordered teams to grab her as soon as they'd established a positive ID.

Worse, Daring had been seen going into a place owned by the legendary Ernesta Hernandez, one of Mexico's only female crime lords, but not coming out.

What was it about females helping?

The thought hit Carter like a freight train. So bad that the gorgeous, Thai flight attendant immediate came aft to check up on him.

Tall. Skinny. Golden skin. Big tits. Utterly beautiful. Dressed in a uniform with pants and a tight tunic that just showed off all her curves and muscles. Even her perfume was lovely. Spring flowers or something equally feminine and alluring.

The general did pick out good scenery. Carter wasn't the least bit confused about her likely role when the general's private aircraft was on the ground.

"Are you all right?" she asked in a delicate, concerned voice.

"Fine," Carter replied gruffly with a tilt of his head. "Could I get a rum and coke, please?"

Anything to distract her. To distract all of them.

Kehoe looked his way. Carter shook his head. General Perez was so taken with himself as a master tactician that he barely acknowledged the two Americans accompanying him to his triumph.

Carter had serious doubts. Joie Daring had kicked his ass and taken him in. Neither of those was supposed to have been possible at the time.

Even today, down an arm, an eye, and an ear, Carter wasn't willing to bet against the woman. Unless it came down to the two of them in a ring with a referee and no tricks up her empty sleeve. Then it might be fair.

He wasn't holding his breath there, either.

The beautiful woman sashayed forward to fix him a drink, chatting quietly with the other one who was only distinct in being a little shorter and bit broader across the hips. Both were incredible.

The general had good taste in women, because both had struck him for their brains, as well as their bodies, but there was no way Carter would get near either of them. Or even flirt them up.

Always assume anybody on the inside is a spy. Including the ones everybody takes for granted as part of the scenery.

Whose spy was the key here.

Kehoe rose and slipped back.

The jet was a hollow cylinder with a table near the hatch forward, and a half-dozen first class seats that could rotate if you needed to turn inwards. Kehoe unlocked his and turned this way.

His face asked all the questions his mouth wouldn't.

"You might finally need to run me in the field again," Carter offered quietly.

"You think she escapes the net?" Kehoe asked, barely audible above the hum of the fans aft.

"Joie Daring," Carter said.

As if that explained it all. It might. Kehoe grimaced.

"What suddenly lit a fire under your ass, just now?" Kehoe asked.

"Maybe a clue as to how Daring is working," Carter offered. "I need to review some of your files when we land in Guadalajara and find out that she's eluded the *Federales*."

"That's a given?" Kehoe pressed, uncertain.

Carter snorted.

A lot of things about Daring left Kehoe uncertain. Carter had been assiduously working to undermine the rest. Anything to get Kehoe off-balance. Especially if he was starting to have a crisis of conscience about working for Bouchard.

"It is to me," Carter replied with a smile for the waitress as she carried a highball this way.

Probably the most expensive top-shelf rum, because General Perez didn't strike Carter as a man to drink rotgut. Carter would make do. He had gotten used to home-brewed hooch, back when he was on the other side of things. Lots of places in Cuba and Central America didn't bother with industrial equipment, setting gallon jars with fermentation locks on shelves and distilling them in old alembics.

Carter thanked the woman and watched her bottom as she returned to the front. He steeled himself and sipped. Yup. Stupidly expensive rum, but Coke was Coke, everywhere you went. And the ice helped cut it down some.

He took a bigger drink and let the coolness knife through the heat that had accumulated in his stomach.

Next to him, Kehoe grunted noncommittally and gestured for the flight attendant to make him a rum and coke as well.

Guadalajara was already burned. That much he was certain. Perez had jumped the gun in his rage and excitement. Daring would elude them.

Except that Carter had an idea now.

CHAPTER 38

Taylor wondered if the General's soldiers had intentionally waited until he landed before telling him the bad news. He and Faulkener were standing off to one side, well out of the way, with the jet behind them and a convoy of armored SUVs alongside, all blacked out and screaming *low-profile assault force* to anyone south of the Rio Grande with half a brain.

"What do you mean?!?" General Perez was screaming at the major in a nice uniform in front of him. "How could she escape you?"

Taylor felt a little sympathy for the man. Obviously, a colonel somewhere had decided to sacrifice this man, rather than a lowly captain or such. He considered placing a bet with Faulkener about the outcome, but that would be rude. Ruder than normal, anyway.

"She engaged in close combat with one of our teams and took them all out, General," the major replied, body rigid, eyes on an imaginary horizon. It helped that Perez was about one hundred seventy and the major over two hundred centimeters tall. Let him see over the screaming man.

"Took them out?" Perez demanded incredulously. "The woman had one arm! Are you people utterly incompetent?"

The major was smart enough not to answer that one. Taylor might have suggested that just about everybody might come up short. Certainly Faulkener had come to Jesus after decades of proclaiming himself the best in the business.

Until Captain Daring came along.

"Where is she now?" Perez demanded of the group.

"We don't know, sir," the major replied, still trying to sound professional and maybe salvage his career.

Perez was an asshole that way. Might decide to break the man just because they hadn't been able to keep up with Joie Daring.

Might as well fire the entire Mexican Army at that point. That might even improve things around here, but Taylor didn't say that out loud.

"Fine!" Perez practically screamed. "Take us to your command post for a briefing!"

Taylor fell in at that point, with Faulkener walking behind him in utter silence. They ended up in the middle of five vehicles. Taylor would have preferred to ride in one of the others, maybe number two or number four, because if he was going to hit a convoy of five with a team, he'd put anti-tank missiles into the odd-numbered ones. Front, rear, and important asshole in the center.

He did not, however, suggest that General Perez was the kind of guy that even his own troops might assist in killing, if revolutionaries or terrorists were to come after him.

Even if it was probably true.

At least the General was a little drunk at this point. Not sloshy, but he'd had more booze than was probably useful, and would need some time to sober up. Assuming the adrenaline didn't burn it all out of him by the time they got where they were going.

Taylor sat across from the man, facing rear with Faulkener next to him. Faulkener, *that tall asshole*, had some scam going, but refused to elaborate while surrounded by Perez's men. Fine.

The ride didn't take long. Across an enormous military post to an office building inside of its own wire and secondary security. The kind of thing that kept the rest of the Army at bay.

Taylor found it almost amusing, how much Perez fell into the perfect stereotype of a corrupt Interior Ministry General. Eerie, really. And predictable.

He could work with that.

They followed the unfortunate major into a briefing room that had maps projected on the walls.

Taylor still remembered sending Daring here five years ago to assassinate the leader of one of the local gangs. Annihilate might be a better term for what had happened, once they tumbled to her identity after she got inside.

As far as he knew, only six people had made it out of the compound alive that day, including Daring. And Perez still looked at the woman and only saw her tits.

Taylor contained the sigh and managed to not roll his eyes as they got seated. How many briefing rooms included a bartender, after all? At least they knew the General's needs, and had a glass to hand him immediately.

Taylor and Faulkener both went for orange juice with nothing in it. The rum had been pushing it, since he never drank in the field, and this was close enough.

"She left the building via a back door somewhere," a captain stood up now and spoke, tapping the projected map with a pointer stick.

Downtown Guadalajara. Nice place. Money and culture in ways that places farther north didn't always understand or emulate.

"One of our teams encountered her here," the man went on, tapping an alleyway about three blocks from the initial spot.

It was all alleys around there, so Taylor knew exactly what she'd done. Standard procedure evasion.

These pimps in black armor didn't like to get their boots dirty in places like that.

"How many men on that team?" Faulkener spoke up, his voice sounding melodious and polite, which would be a dire warning to anybody who actually knew the man.

"Four," the captain replied in a professional tone. "Body armor and control wands, with firearms in the back of the vehicle where they were accessible if needed, but not immediately at hand."

Taylor watched the man nod and lean back again, as if that was the only question he had.

It might be. Four men weren't enough to take Daring down if she knew trouble was coming.

"How badly injured were they?" Taylor went ahead and asked now, since Faulkener wasn't going to.

"Two suffered concussions," the captain said. "All four were hit with control wands she had taken away from one of the men and rendered unconscious. She was also armed, as one of the men said she pulled a revolver on him. She also stole the keys to the vehicle, dumping them down a sewer grate until we could trace the radio tag to recover them."

"And her whereabouts are no longer known?" Taylor pressed.

"That's right, sir," the man said. "We have all of our teams out at this moment looking for her. Local authorities have been alerted and given her description. Computer forces are tracking for any sign of her on the internet."

Taylor smiled and leaned back.

Good luck with that. She got away from us in DC. You'll never find her in Mexico.

Perez had already finished his first glass, possibly without stopping to take a breath. He staggered to his feet now and began screaming insults, threats, and obscenities at his own men, avoiding the two Americans.

Taylor tuned him out and waited for the booze to kick his ass.

Then—and only then—would he finally ask Faulkener what the man thought he knew. Not in front of the locals, though.

CHAPTER 39

Joie studied the scene. Private airport on the edge of the main commercial district. Fifty years ago, the place had been a slum. Almost a *favela* like the Brazilians still did them. Then a local government had decided to do something useful and started building adequate housing on the other side of town, with modern amenities.

To keep people from coming back here, they eventually bulldozed this place flat and sold it to a group of local investors who had turned it into a private airport with high-end facilities and several nice restaurants.

Not quite a country club, but nobody down here played golf anyway. Too hot to keep grass green without wasting so much water that you ended up with a revolution. Wealthy folks around here just wanted some peace.

There was a fence all the way around, but nothing insurmountable if she needed to raid the place. Still, the sun was only on the verge of going down, and she didn't have the right equipment to cut a secured fence and penetrate the place unseen.

Instead, she placed a call.

"Hello," Ernesta said. "How are you, dear?"

Dear? Sure, why not? Sisterhood sort of thing, maybe. Go with it.

"Just outside the main gate and down a block or so," Joie replied. "Wondering if perhaps it might be more helpful if someone could pick me up, instead of me walking through a mass of people that might include federal operatives."

"Lovely idea," Ernesta said. "Where are you?"

Joie described the strip of shops, including the place selling tea and chocolate where she was currently engulfed in rich, warm smells.

"Yes, I know the spot," Ernesta said. "We'll be right there. Could you pick me up some of the eighty-two percent dark caramels?"

"Will do," Joie replied.

The line went dead and she went inside. Chocolates on her right behind glass. A wall of teas in flip-top jars on her left, plus individual satchels. They even had ice cream available. She considered it, but settled for getting some of Ernesta's desired chocolates, and a few flavors of tea for herself that just smelled lovely when she sniffed at them.

Mexico always got a bum rap in American pop culture as a backwards place. Mostly because they were more honest about the social stratification of their culture than *del Nortes* were. This shop could have been dropped into any quaint little tourist town in the United States and not missed a beat. Probably upscaled the neighborhood on the way.

Joie stepped outside with two bags in her hand as a blacked-out sedan rolled sedately to the curb. The rear door opened and Ernesta peeked out with a smile on her face, so Joie joined her.

"Thank you," Joie said. "I know I'll end up owing you for all this later, but my need is great right now."

"And the sorts of people I hate are chasing after you, dear," Ernesta replied. "That helps. You've caused a tremendous ruckus around here and uncovered a spy in my organization that I didn't even know existed."

"Oh," Joie said, surprised. "Good."

Until the government was cleaned up, they really didn't have a lot of ground to complain about the rest of society. The *Federales* were, at the end of the day, just the biggest and best-armed gang. Not necessarily the good guys.

Joie wasn't even sure she could apply that to the folks back home, particularly after the way they'd been treating her for the last two years. Maybe longer.

When had she gone rogue, mentally and emotionally?

Except that she knew the answer to that. The sound of her arm clicking, dying, sliding out of her sleeve, then rattling around on the floor. The sound of the electronics in her ear cooking. The smoke coming out of her eye socket as her cybereye committed seppuku.

Burned, in more ways than one.

Joie handed the other woman the bag of chocolates she'd picked up, resting the other bag in her lap.

"Ready for your vengeance now?" Ernesta asked as they started driving again, the driver on the other side of a panel that was dimmed.

"I don't know that I want revenge," Joie replied, opening her own bag for a chocolate caramel to nibble on as Ernesta did the same. She'd lived on heavy, peasant food for several days, with almost nothing sweet since she'd fled Virginia, so the chocolate was a heavy, sugary treat right now.

"Then what do you want, Daring?" Ernesta asked, turning serious.

"I want to be free of people knocking on my door or walking into the shop to bother me," she decided. "I could burn everyone back home if they really pushed me hard enough, but they haven't ever crossed that line. Not yet, anyway. I'm trying to find some answers about Romana and why she disappeared, but I only have one, slender thread to pull on. If it fails, then I have nothing except jackasses with pomposity and heavy weapons. *Mithras* went rogue, but I always wonder if he's gone back into the fold and I'm being pushed out."

"And how does that make you feel?" the woman asked, also nibbling. They were exceptional chocolates.

"Angry," Joie concluded. "They are acting like an ex-boyfriend who won't admit he made a mistake dumping me, but wants to get back together like nothing at all happened before."

"Oh, I know that feeling," Ernesta chuckled. "I have two ex-husbands who thought that being male gave them some manner of authority over me. Being single as a grandma is far better, as I can come and go as I like without having to deal with male ego."

"Is that why you are helping me?" Joie asked, curiosity piqued.

"Part of it," Ernesta turned serious. "Partly to poke a finger in their eyes. Partly because anything that causes them discomfort should be high on my list. For now, I needed to get out of town, lest they try to sweep me up, in spite of my various fixers, and disappear me for a while. Or forever. Those were Interior Ministry troops that you stomped on, not locals."

"Oh, shit," Joie groused.

She'd been hoping that they were just a local riot squad. *Federales* meant that Kehoe had called in some favors when they lost her and maybe found Celeste in Arizona. Interior Ministry goons meant they had brought out the heavy firepower and would turn all of Mexico into a trap.

Good thing she was hopefully on her way out of town.

Outside, the car rolled quickly through a security checkpoint that would have remembered Joie Daring passing. How often did you see a one-armed woman these days? Tall and muscular would have just doubled the odds.

The car took them around a central area that was less terminal and more country club proper. Joie remembered it from previous missions and visits. Six major restaurants plus something like one hundred little shops, but heavy security like stories of American shopping malls from a century ago.

Instead of pulling up there, they ended up inside a hangar, next to a big Dassault jet that was only a size down from a commercial airliner. Flying in luxury, as it were.

Inside, they were greeted by a pleasant and friendly staff. Joie found it telling that both pilots as well as both flight attendants were female. The only males present were two of the men who had been at the table a few hours ago when Joie Daring stepped into their lives.

She got seated and looked around. The inside was maybe six meters across, with the top and bottom chopped for storage. Deep, tan carpet on the floor. Comfortable leather seats and a pair of tables that could be desks.

Joie settled for and apple/orange juice blend, rather than anything with alcohol in it. Too long without drinking anything because she hadn't wanted to fall into a bottle with the rest of her depression. One glass of wine would probably be enough to knock her on her ass today.

Ernesta sat directly in front of her, but spun her seat around like two ladies in a coffee shop. The lawyers sat forward. They could still hear everything over the electric fans, but it provided an illusion of privacy.

About as good as Joie figured she could get right now. She kept wondering if she'd jumped out of the frying pan and into the fire, except that Ernesta Hernandez's organization had been around for more than a century today. It had almost turned into the Mexican equivalent of a Chinese Benevolent Society in many ways.

Same reason, too. Corrupt governments with racial caste overtones and strict limits on most of the population.

Did the whole world need to be burned down? Rebuild it from the ground up, without the various governments currently in place? Joie had been in enough places to know that crime, violence, and corruption had gotten even worse in her lifetime, in spite of the number of people she'd killed or apprehended.

Or was it because of those killings? Had she spent a decade upholding a crooked system? Making it worse? Or just trying to hold it all together so the punks at the top could continue looting countries for a bit longer?

She wasn't sure where they thought they might go if a true revolution broke out. Maybe build a space ship and fly to Alpha Centauri or something?

Joie blew out a heavy breath and drank half of her juice in one gulp.

"Sorry," she said as Ernesta looked concerned. "Heavy thoughts."

"I could see that," Ernesta replied. "Anything good?"

"Crisis of conscience at a career of mayhem, maybe?" Joie said. "I used to do a thing, and do it better than anybody. Not so sure now that what I was doing was righteous. Wondering if I was making it worse."

"We all have those days," Ernesta nodded, sipping more sedately at her drink. Joie hadn't inquired as to what was in it. "Some of the people you destroyed needed to be killed. I'd agree with that."

"But not all of them," Joie completed the thought, studying the woman.

Not as tall as Sarah. Taller than Celeste. Gray, mostly. Average build, so in between the other two women there as well. Dark eyes full of intellect. And laughter, if Joie was reading it correctly.

"Not all of them," Ernesta agreed. "Some were folks who just wanted to share the wealth around, instead of a small group of trillionaires having it all to themselves. They threatened the system, so those people brought in killers like you."

Joie nodded. Tool of oppression, when West Point taught that you were the freedom fighters.

But how many liberation organizations had she smashed? At how many places were elections a sham, returning someone to power again and again with ninety percent of the vote?

How much better had the world gotten, just in the last two years, without Captain Daring stomping on people who just wanted to be free?

She finished the juice and set the cup down as the jet started down the runway with a hard whine, then leapt into the sky.

"So what do you think you'll find in Argentina when you get there?" Ernesta asked after a few minutes when the plane leveled off.

Out the window, Joie could see ocean approaching, so the flight plan was apparently to get over international waters before the Mexican Air Force could give chase? Run out over the Pacific, avoiding Central America while headed to Chile, more or less? Radar and satellites could follow them, but you had to know which aircraft to be looking at.

How many enemies might be looking for them right now?

Joie sucked in a breath. Ernesta had asked a question.

"Something somebody said," she replied, leaving Mitch's name out of it. "I tracked *Mithras* to Argentina two years ago. Fought him there and captured him, but it was a hostile country to my kind, so I just loaded him onto a helicopter line and we rode out to a freighter off shore."

"That was your last mission?" Ernesta asked.

"Correct," Joie nodded. She waved to the flight attendant and gestured for more juice. More dehydrated than she had thought. "When we got back to DC, I got called into a meeting, where they…*decommissioned* me."

Joie hadn't meant for the amount of rage in her voice to slip out, but it had. Obviously, she felt comfortable around this woman, in ways that she only had with Sarah and Celeste.

Folks helping her because she was in need, rather than the men chasing her.

What did that say about the state of the world? Or at least her world?

"What a bland term," Ernesta replied, concern on her face. "They took your arm and your eye. Turned you out into the street with no explanation save threats to keep your mouth shut. Abandoned you. And now they want you back?"

Ernesta Hernandez's voice was filled with anger as well, but Joie didn't pretend to understand what might be causing it. Ex-husband, perhaps?

Joie nodded.

"So the only thread I have left at this point is the suggestion that maybe I must have seen something when I was stalking *Mithras*," Joie said. "Maybe I said something innocent at the time that led them to believe I knew more than I did, because the reaction was swift. Boom."

"And you don't know?" Ernesta asked.

"No clue," Joie acknowledged. "Romana vanished four months ago and everyone thinks I know something about that as well, even though I haven't seen her in nearly a year. Even the ex that we share last saw her six months ago."

"Ex you share?"

Joie spent a few minutes delicately editing out her last three years, covering her relationship with Mitch and how it fell apart when she couldn't drag herself to care anymore. Then how he and Romana got close, then parted.

"Sounds like a *telenovela*, Joie Daring," Ernesta said seriously. "Soap-opera-romance levels of crazy."

"I never claimed to be sane," Joie laughed. "And I have been on the outside for two years now, until Kehoe showed up to *chat* a few weeks ago."

"Which you wisely refused."

Joie nodded and shrugged. She wasn't certain on that one. Not anymore. Would they have just sweated her for a few days and then realized that she didn't know?

Or would their questions have given her the clues she needed to understand?

"That would have been the end of it, but *Mithras* walked into my coffee shop the next day," Joie said, watching Ernesta's eyes get big. "Middle of Arlington, Virginia, and he just bips in to say hi. Just like that."

"It was a trap," Ernesta breathed quietly.

"Yes, but whose?"

"You captured *Mithras* in Argentina and hauled him to prison, yes?" Ernesta pressed. "Colorado, or wherever they put people like him."

"Probably," Joie agreed. "I was having my own issues at that point."

Ernesta surprised her by reaching a hand and taking Joie's. Just held it with a squeeze, but Joie realized how much she had been craving human touch in that instant. Something melted in her stomach that she hadn't even been aware of.

The band of iron around her chest loosened.

"How did *Mithras* escape?" Ernesta asked. "I cannot imagine something that big could have possibly been kept quiet."

Joie nodded, finding her emotional balance a little wobbly right now and unwilling to speak.

"Absent any other evidence, I would presume he is working for Kehoe now," Ernesta continued. "Filling your shoes, as it were, though not as well. Nor as publicly."

"Not as well?" Joie squeaked.

"You took him down," Ernesta reminded her. "Nobody else had ever been able to do that."

"I'm half the woman I used to be."

"And they still fear you, Joie Daring," Ernesta pronounced. "Why else go through everything they have done? They wanted to prod you into motion, to see where you would run to. To find out what you knew."

"Nothing."

"Which they do not believe, because they are men," Ernesta growled. "Will us fleeing to Argentina draw them after you too soon?"

Joie stopped and considered that.

She'd been trying to get far enough away from Kehoe and Faulkener to breathe. She could have largely disappeared in Mexico had she wanted. Argentina, if she really had seen something, would draw them after her like hounds finally spotting the fox.

It helped, though, that Argentina as a culture hated nearly everything the US stood for. Too many years of attempting autarky and finding that you really did need to trade with the rest of the world. American banks and bankers. Still, they had a reputation going back centuries of borrowing money and then stiffing those same banks. Juan Perón's ghost still ruled over the place, however long it had been since the man had died.

"A wise woman once told me that hurt dogs howl," Joie said quietly. When Ernesta looked quizzical, she explained. "Only the guilty have a reason to react badly to an accusation. They want to distract you from learning too much. And keep everyone else from knowing that it's true."

"So if they chase you hard…"

"Then we're right that something down there caused it," Joie nodded. "Something they don't want the world to know about. What, I have no idea, but if they ignore me at that point, then I have nothing. And no idea what to do next."

"Next, you go on with starting your life over, Joie," Ernesta said. "You have already begun doing that, but it sounds to me like you only started in the last few weeks, after wasting two years."

Joie had nothing to say to that. Mostly because it was the honest truth.

Now, though, maybe she had something to look forward to.

CHAPTER 40

Carter had sat, sipping orange juice or Italian sodas, while the Mexican Army proved that nothing much had changed in the last ten years. Or maybe four hundred. They'd lost multiple wars with the United States, and hadn't forgotten that. At the same time, they were in no shape to try again, unless they wanted to add several dozen new stars to an American flag.

General Perez's screaming and ranting was finally winding down. Man had a stupid tolerance for alcohol, once he got a good head start. Carter had been sitting next to Kehoe for nearly two hours, quiet as church mice in a corner while messages and messengers came and went. The verbal abuse hardly wavered in that time. Up until now.

At one point, Kehoe had leaned over to ask something, but Carter had just waved him off. The extra time wouldn't matter, because there was no way in hell these incompetent fools were catching Joie Daring at this point.

Carter kind of felt like rubbing their noses in it.

General Perez finally yawned and departed, no doubt to discuss business with his two flight attendants from the plane. As one did.

Carter checked the time on his phone. Coming up on midnight, when they'd spotted her around four this afternoon.

He rose from his chair, mostly to make a physical statement when he spoke. It helped that he was thirteen centimeters taller than the next soldier in here. And ninety kilograms heavier.

He cleared his throat meaningfully at a nearby major. Not by chance the one who had briefed them when they first arrived.

"Sir?" the man looked up from where he and some enlisted men had been making marks on a paper map.

"I'd like a chance to shower and maybe have a nap while the pursuit boxes her in," Carter said, suggesting that they might really be in the process, rather than keystone-kopping their way around Guadalajara in Joie's wake. "Who would I need to talk to?"

The officer gestured to a corporal and the man stepped closer.

"Put these two in officer's quarters and make sure they have badges for everything," he ordered.

"Yes, sir."

Carter glanced back at Kehoe, but the man was already moving. They followed the pudgy corporal out into the cool, night air and across a quad covered over with grass rather than another parking lot. Almost felt like he was back walking around West Point, though he'd never attended the place. Still, military school campus. Calm, quiet, and green.

They got settled into a pair of bedrooms on the second floor, which was Carter's preference anyway. Easy enough to jump out a window in a hurry, but hard for someone else to climb in quietly.

They were alone as the corporal went off to find someone to get them badges. They would, after all, need to get into the gym, the kitchen, or the command post later, you know? Gotta be official.

For now, they were alone.

Kehoe closed the door and leaned against it as Carter tested to make sure the bed wouldn't collapse under him. They did that, occasionally.

"So we're probably about as alone as we'll get," Kehoe said. "What lit a fire under your ass, back on the jet?"

Carter nodded and relaxed. Bed probably wasn't going to shatter under him.

"We have been chasing Joie across country and now down into

Mexico," Carter said. "You did not have Celeste Graydon arrested in Arizona, but we presume that she drove Daring down from Seattle."

"We have not declared Daring a fugitive from justice," Kehoe said bluntly. "Perez is being an asshole for personal reasons, but I got overruled by Bouchard on that one. Graydon wasn't committing a crime."

"Just so," Carter continued. "But we know that Joie was also assisted by a conductor on the train. And the dispatcher at the station. And even the driver. That's before she gets to Graydon's mother and borrows first a car, and then the woman herself."

"So?"

"So with the exception of Mitchell Graydon, every single person that has helped Daring from Day One appears to be female. Including Amy Watanabe, that, cute, dangerous pixie manager of the coffee shop in Arlington."

"I still don't think Watanabe could kick your ass in a fair fight," Kehoe grinned at him. "But she has access to boiling water and coffee grounds, so she wouldn't fight fair."

Carter let that one go. Physically, the tiny woman was no match. At the same time, she'd impressed the hell out of him that day in her store. Not an easy thing to do.

Not a woman you wanted to cross. At the same time, maybe the kind he'd like to date. Carter liked them feisty.

"What conclusions have you reached?" Kehoe inquired, sounding more like a professor now.

"One, she doesn't trust men," Carter replied. "Excepting Graydon, and even then she got help from the man's mother. She somehow got to Guadalajara to ask Ernesta Hernandez for help. And apparently got it, because I seem to remember someone back in the other room saying that their source inside the Hernandez organization had suddenly gone dark. Plus, the woman in charge disappeared before the *Federales* could arrest her."

"You think Hernandez is helping her escape?" Kehoe asked.

"I think Hernandez escaped, and took Daring with her," Carter fired back. "Different scope. Plus, I'd like to know how Joie got across the border in the first place. I think Yuma was a red herring. Who else does she know across the California border that she might have contacted? Those are the things that I want to look up in your database."

"Hernandez helping Daring?" Kehoe asked. "Just like that?"

"Oh, the woman might think that Joie is some sort of deep cover agent trying to infiltrate," Carter allowed. "Hernandez wouldn't necessarily trust her up front, but might be running her now to establish her bonafides. I think you need to quietly go around Perez and ask Stone, back in Virginia, to put some resources on Ernesta Hernandez. Find her. Or at least see where she's going, so you can find Daring."

"Where would you go, if you were running from this scenario?" questioned him.

Kehoe moved to a chair. Carter had been rebuilt to not need a lot of sleep, because his muscles didn't build up toxins like a normal human's did. Mostly, four to six hours so the brain reset. However, Kehoe looked as though he'd been pulled backwards through a knothole at this point.

That was to Carter's benefit, though, as the man wouldn't be as sharp as normal. Nor as tight-assed.

Maybe even useful.

Carter smiled.

"She left DC and went straight to Seattle," he replied. "Contacted Mrs. Graydon, drove her car out to see the son, spent the night, and left. Immediately the next morning, both women started driving south, as Stone has tracked the license plate through Oregon and all of California. Then Daring crosses somewhere between Tijuana and Yuma, disappearing until she suddenly shows up in Guadalajara, which is one hell of a run, especially in a car."

"Away from us," Kehoe mused. "West when we were east. South when we were north. How much farther south does she go?"

Carter wondered if he'd just been struck by lightning from the jolt of insight that hit him. The bed frame squeaked so badly he thought it might rupture and dump him on his ass. Kehoe perked right up.

"What?" the man demanded.

Carter struggled to open his mouth and force the words out. It took three tries.

"How far south?" he finally managed to ask. "I've burned most of my former South American contacts in various outlaw and terrorist organizations in order to get back into your good graces, Kehoe. Your people are watching folks everywhere and she has to know that. I can only think of one place that stands out better than everywhere else south of Mexico City. La Plata, Argentina."

He watched Kehoe flinch now. Unconscious recoil he couldn't control fast enough. Fear. And guilt.

Carter played stupid, though.

"Returning to the scene of the crime?" Kehoe asked in a voice full of false bravado and *bonhomie*.

"As good an explanation as anything else I can come up with," Carter lied.

Kehoe knew something about the town. Something Carter had missed while he'd been there. Something that maybe he thought Daring had seen.

Granted, Carter had been hiding out from any number of folks while he'd been there. Lying low because La Plata was close enough to Buenos Aires to be quiet and relaxed, compared to the big city just up the coast. Thinking back, there had been a lot of interrogation centered on those two cities. Far more than Carter had felt was justified at the time.

Carter had gone there intending to disappear.

What the hell was TRC hiding in Argentina?

CHAPTER 41

Joie woke with a start from ugly nightmares. Being chased through a maze of hallways by monsters she couldn't identify, nor fight.

Ernesta had gone to a small aft cabin that Joie had originally mistaken for storage, but turned out to be an executive bedroom. Joie had passed on sleeping next to the woman, even though the bed looked comfortable.

She and the two lawyers without names were stretched out in chairs that mostly moved flat. Too many years on military transports, so she could rack out anywhere.

Usually without the nightmares, though.

One of the flight attendants approached, concern visibly etched on her face even with the lights in here dimmed so far.

"I'm okay," Joie told her, trying to convince both of them. "Maybe some water or a soda to drink?"

The woman left her alone and did something in the galley.

Outside, the sun was starting to come up, and all the shades were currently drawn. Joie lifted one just enough to know that dawn was approaching. They were over land now. Presumably Chile, if she cared enough to ask someone.

Buenos Aires was roughly ten or eleven hours flying time from Guadalajara. That much she knew. There was a relatively new airport, located near the old town of Cañuelas, southwest of downtown but not that far out. Buenos Aires had always struck Joie for how densely it was populated. Far more than anywhere in the US. Or even most cities outside of Asia, for that matter.

Good place to vanish. To hide.

Carter Faulkener had thought that it would cloak him from TRC, but Kehoe had gotten a tip from someone.

Who?

Up until now, she'd never really considered who might have been able to contact Kehoe or a TRC source to tell them that the infamous, wanted criminal **Mithras** was in town. Whoever it had been had seen the man, recognized him without being recognized themselves, then laid low long enough for Captain Daring to be called in.

That suggested someone in deep cover. Or also hiding out.

But Argentina had always been like that. After the second World War, one hundred and fifty years ago, a lot of Germans had emigrated down there. The running joke for generations had always been Nazis on the run from Israeli hunters and others, such as the old Soviet Union who had hated the fascists so much, back when Russia and the others had been a single place.

Now the nations of the former Soviet Union were mostly either happy, little European suburbs, or Chinese subsidiaries.

But there had always been a kernel of truth about people going to South America to hide.

She doubted that Romana would be there, but at least Joie could go back to the place where she'd found Carter. Look around and see what she saw.

But could she? If whoever it was had known *Mithras* on sight, they would likely know her as well. Worse, it wouldn't be that hard to capture her, if they really knew who she was.

And it wasn't like the old days, or even the movies, where she could allow herself to be captured, confident that her cyberware was deadly enough to help her break out.

After all, if you didn't know she had a fusion rifle hidden in her right palm, you'd be infinitely surprised. For about a half second.

She missed having two hands. Not enough to ever trust Kehoe again, but maybe *Uno* could find or commission something for her. Kehoe was making more warriors like her these days, which would mean more research, and technology like that wanted to be free.

Maybe it should be.

But walking around the streets of La Plata sounded like a slow and stupid way to commit suicide. Especially after coming this far.

Could she ask an even bigger favor of Ernesta? She was already going to owe one of the middle-tier of Mexican crime bosses seriously for this. More would be adding interest.

Except that Joie might finally be angry enough to burn it all down. Destroy whatever TRC was doing in Argentina. Maybe with the help of the Argentine government if it was a secret from them, too.

The woman returned from up front with a fizzy, yellow glass.

"Thank you," Joie said as she accepted it. "I didn't catch your name earlier. I'm Joie."

"Ximena," the flight attendant replied with a smile. "Just wave or yell if you need anything. We should be arriving in about three hours now. Breakfast will be in about an hour."

"Thank you, Ximena," Joie nodded.

Mitch had helped. At least as much as she'd allowed. The spark that had been there wasn't anymore. She wasn't sure she wanted to pursue it, either. Might be a burned bridge.

The *Pedros* had helped, but she'd always been closer to Sarah than even *Uno*, staying that first time at the hacienda under Sarah's invitation.

At each step, she had been helped by a woman. One seeing another woman in need.

The thought was still so alien that Joie found herself marveling at it. Too many years in green, obviously, where you trusted your team and nobody else. Not enough thinking like a civilian.

Joie flipped her seat upright. She'd slept enough. More would tempt her to fall back into that nightmare, and she had better things to think about.

Like, how could she convince a relative stranger to help her take down the entire United States military.

CHAPTER 42

Joie looked up as Ernesta emerged. There was a small shower back there, but Joie hadn't invited herself to use it. Ernesta, however, looked ready for a catwalk, even wearing simple blue jeans and a silk blouse in a soft mustard color that really brought out the olive tones of her skin.

The smell of bacon, chorizo, and eggs frying filled the aircraft with a taste of home that had Joie's stomach rumbling and pangs of homesickness poking her in the shoulder.

She didn't have a home. Instead, she had an apartment where she kept some stuff and slept. Sifu Wěn's dojo. The coffee shop.

No place with roots.

Taylor Kehoe had done that to her. Burned her and kicked her out of the Army, which had replaced the family she'd mostly cut ties with in the first place.

She owed him one.

More than one.

Ximena delivered a mug of coffee. Joie could testify that it was good coffee after a single sip.

"You're welcome to the shower," Ernesta said as she took a nearby seat.

Joie considered it. She had spare clothes in her messenger bag, scrunched down for travel. It was fall in the southern hemisphere, so she'd kept the jacket.

"After breakfast," she decided aloud, letting the scent overwhelm her a little.

Ernesta smiled.

"Did you sleep well?" she asked.

"Some," Joie admitted. "Stress nightmares, but that's nothing new. I have a different issue, once I put my waking brain to it."

"Oh?"

"*Mithras*, the agent Carter Faulkener, was spotted in La Plata, a suburb a little south down the coast from Buenos Aires," she explained. "Whoever spotted him was not seen themselves. When I got there, Carter wasn't part of a group, but hiding on his own, so whoever tipped off my bosses wasn't a disgruntled employee turned mole, like you had yesterday. I was hoping I could ask a second, possibly bigger favor. I'm not sure how I'd be able to pay you back, but without your help, I don't have any freedom left, so I'm verging on desperate."

Ernesta studied her for a long moment, then got interrupted when Ximena and Consuela, the other flight attendant, delivered plates of food with huevos rancheros like Mom used to make. Joie had missed the smell of potato cubes frying, or flour tortillas, possibly freshly made this morning.

On an airplane.

Joie mentally took a step back and considered just how much money and power a woman like Ernesta Hernandez must have, to be able to do all this.

To just fly to Argentina to escape a manhunt, on her own, private jet airliner, taking a couple of lawyers with her at the drop of a hat.

Captain Daring had existed inside the bubble of the US military for a long time, first as the daughter of two soldiers, then as one herself. When all that had been taken away from her, she'd had a pension and a job cleaning and stocking a coffee shop, because even making most drinks required two hands that she didn't have.

Money. And power.

Joie was watching the woman eat and realizing that Ernesta was possibly in the same league as Kehoe, bizarre as that might seem.

"What favor would you like to ask, Joie?" Ernesta replied as they ate.

Joie decided to gamble for everything. It might be a deal with the devil, but what did she have to lose at this point? Her freedom was at risk for as long as Kehoe thought he could run her or mess with her head. She didn't know anything today with which to force them to leave her alone, but maybe, just maybe, there was a piece of the puzzle in La Plata that would help.

"If I'm right, the same people who knew Carter Faulkener on sight in La Plata will know me as well," Joie said, consigning herself to the gods who might find favor for her. "Worse, I probably won't recognize them."

"You'd like me to go looking around?" Ernesta asked with a slight grin.

"Someone who works for you," Joie corrected. "You shouldn't be out there risking yourself for me. Doubly so if they now know we're associated, at least enough for your picture to be circulated."

Ernesta smiled. She had dimples that Joie had missed earlier. Perhaps this was the first honest emotion Joie had seen?

"I don't have anyone with me good enough," she said mirthfully. "But I have an idea. Let me make a few phone calls and we can have some people waiting for us who will help."

Joie started to interrupt. To say something. Anything. Ernesta waved her to silence, still smiling.

What had Joie gotten herself into?

CHAPTER 43

Taylor had brought a laptop computer with him from DC. It had enough signals encryption to receive files from Stone without Taylor worrying about man-in-the-middle attacks. Or someone accessing the data, even if they stole the machine itself when he wasn't looking.

He was back in his barracks room, wracking his brain about Argentina and trying to remember how much Faulkener knew. He was pretty sure he'd covered that momentary blip when Faulkener mentioned the place.

Taylor was certain the man didn't understand why La Plata was so important to TRC. Nobody knew. Closed secret you had to practically be initiated with a branding iron to even know about, let alone learn about the innards.

He slowly and methodically worked through connecting with the servers back in DC to pull some files. Those were even more secure than CIA Headquarters at Langley, but it was necessary.

Even Presidents didn't get to know about this stuff. They were politicians. Nobody in their right mind trusted those folks.

Taylor pulled down the files on the *La Plata Incident*, as it was generally known, and opened them to review. Carter Faulkener spotted, which had turned out, near as Taylor and anyone else could figure, to be one of those bizarre, random coincidences that caused gamblers and fiction writers to throw up their hands in disgust.

But the facility was so critical, so sensitive, that Taylor had thrown Daring at him immediately. *Dead or alive* had been because nobody honestly believed that the latter option was possible. Not even with Joie Daring.

She'd proved them all wrong.

These days, he wasn't sure if she had lied during her debriefs after bringing *Mithras* in. Did *Mithras* somehow know the truth? Had he told her, and used that as leverage to be taken alive?

That had been the crux of the decision from the top to burn her. And to throw Faulkener's ass into a concrete box with zero privileges save cable television until he broke or talked.

The man had ended up talking. Burned all of the organizations he knew about in South America. There were a lot fewer freedom fighters and independence movements down there these days.

Taylor still didn't know if he'd broken the man. Carter Faulkener was designed, physically and mentally, to be an escape artist. To lie and mislead until he could penetrate your organization and destroy it.

Right up until the day he'd changed sides and gone into private business.

Did he know about La Plata?

Taylor sighed and checked his watch. Two in the morning. Faulkener was probably napping. Taylor would need sleep soon, and a lot of coffee in the morning.

And help.

He typed a message to Bouchard and almost felt the first stirrings of the avalanche start down the mountain.

Faulkener might go rogue again. And he might discover things he wasn't supposed to know.

Taylor Kehoe wanted an insurance policy in place.

CHAPTER 44

Joie studied the woman as Ernesta came into the hotel room and felt her jaw drop open. Ernesta grinned.

"You see?" Ernesta asked. "Magic."

Joie had to agree.

Ernesta had called a stylist. Not just any stylist. A sorceress.

Her hair was now the same rich black that Joie's was, at least for a few more years. Makeup had done things to change the shape of her face. And make her look forty, instead of the sixty that she'd been a few hours ago.

She had changed into jeans that did something to the way her legs and rear looked. Joie was tall and muscular. Sarah was tall and lean. Celeste short and squishy.

Ernesta had transformed like a rich tourist, a divorcée perhaps, out for some fun with the way her hair had been pulled back and held in place with a gold-colored band.

"I wouldn't recognize you," Joie admitted.

Ernesta smiled.

"I haven't always been in charge of things, dear," she replied. "My grandfather got me started in the business when I was fourteen, running errands and small missions as I learned the ropes. I didn't really have a desk job until my father took over when I was twenty-four and had a degree in accounting and two children."

Joie laughed at that, wondering what that woman must have been like.

They were in a hotel in Buenos Aires proper. A nice place down on the waterfront, with a view of the Atlantic in the distance, more or less. The plane was back at Cañuelas being refueled and serviced for departure on short notice.

Both women agreed that Kehoe would be along just as soon as he could track the aircraft down here and find a plane himself, so they might need to go right back to Mexico where she had the resources to hide better.

Joie figured that they had about sixty hours at this point. At most.

Joie was sitting on the bed closer to the window, where she had been watching television for any news. Ernesta had a spot on the other bed.

Someone knocked.

"Oh, good," Ernesta said, popping right up and walking to the door with no explanation.

Other than she had apparently been expecting someone.

"Come in," Ernesta said to whoever it was.

Joie watched her lead a well-dressed, middle-aged woman in, holding an anvil case similar to the ones her cyberarms had been transported in. Ernesta gestured Joie to stand.

"Take off your shirt, dear," Ernesta ordered.

Joie was confused, but complied. She wasn't wearing anything under it right now, mostly because bras were a pain in the ass, even if she generally didn't need one to hold hers up. They were fake, after all. Inserted at the same time she'd gotten the bullet-proof lining to go from a B cup to a D.

She'd have almost preferred if Kehoe had found a way to remove them, too, but she'd learned to live with men—and women—staring at her chest a lot.

The stranger opened her case and Joie gasped.

It held an arm.

"Is that…?" she managed.

The stranger moved around to look at Joie's stump. The dock that contained anchors to her ribs and clavicle, plus all the electronics. Ten centimeters of matte black plastic with gold rings and connectors.

"US Army issue?" the woman asked in a voice with an Italian accent.

"That's right," Joie said automatically. "Experimental program."

"Yes, I can see," she replied.

The woman pulled a pocket scanner and began analyzing Joie's stump as Joie fought not to fidget.

"Okay, I think I can make it work," she announced after a few moments. "Won't work well. Won't fool anyone, so don't get naked unless they are expecting it."

"What?" Joie gasped. "How?"

The stranger ignored her and started tinkering with the arm. Joie turned to Ernesta.

"There is a lot of technology research going on around here," Ernesta replied. "It won't be, as she said, as good as your old arm, but if it works, even a little, you don't stand out for being Joie Daring."

Joie felt tears just pour down her face. Her brain turned to white noise for a few seconds, and she found herself in Ernesta's arms, sniffling and blinking as the woman held her and made comforting noises.

"Thank you," Joie managed to hiccup. "I…"

"Hush," Ernesta said. "Let's see if it works first."

Joie dutifully stood still as the other woman lifted the arm out of the box and approached. She fiddled with it for a second and then socketed it with a loud snap that seemed to ring all the way through Joie's soul.

Automatically, she glanced up and right for the heads up display that no longer existed. It would have initiated a full diagnostics check of a new arm before she went out into the field.

Could she get a new eye on the black market, one of these days? What would Ernesta ask for such a favor?

What would Joie offer?

The scientist woman pulled an impact hammer now and screwed in anchor bolts with a loud whir and a hard ratcheting clank. Joie watched her open up a panel on the inside of the wrist and toggle a switch.

All of a sudden, her hand twitched, like it had fallen asleep and was waking up with that nasty tingle she only got with her left one now.

"Pain?" the woman asked.

"Discomfort, centered on the middle two fingers and ranging over the back of the hand," Joie said automatically.

Just like the old days with TRC when they were tuning her arm.

Shit, she was ambidextrous again?

The woman started adjusting things. The pain increased so sharply that Joie yelped and flinched, then dialed down to nothing other than the woman holding her hand.

Joie was crying again. Or still. It was hard to tell.

Both of the other women were sniffly as well.

The nameless scientist woman pulled a racketball out of the case and put it in Joie's hand.

Joie squeezed it a few times, reveling in something so simple as that. It had been two years.

"Lift your arm," she commanded.

Joie did. It didn't move as naturally or as fluidly, but it actually moved. Good enough to eat. Maybe even to put her hair in a braid.

Hell, trainers with laces instead of velcro or inflatable bladders. The future was bright.

Joie wondered if her face would crack from the smile.

"Okay," the woman decided. "This is about as good as I can get it without custom building a new one. There is a charger in the case. Your batteries should last about two days of normal use. I'll leave the impact hammer in case you need to take it off for some reason, but I doubt that you'd be able to get it back on correctly if you did, so only in an emergency, or she can call and I'll come out. Assuming you are still in Buenos Aires and not north. Questions?"

Joie opened her mouth, but nothing came out. All she had at this point was tears.

The woman finally smiled at her. An honest smile. Then she turned to Ernesta when it was clear Joie couldn't speak.

"This is why I do it, madam," she said, pointing at Joie. "That right there makes all the frustration and late nights worth it."

Joie hugged her. With both hands. Hugged Ernesta. Boggled.

After the nameless scientists left, Joie remembered to grab her shirt and put it back on.

"Ernesta, I don't know…" she started to say.

"Hush, Joie," Ernesta said. "Just the look on your face made it all worthwhile. Now, it's mid-afternoon. Let's go have an early dinner to celebrate and we can plan how we'll go after your two-timing ex-boyfriend."

Joie wouldn't have classified Taylor Kehoe that way, but when you did, suddenly it became two angry women looking for the sorts of revenge that went well with ice cream sundaes.

Joie found herself looking forward to the future again.

CHAPTER 45

Ernesta enjoyed the transformation that almost made her look like Joie Daring's older sister, rather than being old enough to be the warrior's mother. She'd been hesitant at first, assuming that the US government was attempting some bizarre infiltration of her organization, after ignoring her for so long.

But if that was their mission, Ernesta really couldn't imagine a less competent method for doing it. No, at this point she was more convinced that the Americans were hunting Joie for the sake of what she might know. In that case, how quickly would they race to Argentina?

Ernesta smiled. Her jet could be impounded, but she doubted that the Americans would get far, making such demands of a nation that had spent centuries angrily thumbing their noses at the United States. Even Mexico would be told off as the American's yappy lapdog this time around.

She should be safe for now.

So she had brought the newly re-invigorated Joie Daring with her today, walking the streets of La Plata as they slowly worked their way inwards. Joie's makeup was intended to make her look like a niece, with her hair up and colors overdone enough to suggest a woman in her early twenties, instead of mid-thirties.

They both wore jeans and T-shirts like Spaniards on vacation, along with light jackets against the bit of autumn chill gathering.

Hopefully, nobody would take notice of two women out being tourists. Especially when they had four arms between them. The morning was waning. Folks would start thinking lunch thoughts soon, perhaps wandering into one of the sidewalk cafes on both sides of this street. Or the coffee shops where retirees and middle-class mothers with young children were meeting to bitch about their lives, their families, and their spouses.

It was a thing as old as civilization.

Ernesta walked with Joie's flesh hand in hers, just like two friends or close relatives.

She'd almost forgotten how much fun field work could be.

"How close?" she leaned over and whispered to the taller woman.

"About three blocks up on the right," Joie replied quietly.

The place that *Mithras* had originally gone to ground. A bit past the pedestrian and cultural center of things where she was standing. Where buildings started being commercial on the ground floor and residential above. Ernesta had invested in enough such developments in Guadalajara to understand the cultural impact of anchoring neighborhoods. The Americans had forgotten it in the twentieth century, then spent most of the twenty-first recovering it.

Around them, Ernesta studied the ebb and flow of human need. Several governments might accuse her of being a smuggler and a criminal, but she was a businesswoman. If they hadn't made things illegal, the regular market would have supplied folks with their needs. Unlike her old nemesis Obrador, she had never felt the urge to get into guns and armies. And Joie herself had seen to that man.

Ernesta just met people's needs. Drugs, booze, pirated videos, imported luxury goods nobody had paid taxes on. La Plata seemed to be doing a relatively decent job of things, but even the last few blocks Ernesta had been able to spot a number of ways she could improve things around her, if she chose to invest.

Maybe she should. The Mexican government might decide to be

shits to her for a while. At least until the Americans stopped complaining again and everyone could get back to business as usual. So it might be worth investing some funds down here. All manner of organizations had been broken up by government crackdowns over the last year or two. The locals might be open to foreign money again.

Even aboveboard.

"Let's get some coffee," Ernesta said, mostly to give them a chance to edge out of the crowd of pedestrians on the sidewalk and just stand, watching for trouble.

Ernesta found all her old skills suddenly percolating again, even though it had been more than thirty-five years since she'd been in the field running missions and agents with a pistol in her pocket. Old dogs and new tricks? Maybe it really was like riding a bicycle. Joie would have been in diapers then.

Ernesta pulled the woman to a coffee stand and laughed out loud for the sheer joy of being alive today. Others looked at her a little sideways, but she always considered their type to be *little people*.

Little lives. Little dreams. Little merit. Bitter and sour.

She had dreamed big, and been able to achieve them. Having a lot of money helped.

Most of the folks in earshot wouldn't have known how to dream.

Maybe that was why she was helping Joie? Everything that the woman had been through, all that they had done to her, hadn't broken Joie's spirit. Just her body, and that could be repaired.

And what good was it having money if you couldn't do crazy shit with it every once in a while?

She ordered them drinks, refusing to allow Joie to spend her dollars or pesos. She might yet need them, if they got separated.

Ernesta got to watch the sheer joy in Joie's face when she was able to pick up a mug of coffee with her new arm and take a sip without spilling any. It didn't have the strength or capabilities that legend had assigned to the woman, but she had two hands now.

What could she dream?

After they got their drinks, Ernesta moved them off to a low wall nearby where others were resting. It wasn't yet hot. Might not get there with the ocean so close on a pleasant, autumn day.

"So how did you approach?" Ernesta asked her new partner in crime.

"We couldn't do a lot of scouting, but I did my standard walk-through of the neighborhood, just to get the feel for the geography and geometry," Joie replied, sipping and flashing back from the way her good eye flitted about. "Started back a little, and circled in. Mostly people spotting. What are you expecting?"

Ernesta tried to find the words to explain it. She'd never met *Mithras* in person, nor even hired him for anything because he'd been in the violence business, and she rarely ever needed guns to achieve her goals. Bribes always worked so much better, once you took the time to understand what the person across the table really wanted.

"He was seen," Ernesta said. "That means *someone* saw him. The better restaurants and shops are on this *avenida*, where we are right now. He would walk from there to here and back. Whoever saw him most likely saw him along this stretch."

"Agreed," Joie said carefully. "When I walked it, both streets out from here sideways are more residential, as are things beyond where he was. How do we tell?"

"I don't know," Ernesta admitted. "But they thought you saw something, whoever they are, so I expect it to be along this stretch of road."

"What's around us?" Joie asked.

"Offices for the most part," Ernesta said, looking around while she sipped. "But this feels right."

Ernesta pulled out the burner phone she had picked up yesterday upon landing and dialed. She waited for an answer and gave her location.

"Pull the business records for everyone within three blocks that is not a retail shop," she ordered. "Lawyers, accountants, insurance, anything. Specifically, second story offices or higher, then assemble them for when we get back to the hotel… Good. Thank you."

Ernesta hung up and smiled. Joie's eyes were a little big. That poor girl really didn't understand what those two men did for her. The ancient term for them was *Fixers*. Whenever she had a problem with the law, they *fixed* it, whether it was a beat cop who might be honest, all the way up to a Governor who was getting greedy or had the wrong minions serving him. Today, they would be bribing folks for records that might not be readily available.

Because they had all manner of connections they could contact, even in foreign countries.

"Now," Ernesta smiled. "Let us go down and see about the so-called scene of the crime."

CHAPTER 46

Taylor studied the morning sun out the briefing room window. Gray and hazy. Kind of like how he felt, at the end of a long, restless night. He held an oversized mug of black coffee and listened to the major from yesterday update everyone on the fact that they'd lost her.

He wasn't surprised. Joie Daring. Reactivated herself. Enough said?

Ernesta Hernandez also disappearing was a novel wrinkle, but Taylor understood Faulkener's theory about the two of them heading south. Hopefully, Stone would be able to confirm it, sometime this morning. The man had been up early and was an hour ahead of him.

Faulkener sat like a prize student in the front row, looming over the other officers by half a head at least. Taylor assumed it was the man's way of saying *I told you so* without saying it.

"That's it?" Perez demanded.

At least he was just peevish this morning, and not screaming or ranting. Must have gotten a visit from his mistresses last night. Taylor made a mental note to thank whoever that was when he had a chance. Otherwise, he might break down and punch the stupid fucker in the mouth at some point.

"All avenues have come up empty, General," the major replied, carefully rigid so he didn't flinch. "The woman, women, have disappeared. I have alerted local garrisons to be on the lookout and contacted our various spies. It remains to see what they can discover."

Taylor watched Faulkener turn, slowly and deliberately, looking over his shoulder until they made eye contact.

"So that's it, then?" he asked in a mild voice. "Maybe we should return to DC where we can engage all our resources there to help? What do you think, Kehoe?"

Taylor bit his tongue. Faulkener already knew that most of TRC and friends in the CIA were turning North America upside down looking for the woman. He didn't need to be there to hold their hands.

Faulkener wanted out of this room. Out of this city. Out of this country. And he was even asking politely, wonder of all wonders.

Taylor started to reply when his phone chirped with a message.

* *Transport inbound Guadalajara.* Pakhet *aboard. Mark II.* — Bouchard *

Taylor read it again and did a few translations in his head.

Pakhet was the code name of Lt. Freya Malik, the cybernaut woman who had accompanied him to visit Daring that first time as a bodyguard. Mark II meant that she was equipped with the cyberarm that had a fusion rifle in it.

Faulkener might be all that and a bag of chips in close combat. Bulletproof for the most part. A XM24E4 *Sunbolt* Cyberarm rifle would still fuck the man up seriously at anything less than forty meters. All the Argenite plating protecting his skull would still melt if you got it hot enough.

He wondered if she had packed along her Mark III arm. The XM29E1 *Supernova* Heavy Cyberarm cannon that made no pretense of being an arm at all, as it was just a barrel attached to the shoulder.

That one would blow daylight all the way through Faulkener's internal armor. Maybe any civilians standing too close behind him, too.

Taylor rose. All heads had rotated at the sound. All eyes were now rapt.

"I've just gotten a message from DC," he said, rather unnecessarily. "General Bouchard is sending a transport with a messenger aboard.

Obviously, something so top secret that he can't even transmit it, so I'll meet with that person when they arrive and update everyone. Until then, we'll get out of your hair and let you run your operation, gentlemen."

Faulkener hadn't even waited until Taylor was finished to pop up out of his chair. He got to the door faster than Taylor could and was gone without even a cheery wave. Taylor followed.

But then, Faulkener knew how good DC's signals encryption was. Bouchard could have simply told him to check his mail and let Taylor log into their computers from here to read it. Faulkener understood. Perez probably didn't.

You didn't need a messenger.

Unless she was a killer.

Then the message was perfectly clear.

CHAPTER 47

Joie fought to keep her emotions balanced. The last month had been a complete whipsaw that way. She was just glad she was menstrual mid-cycle right now. Everything *plus* her period and she'd either be randomly crying or ranting right now.

La Plata brought with it flashbacks and nightmares that had plagued her for years. She'd fucked up here, somehow, in taking Carter alive. However insane that was, just to contemplate. The Brass had assumed she'd cut a deal with the man to let him live, when really she'd been proving to *everyone* that she was the best in the business.

Nobody had ever been able to take *Mithras* out. She'd taken him down instead. Even better.

The rest of you were junior varsity.

And it had destroyed her life.

Cast her into the abyss. Into purgatory.

Maybe into hell itself.

All of that emotion wrapped cold, slimy fingers around her soul as she walked. If not for Ernesta, holding her hand, she felt like she'd be swept out to sea on an irresistible tide at any moment.

Worse, she could feel a paper cup of coffee in her new hand, which awakened all manner of joy and wonder, at odds with the darkness, until everything was kind of gray inside.

The revolver under her jacket was both an anchor and a balloon. It held her back, but stopped her from flying randomly away.

Joie was willing to admit that she was a little fucked up emotionally right now.

She walked with careful deliberation, trying to look like nobody in particular.

"You okay?" Ernesta asked.

"Holding it together," Joie admitted. "Not going to push much beyond that."

"That's fine, Joie," the woman nodded, leaning her weight inward a little onto Joie. "I've got you."

Joie opened her mouth. Closed it again.

"What?" Ernesta asked.

"Why?" Joie finally asked. "That's the part I don't understand."

"Why am I helping you?" Ernesta replied.

"Yeah."

"It's complicated," the woman said. "But partly, because everything they did to you didn't break you. Didn't make you bitter. Didn't cut short your dreams. On the personal side, you want to hurt the same people I do, so that makes us allies, at least for a while. Mostly, because you needed a friend."

Joie felt those words hit her like a garbage truck.

She hadn't had friends.

Ex-lovers like Mitch. Former partners that had given up on her in Romana. A fantastic boss in Amy. Pretty nice co-workers, but they were all a decade younger than her, so she didn't hang out with them outside work.

Even Sifu Wěn was her teacher. A sculptor who saw her as a block of granite that might be formed into art, given time and patience.

She didn't have friends.

She didn't have friends.

Joie choked back a sob. Ernesta felt it, because she suddenly dragged Joie off to the inner edge of the sidewalk through the other pedestrians. Got her up against the building and wrapped arms around her. Joie did the same, letting the woman hold her upright for a moment as she tried to find a new center of equilibrium.

The only way to do that was to let everything go.

Everything.

Mitch. Romana. Even that asshole Kehoe.

Dare she just walk away? Throw up her hands and let La Plata go?

She could start building a new future, but in her soul Joie knew that they would never stop chasing her. If she came to rest, Kehoe or Faulkener would show up, maybe kicking in the door next time, to drag her into custody and strip her mind and soul bare.

Fuck that.

Joie sucked a breath deep and hard into her soul and felt it fan a bed of coals she hadn't even known were there until they suddenly came alight.

She went from shivering to burning up in a heartbeat.

Ernesta felt it as well, because the woman released the hug and stepped back, studying her face.

Movement to Joie's right caught her attention.

Or rather, lack of movement. A still point in the middle of the sidewalk, where a man had suddenly stopped walking, with other pedestrians brushing or jarring against him until they adjusted.

He was staring at her, eyes wide and mouth open.

"You," he mouthed, no sound coming out.

The man started to turn, to flee her.

"Stop!" Joie barked hard at him.

It was just natural for her right arm to come up, fist closed and finger pointed at the man.

"Do not move!"

He froze in place like a granite statue and turned gray.

Gray?

His natural color was more Anglo-German than most of the traffic around here, but Argentina had just about every color under the sun, after so many centuries of immigration.

An Anglo like him was really pink with a brown tan normally, compared to her more olive-red tones. Shock should cause all the blood to drain out of his face, making everything more white.

His skin had a gray pallor that was utterly unnatural.

Unnatural?

What the hell was going on around here?

Three steps and Joie had hold of the man's wrist, using her replacement arm. It didn't have the strength to crush bones, unlike her old one, but it was good enough to pin an unresisting man in place.

"Come with me," Joie growled in an ugly tone, tugging now to drag him back into the eddy by the wall.

Ernesta was there suddenly, politely picking the man's pockets. They got him into a doorway.

The man was a little shorter than her. Broad but not fat, like a martial artist who added bulk when he wasn't going to have height.

Brown hair clipped short, but that English brown rather than her Hispanic roots. Blue eyes that wanted to fade over into sea gray. Still wide open with shock. Looked right about fifty, but a well-preserved fifty, rather than the used-up kind.

"If you move, I will hurt you," Joie promised vengefully.

She had no idea who the man was. None whatsoever.

Anyone suddenly recognizing her on the streets of La Plata, Argentina, however, worked for Taylor Kehoe and Technology Research Command.

Had he been the one who had accidentally seen Carter walking these streets, two years ago? Not been spotted in return, so he had been able to call in for a strike team that consisted of Captain Daring?

To take down one of the most dangerous criminals in the world?

And her as well.

"Sal McKenzie," Ernesta said, flipping his wallet open in one hand to read the name.

In her other hand, Ernesta held a…

It screamed weapon. Shaped vaguely like a pistol, with a handle, a barrel, an upper receiver, and a trigger assembly. Everything done in a dull, matte gray that wanted to absorb sunlight. It felt more like plastic than metal. Ernesta had it pointed at the man, so she thought it was deadly.

Joie made a snap decision.

"Sal, I'm Joie Daring, but you already knew that," she said. "Nod if you understand me. Do not speak at all."

Still gray. Still on the verge of hyperventilating as he watched her.

Captain Daring had two hands again. Did that mean she had her *Sunburst* fusion rifle ready to shoot someone?

Sal nodded. It was more like a spasm, forward and back, but it conveyed what she needed.

"He have anything else?" Joie asked her partner in crime.

Ernesta pocketed the wallet and braced the fellow rather expertly. Better than Joie could have done it as a matter of fact.

"Phone. Pocket change."

The woman pocketed it all, then tapped his shins with her foot, checking for an ankle holster.

"He's clean, at least until we get him someplace quiet enough to be thorough."

Sal turned to look at Ernesta. His eyes got even bigger.

"Don't give me a reason to shoot you, pal," Ernesta smiled at him.

Again, the spasm of a nod.

Shock could be a bitch.

Joie took his right hand with her left. Flesh on flesh. His felt clammy and cold, but she put that down to his emotional signature.

And all the rage coursing through her body right now.

Josefina Dearing didn't really believe in angry, vengeful gods. Right now, however, she had to consider the possibility that one of them had a black, almost English sense of humor.

"You are going to accompany us back to our hotel, Sal," Joie instructed him. "It's not far. You are going to behave. You are going to answer some questions. In return, we won't hurt you. Is that clear?"

At least he was starting to recover. The nod this time almost felt natural.

Joie started walking, dragging her newest friend along like a boyfriend who didn't want to go shopping for shoes but was going anyway.

Ernesta fell in behind them, no doubt prepared to unleash mayhem if she had to.

Joie hadn't planned on turning her new friend into another field agent. At the same time, the woman had been doing it since before Joie was born, so she might remember a few things.

Joie just wanted to get some answers.

She smiled over at Sal to convey the simple understanding that this could go two ways.

Only one of which he would like.

CHAPTER 48

Carter held his peace. Something had gone a little wrong, but not terribly so. Freya Malik, the nasty piece of work known generally by the codename *Pakhet*, was good. Maybe exceptional.

Not Joie's match.

Still, her being here meant that Kehoe didn't trust him to be the heavy when it came time to take Daring down. Or, more likely, Bouchard or someone at a senior level. Kehoe had been playing things pretty straight up until now. And he hadn't seemed all that pleased with developments, either.

They had gone across the airport to meet the plane. One of those long-range military jobbies that could fly seemingly forever, because they had hybrid engines burning fuel to generate power on top of the immense battery packs.

Carter was seated in a comfortable chair about as far forward, as far from *Pakhet*, as he could get without being rude about it. She smiled at him like she knew he was uncomfortable.

He wasn't, but it made a good game to play on the woman. She was just a soldier. A tank on two legs with a cannon in her right arm. Just like Joie had been. Even when she'd been better.

Malik wasn't his match, let alone hers.

Still, he let himself appear even a shade nervous as Kehoe got settled and the hatch closed. Unlike Perez's plane, this one had a couple of Air Force punks handling things. Both male. Grumpy E-6s, but they were all smiles when looking this way. Like they knew Kehoe was more than just a civilian.

Outside, a fuel truck was filling the wing tanks to make the run to Argentina.

Carter was all ears as Kehoe turned to include him in the conversation with *Pakhet*.

"So we all know that they'll likely never find Daring," he told the woman. "Hernandez's jet is currently on the ground just outside Buenos Aires. As soon as we can get clearance, we'll be joining them."

He checked his watch.

"We should hit the ground there around 10 pm local time," Kehoe continued. "If we assume they went straight there from here, that means they've had a full day head start on us, but only one."

"They going to ground?" Malik asked.

She'd been out of this loop, while Carter had been inside from the beginning.

"We think they will be heading to La Plata," Kehoe replied.

Carter caught the meaningful glance the woman gave Kehoe. She was assuming scene of the crime kind of thing. Like he would have, had he not caught that moment of falseness from Kehoe last night.

There was something in La Plata that Carter wasn't supposed to know about. Daring, either, but her going there suggested that maybe she did.

She'd been entirely out of the game for two years. How had she figured it out?

Carter didn't give voice to his frustrations. Just scowled at Malik and watched her ghost of a grin in response.

"Once in La Plata, we'll get rooms at a hotel downtown," Kehoe said. "Much of the city is walkable, like New York, so we won't bother with a car immediately."

"Can we get transport in a hurry if we need it?" Carter asked anyway.

"We can," Kehoe nodded, confirming that they had far more resources in that town than he'd ever imagined.

Shit, had he known that, he'd have stayed in Bogota.

"What are we looking for?" Malik said now.

"I have recent surveillance pictures of both women," Kehoe said, pulling things from the travel bag where he kept his computer.

Must have gotten them from the Mexicans when Carter wasn't looking. He reminded himself to pay closer attention. Taylor Kehoe was still an exceptional spymaster in spite of the fact that Joie had made him look bad. She made everyone look bad.

Captain Daring.

Malik was just a killer with a heavy shotgun. Not even all that dangerous if he could get far enough away from her. Say, one hundred meters over iron sights with armor-piercing ammunition.

Kehoe passed them each a pair of printouts.

Joie, looking worn and tired, standing next to a punk in a badly-tailored suit in front of Hernandez's restaurant, at the place where she'd shown up on everyone's radar again. The zoom was good enough to see her dead eye, a gray orb that didn't move. When it had worked, you couldn't tell that it was mechanical and electronic.

When it had worked.

Hair was longer than the old days. He'd wondered if she would cut it while on the run, just to throw things off. One arm, with the sleeve of her jacket awkwardly tucked into a pocket. Wouldn't fool anyone looking, but it might not immediately draw the eye.

Ernesta Hernandez, in the other picture, didn't look all that impressive, but Carter assumed that was by design. She had gray hair a little past her shoulders. Thick and rich. Medium height. Medium build.

From the lines on her face, he would assume her to be around sixty. Hard to tell down here, compared to the States, where many people spent a lot of money on cosmetic treatments to try to look thirty forever.

As opposed to subjects of Project Herakles like him, who might live for two hundred years, most of those looking thirty to forty before it all broke down at the end. Assuming the original calculations were correct.

She looked like a grandma, though. Harmless. The kind who might bake you cookies when she knew you were on your way over.

Carter wasn't fooled. All the best crime lords looked innocent. Right up until the point they pulled the trigger on you.

"How big is La Plata?" Malik asked.

She was asking Kehoe, but eyeballing him, so Carter went ahead and answered her.

"Not big in size," he replied. "Compact. Extremely dense, in terms of bodies per square kilometer. High walkability score, like the best parts of Seattle or Manhattan. Lots of restaurants for takeout."

"How long did you live there?" she followed up.

Carter could tell that Kehoe was going to let him do the talking. Call it yet another interrogation about what he'd seen and done in the town.

The bitch of it was that Carter still didn't know what was the one thing that had burned him last time.

"I was in place for a little under three months when Daring took me," he said with an honest sigh. "Late summer into fall, but the city is extremely mild and pleasant that way. Couple of really nice places for Japanese or Ethiopian food, both on side streets off the main drag, about a block apart."

He turned to Kehoe next.

"We're going in cold and dark tonight?"

"Correct," Kehoe said. "We'll be met at the airport and transported in a black car to the hotel. I expect that we'll check in about midnight, sleep, breakfast early, and then see what intelligence Stone and the others in DC have been able to locate."

Carter had no doubts that TRC was currently scoring any number of false positives, just because they would have turned the sensitivity on all their camera search routines all the way up. Hundreds of hits on any woman even remotely close would be shown to a live person to confirm.

Exactly the opposite of how you were supposed to handle these sorts of things, where patience and building up a case like an oyster did with pearls was the key.

What was Kehoe so afraid of? What had Pham supposedly seen?

Or was it enough that Pham had been partners and friends with Daring? Had that been the spark, so that when the woman vanished, all the old farts at the Pentagon had freaked the fuck out?

At least Carter was in a position to learn the truth now. Or more of it, at least.

Whether that meant he could be fully reinstated, or cast forever into darkness remained to be seen, but disappearing like Pham had was always an option. Not as good as it used to be, before he'd burned everybody he knew down here, so he'd need to be somewhere else when he ran.

Mithras had no friends in South America. Unfortunate, but true.

Which was maybe why Kehoe was willing to bring him along?

Oh, you prick!

Carter looked at Kehoe with the blinders maybe removed for once.

He doesn't think I can run, because I have nowhere to hide. And I don't.

Yup. Malik was second string, at least in this game. Kehoe was the one Carter needed to worry about. The one that could burn him.

They had lapsed into silence. The fans suddenly came on and began to whine as the plane started to roll. He caught the eye of one of the Air Force punks.

"Lunch?" Carter asked.

He was always hungry. Side effect of his enhanced metabolism.

The man had apparently been briefed, as he was already moving this way with a cold plate. Not quite anti-pasti, but close enough. Redneck dim sum, maybe. Meat, cheese, fruit slices, crackers, vegetables.

"All hands, we will begin taxiing shortly," the pilot announced over the intercom. "Please fasten your seatbelts. Next stop, Argentina."

Yes. Next stop, Argentina.

And some answers.

CHAPTER 49

Joie got Sal up the stairs to their floor without running into any civilians. Into the room quickly, Ernesta following behind. She sat him on the bed closer to the bathroom. Farther from the window, but she was standing there, with Ernesta between him and the door.

"How?" he managed to gasp, hands shaking a little.

Joie scowled at him for a moment before answering.

"How what?" she fired back.

His hand started to come up. Ernesta's did, too. She had the gun in it. Sal recoiled back into himself.

"Your arm," he whispered.

"Replacement," Joie said, leaving it at that.

Didn't work all that well. Only supposedly held two days' worth of charge. Weaker than her left arm.

But two hands. Drinking coffee while holding a book. Maybe riding a motorcycle again.

Sal blinked too slowly. Even for shock, which should have worn off.

"What are you, Sal McKenzie?" Joie asked.

He flinched so hard he almost fell off the bed.

"How did you know?" the man stammered.

Joie stopped cold and wrapped both arms—good and replacement—around her anger, boxing it up and putting it to one side.

She'd meant to say *Who* instead of *What*, but the *what* here meant the larger organization behind him. Whatever TRC was doing.

Joie had to play a bluff now.

"Answer the question!" she snapped at him, cracking the whip of her voice across his head and back.

Sal did not strike her as someone who had gone through interrogation training like her. Didn't know how far he could go before he cracked. Hadn't been rebuilt with steel rods inserted into his psyche.

Not like her.

"My species is called Danorak on Earth," he said, breathless and awed. "My real name is Bandi Algom. At least as close as your tongue could pronounce it."

Joie let her scowl etch steel. Ernesta had blinked hard and almost fired a shot into the creature's back when the spasm passed through her entire body.

Not human? Not from Earth? What the ever-loving fuck?

"How many of you are here?" Joie asked, just playing a hunch. She had no idea what the words really meant, but he seemed to think that she had already penetrated his organization and was on the verge of discovering everything.

Whatever *EVERYTHING* might be.

Sal/Bandi stared at her. His eyes had gotten so huge she wondered if she had fallen into a Japanese anime show of some sort.

"Bandi!" she snapped.

"Three," he said, fear suddenly—finally—evident in his voice. "More is a risk, as this planet is scheduled to be embargoed for at least another five hundred of your years. By then, the elder races believe that you'll either have evolved, or wiped yourselves out."

"Then why are you here, Bandi?" Ernesta asked from the other side.

His head snapped across his body like a dog chasing a ball. It was so bad he nearly fell off the bed again.

Didn't look like his hold on reality was all that stable, right this moment.

Joie could commiserate. If she wanted.

The creature's mouth opened. Closed. Opened again. Nothing came out.

"Answer her!" Joie growled, shifting fully to bad cop so Ernesta could be the nicer one.

Nicer.

Not nice.

Fucking alien on my planet? A real spaceman? Fucker.

"We want to bring your technology base up sooner," he finally sighed. "My superiors believe that humans would make the perfect warrior species with which to conquer the rest of the galaxy."

Joie wanted to punch him. Bite him, maybe. Anything.

She couldn't, though, because he was right. Wasn't she proof of that?

The perfect soldier, doing whatever she was ordered.

Why had she never asked how the US was the only nation able to create soldiers like Carter Faulkener and the rest of Project Herakles? Or insert parts into her broken body that made her better than she had been? Stronger. Faster.

Was she full of alien parts?

"How long have you been here?" Joie asked, letting her voice soften a little.

Sal/Bandi felt like a scientist. Or maybe a shopkeeper. Not a hardened veteran. That guy who thinks that he can explain everything because the truth will set everyone free.

Or some shit.

Didn't feel like a con artist pulling a grift on her. She'd dated one of those folks accidentally.

The creature even sighed again, turning back to focus his attention on her.

"Nineteen Twenty-Eight," he said. "You were on the verge of truly advancing, so we wanted to help."

"Help?" Joie snarled at the man. "The Great Depression? The

Second World War? The Great Cold War? The Era of Terrorism? That's helping?"

Sal/Bandi shrugged.

"I was just following orders, Daring," he said. Then his head fell and he looked at the floor. "A lot of them said that, afterwards, I appreciate. But only in American courts. I'd been captured by the Soviets and spent the next fifty years, first in one of their camps, then working with their scientists instead of the Germans."

Just following orders. The phrase that many Nazis had used to justify why they shouldn't be held accountable for all the vicious, racist shit those fuckers had done to anybody that wasn't an *Aryan Übermensch.*

Joie really wanted to kill him. She knew enough history of the last two centuries to wonder if the Second World War had been them *bringing up a technology base.* Certainly, ten years had leapt everyone forward a frightening amount, from cloth airplanes to aluminum jets. Toy rockets to ICBMs.

Atomic bombs.

Evolve into a better form, or wipe themselves out.

"How far ahead of schedule are humans with their development?" Joie asked in an offhand tone, still playing longshot bluffs that kept hitting. Like a roulette machine throwing you sevens with every pull of the lever.

Casual. Two dudes in a coffee shop, shooting the breeze.

"About one hundred and fifty years right now," he replied.

Then his head snapped up and he stared at her in awe.

Gotcha.

"Now, answer me this one and answer well, or I will get angry, Bandi," Joie said, taking a step forward to loom over the man. "When those five hundred years are up, the folks coming to check on us are in for one hell of a nasty surprise, aren't they?"

Joie was reminded of a rabbit, staring up into the beam of a flashlight at night. Or maybe spooked by the cry of a hunting owl, until it just froze.

He'd turned gray again. Must be his natural color. Maybe they were close enough to humans that with a little cosmetic work they could pass?

Joie had been rebuilt. All the scars were on the inside for the most part, unless you were close enough to kiss her. And the boobs were after-factory models designed to help distract targets from her face.

"Bandi?" Ernesta asked, sounding like a mother confronting a five-year-old with a hand in a cookie jar.

Not that Joie had any idea what that sounded like. Honest.

"Cataclysmic," he whispered. "They will be expecting you to be somewhere around where you were in the year Two Thousand, in terms of your technological and cultural development. No other species has ever embraced technology and warfare like humans. None."

How many species were there, out there? How many little gray people with big heads, landing in flying saucers in the mid-twentieth-century before they got smart and started stealthing or something?

"And you intend to conquer the galaxy with a Human army?" Joie asked.

Sal/Bandi nodded.

"That is the plan," he said, voice utterly bereft of emotion now, like a computer answering questions.

Technology Research Command. A US effort to develop advanced weapons and systems. Nobody else had anything like it. Project Herakles. Project Cybernaut. Maybe the fusion rifles she'd had in her right arm with the Mark II and Mark III cyberarms?

Joie turned to Ernesta now.

"Check his wallet," she said. "Anything in there that will tell me where we're headed next with our little friend here?"

"That is forbidden," he said, so wound up that he actually stood up.

Joie was so angry that she stepped right into his face, standing nose to nose with the man.

"Sit down or I will make you," she growled.

Gray skin could turn white, if the person possessing it was frightened enough. The creature plopped his ass right back down on the bed before she kneed him in the balls and maybe worked him over a little.

Joie wasn't sure she'd be able to stop hitting him at that point, as emotionally off-balance as she was. Best not to get her started then.

"Sal McKenzie," Ernesta spoke as Joie scowled down on her prey. "Business card for *Elliott Engineered Integrated Logistics*. They have an office about five blocks from here."

"Call your lawyer?" Joie asked.

"Lovely idea," Ernesta replied.

Joie took three steps back, mostly to keep from slapping the alien. She held him in place by pure force of will. He seemed resigned, acquiescing rather than getting a sneaky look in his eyes.

Joie watched the man and listened to half the conversation the woman had.

"You cannot do this," the creature implored her desperately. "You will ruin everything we have worked so long to accomplish."

Joie leaned forward a little to stare at him with her good eye.

"Look at me," she commanded, letting him also see the burned-out gray orb that lived in her right eye socket. "Do I look like I give a fuck what you think?"

He subsided. Deflated a little, even. Curled in on himself.

Ernesta hung up and practically beamed with excitement.

"Founded in Twenty Fifty-Seven," she announced. "Original incorporation papers list a Sal McKenzie as Chief Scientist, along with a couple of other names."

"Fifty-Seven?" Joie repeated, eyeballing the man. He looked like a well-preserved fifty. She'd noted that earlier. "When were you born, Bandi Algom?"

He looked up at her softer tone. More polite, at least, but not any more friendly.

"Eighteen Forty-One, according to your calendar," he said after a long beat. Maybe doing math in his head.

"So you came to Earth when you were almost ninety?" Joie asked, mathing quickly in her head.

"Eighty-seven Earth years, yes," he agreed.

"And you are two hundred and sixty-three years old now?" she pressed.

He nodded. Looked defeated when you caught the gleam of dejection in his eyes.

Assuming alien body language was the same as hers. She didn't trust him. Not one damned bit.

And she didn't dare ask *where* he'd been born.

"How do I get Taylor Kehoe to leave me alone?" she asked him, mostly just to watch the man flinch himself.

"That one," he hissed angrily. "Almost as bad as Bouchard."

"Bouchard?" Joie asked.

The commander of TRC itself?

"Valmy Youri Bouchard," Bandi said. "General in your Army with four stars on his shoulder. Another prick like Kehoe."

"How so?" Joie continued digging, just to see how far she could take this charade.

If the man was lying to her, he was an exceptional poker player. She'd known a few.

"Forever pushing," Bandi groused, sounding like an engineer being handed impossible deadlines. *Again.* "I tell him that it would be better to let our new discoveries out everywhere, to benefit all of your kind, but he demands that we keep everything secret. The fool is as bad as Heppenheimer or Achterberg."

"Who are they?"

Bandi waved a hand.

"Nazi scientists," he replied. "Both long since dead. The Soviets only took a few of us prisoners. I was one because they had found out who I was. Or at least what."

"How did you escape them?"

"The Soviet Union finally broke up in Nineteen Ninety-One," he shrugged. "Funding fell apart after that, so the guards were easier to bribe. I went home for a while."

"A while?" Joie asked, shocked at how casually all of them were discussing such an explosive concept.

Maybe the man had been here so long, with nobody to talk to, that he was bored and lonely? Joie could understand that concept.

"Until about Twenty Twenty," he said. "That big, global plague represented those dumb Chinese fuckers experimenting with bioweapons. I got pulled back in to come do something about that.”

“Project Herakles,” Joie guessed.

“That was later, but yes,” he said. “Human genetic engineering had made a number of hard jumps and so it was easy enough to contact a few folks and throw hints and funding at them.”

“Jesus?” Joie exclaimed. ”How much of modern, human culture is a result of Danorak meddling?”

He gave her a sad smile.

“You might not want an answer to that, Daring,” he offered.

That just made it worse.

“You never answered my other question, Bandi,” Joie said. “How do I get Kehoe, and this Bouchard fellow, to leave me alone?”

“I don’t know,” he said. “You weren’t supposed to know I existed. That was why they decided to burn *Mithras*. All of your agents are to be kept out of La Plata.”

“Too many old Nazis around here?” she asked, mostly as a lark, but he grimaced.

“Those are all dead,” he said. “Their descendants, however, are still around. Nobody down here likes the US or the Chinese, or anybody else, so Argentina is a good place to be left alone to work.”

“Inventing the future?”

“The Argenite alloy in your bones was something we invented, Daring,” he turned serious. “Argen was for silver, but I told them to make up a different word, as it was too close to Argentina and someone might wonder. But I am just a scientist. I don’t make policy.”

“You just invent things,” she growled. “Just follow orders.”

He wanted to jump up again. Wanted to argue with her. Maybe lean in until their foreheads touched so they could really get a good screaming match going.

Something in her good eye convinced him that would be a stupid idea.

A really stupid idea.

“I think we need to see your lab, Señor,” Ernesta spoke up next, breaking Joie and this alien out of the stasis that wanted to descend on them. “Talk to the rest of your people. Maybe convince them to leave

Joie alone. And me, as I'll make sure to tell everyone on the damned planet about you if I have to. And leave documents that will be shared if anything ever happens to me."

That gray skin had started to soften again, because Ernesta's threat caused him to pale.

Publicity was the thing they didn't want. Not just the Chinese or Nigerians, either. Maybe the other aliens were watching, or had their own spies that would suddenly call the mothership if someone started talking about Danorak inventions?

"You can't," he whispered.

"You got a better idea?" Joie asked.

CHAPTER 50

Taylor hated coming to Argentina. Not that it was a bad place. On the contrary, an exceptionally sophisticated place, at least culturally.

It was all the emotional baggage that came with it.

The jet had dropped them last night. Then to the hotel. Nap. Late breakfast for four delivered to his room, so the three of them could eat and talk privately as Faulkener ate six eggs' worth of omelet, along with a kilogram of meat and another kilo of potatoes. Six slices of toast. Seemingly a couple liters of coffee.

And the man would lose weight if he didn't. That was the bitch of it.

"Stone sent us a packet overnight," Taylor announced.

"Anything interesting?" Faulkener asked between bites.

"A lot of women who look like our target, but Argentina doesn't have the sorts of accessible security systems the US does," Taylor replied. "Mostly they are CCTV, with tapes manually uploaded if someone wants to prosecute later."

Faulkener grinned happily. "Good, so they don't trust Americans at all."

Taylor let that one go. The man was both a menace, as well as correct.

"Will I stand out?" Malik asked precisely.

Black woman. West African heritage in the darkness of her skin and the broad shoulders. Folks from farther east still tended to be tall and lean.

"No more than we will," Taylor replied. "Daring knows your face, but not as well as mine or Faulkener's, so you can range a little, but we'll be staying reasonably close together when we head out. Not a trio, but no more than a block apart, because both of you can cover that distance adequately quickly, if necessary."

"And what are we doing?" Faulkener asked. His plates were empty, finally.

"She's looking for something or someone," Taylor replied. "As you've noted, there are almost no underground organizations of any size left, and there hasn't been time for new ones to grow. That means she's likely to be out on the streets casing things. If we keep a low enough profile, we might be able to spot her before she spots us. I've also ordered a team to stay close to the Hernandez aircraft, in case they try to escape us again."

"The government won't stop them?" Malik asked.

Faulkener grinned. Taylor grimaced.

"They don't like Americans," he said. "Officially. Unofficially, it runs hot and cold, but they won't just impound an aircraft belonging to a Mexican national on our say-so alone. And my superiors have decided not to unwrap any indictments as yet."

Meaning that they existed, but that was just so that various intelligence agencies could be brought in to do things without violating any laws themselves. Everyone was willing to fight crime, however tenuous some of the threads might be.

"I presume my old flat has been taken?" Faulkener asked.

"Why?" Taylor barked back at him.

He was starting to get tired of the way the man was always pulling at his leash. Like he was waiting for Taylor to lose his grip on it and the mighty *Mithras* could run free again.

Not going to happen.

"Because it had one of the most perfect vantage points in the city," Faulkener said. "A private balcony on the corner that wrapped around and let you see up the one side road with the Japanese place, but more importantly the entirety of the main boulevard. I'd presumed that you were searching for me. That balcony allowed me to watch much of my perimeter without really being seen. That was why I rented the place."

"I'll have Stone check and see," Taylor replied, a little grumpy and testy. Even when Faulkener was right, he was still something of an ass.

Faulkener's smile didn't help.

Instead of dealing with it right now, he handed them each a data chip.

"This contains the current briefing packet," Taylor said. "Spend the next hour studying it, then we'll move into the field. Questions?"

Faulkener bounced right up and headed for the door. Malik scowled at the man's back, but didn't speak. She didn't have a much higher opinion of that one than he did.

Quickly, he was alone. A couple of questions sent back to DC to get Stone onto the next task, then some time to think.

What the hell did Daring know that had brought her here? Would she be headed to the same flat that Faulkener had lived in, looking for answers?

They weren't there. There was nothing there, as far as he knew. Instead, the key was about three blocks closer to downtown, off on a quiet side street that Taylor had visited any number of times over the last decade.

The biggest secret in the world.

And the most dangerous.

What was Daring going to cost him, if he didn't stop her?

CHAPTER 51

Ernesta was going to need to visit the priest after this. And it would involve a rather lengthy and complicated confession this time. As Joie might have said, the shit had gotten weird.

She held the alien's pistol low at her side like you were supposed to. Joie had the man's hand. Could she call it a man?

He presented as male. Even when his color was off. Right now, he seemed exhausted by it all. Ernesta could sympathize some.

But only some. This person was likely responsible for some of the things done to Joie. In that, he qualified as some sort of alien Doctor Frankenstein, when you framed it that way.

Ernesta would collect some of that personally, if necessary.

She didn't think that breaking the Americans' unique hold on this technology would help much. It was likely to ooze out anyway. Like being able to make a few calls and locate someone who was doing research into cybernetic replacement arms. And buy one.

Buenos Aires had a reputation for scientific research. How much of that wasn't because of the Americans, but the aliens? Well, the Americans had the most money, but their funding would spin off, as the lab this person supposedly came from would need things, which other places would craft for them.

Like cybernetic components and electronics.

Ernesta really needed to invest down here. There was an upside of potential profit around her that she'd never imagined.

Or was there? Would it be necessary to blow the cover of secrecy around this place? The alien seemed to live in terror of other aliens finding out what was being done here. Would those people put a stop to it? Throw human civilization down to what it might have been?

Could that genie be stuffed back into the bottle? Or would they just freeze everything at the present status quo? Even without the aliens, could humans still progress as madly as they had?

Ernesta had no answers.

And they had arrived.

"Up these steps into the courtyard," the alien wheezed quietly, still holding hands with Joie like lovebirds on a date as Ernesta followed a few steps back.

Ready for any surprise and willing to shoot things with her new gun if she had to. Joie had the revolver, and Ernesta had no doubts how dangerous that woman was. Everyone knew about Captain Daring.

She followed them up the stairs.

"What's up there?" Joie asked the man.

"We have several floors, where they are accessible from the back without having to go through the building itself," he said. "Nor interact with locals, as the special operatives coming around like to keep a low profile."

"Kehoe," Joie nearly spat the name out.

"Him," the alien agreed. "Only rarely. Others more frequently. Bureaucrats, the lot of them."

He said that with such disgust that Ernesta almost laughed. She understood the disdain for the paper pushers, even as she recognized the need. They really did make the world go around, which was why she kept them with her.

So they could do those little things and leave her free to plan forward.

The stairs debouched onto a small, tree-lined courtyard, tucked away from where anyone might look for it. A door on the left opened into the building itself, but that was the only access, making it a dead end, unless you were going to *Elliott Engineered Integrated Logistics*, the name on the door.

The man led them to it, opening it and stepping in.

There was a secretary sitting behind a desk. Receptionist, basically. Simple room with a sofa on one side and a couple of chairs. More plants in pots. Hallway behind the desk, presumably leading deeper into the facility.

The girl behind the desk looked up a bit surprised, then concerned when Ernesta pointed the pistol at her from the doorway.

"Come with us, please," she announced.

"That's not necessary," the alien said in a grumpy voice.

"Yes, it is," Ernesta replied. "We've already got your friends chasing after us with guns and soldiers. I'd prefer to be able to slip quietly away afterwards without the building being completely surrounded in the next five minutes."

"You think I want…outsiders in here?" he demanded, actually tugging Joie's weight around as he turned and snarled back at her.

Ernesta smiled. He'd almost said humans instead of calling them outsiders, which suggested that the woman was human herself. Probably a local hire who didn't understand why none of the scientists would hit on her.

She was young. Ernesta would have said twenty. Short and slender. Darker skinned than a European, but not as dark as you might get out of the northeast. Pretty. Obviously smart enough to rise immediately and move off to one side.

Ernesta paused to lock the outer door. It was glass, but it would at least slow anyone down following them, unless they already had a key.

"Through here," the man sighed, gesturing the secretary to follow him and Joie. Ernesta brought up the rear. "Genevieve, please join us."

"What's going on?" she asked nervously.

"A complex misunderstanding," the man said over his shoulder as they entered the hallway behind the desk. "Can I ask you to go up to three and just have a long coffee break? Don't call the authorities while I contact this woman's superiors and get all this sorted out."

"Yes, Doctor McKenzie," she said. "If that's what you want."

"Genevieve, you know how secretive this facility is," he told her. "Someone talked to someone they shouldn't have, and now the three of us need to meet in private. They are obviously concerned that we've gotten them into trouble, when it is not the case. I promise you, I'll be fine. You'll be fine. And if you see Camilla or Franco upstairs, could you ask them to join me in my office? I'll intercom them shortly if they aren't in theirs."

"Yes, Doctor McKenzie."

Give the woman credit. She paused and turned to look this way. Ernesta smiled and nodded, so Genevieve moved past the other two and turned up an open staircase.

The man sighed heavily and looked at both of them.

"This way, please," he said.

Ernesta wondered what other surprises might lie in store.

CHAPTER 52

Carter was pleased. Not that he would ever move back to La Plata, but that lovely corner flat he'd rented out was vacant at present, the previous tenants having been a Canadian mining mogul and his family that came south for the summer while Canada was undergoing the usual weather insanities they took for granted. Nobody had rented it this month, so the landlord was willing to let them tour it for a quick bribe.

Kehoe had apparently come in with a team after Daring had wrecked the place and him, fixing what they could and paying cash for damages for the rest. Carter was not *persona non grata* around here.

At least not with the landlord.

So he was standing on the corner of the balcony, breathing the sea air and enjoying the cool breeze coming off the land behind him. Below, the mid-day crowds were swirling to and fro. He'd really loved his time around here.

Maybe he could talk Kehoe into getting sushi for dinner.

Something below caught his eye in ways that Carter couldn't identify consciously. Lizard-brain that had kept him alive more than once had kicked in, poking him in the kidney and pointing to a couple walking five floors below, moving to his right.

He blinked. Leaned forward. Cursed under his breath.

"Kehoe, come here immediately," he barked over his shoulder.

Both joined him in seconds. Carter hadn't taken his eyes off the couple below, certain he would lose her if he did.

"What?" Kehoe demanded.

Carter risked it and pointed.

"That's Joie Daring," he said.

"Can't be, she has two arms," Malik interjected.

If they were only on the third floor, he might have risked just jumping, but the crowd was heavy down there and chances were he would land on someone accidentally. Yelling for them to clear a path for him would spook Joie. As would him starting to climb down the balconies.

People would yell and scream at him.

"Shit," Kehoe muttered, so he'd seen it.

There was a way the woman walked. Carter didn't have any other way to describe it. He hadn't seen it in Arlington, but she had it now.

Lethal.

"We've got to track her," Carter said. "Shit, they just turned and went up some stairs. Come on, let's move."

"That's unnecessary," Kehoe said, almost glumly. "I know where they're going."

Carter wanted to shriek. He'd been living two blocks from whatever the hell it was, all that time?

Fuck.

He turned to Kehoe now, and watched the man go through the stages of death, from the way his eyes changed.

Finally, the man settled on *Acceptance*.

"Faulkener. Malik. I need to tell you a few things," Kehoe admitted.

And then he did.

CHAPTER 53

Joie felt the tension in Bandi's hand, which was why she was holding it. He wasn't about to start anything. Seemed more concerned that the receptionist would gossip, which might just make it all worse.

The alien just sighed and led them through a door into a larger room with what Joie took to be workbenches around an open space in the middle, and offices around that. Maybe fifteen meteres across the square. All the surfaces had gear or computers on them, sometimes haphazardly stacked. Others carefully arranged.

One woman looked up from a board she was apparently studying with a microscope. She turned this way, flinched, and her jaw dropped open.

"Camilla, I need to talk to you for a few minutes," Bandi called before she spoke. "Is Franco around?"

"Here," a male voice sounded from their right.

A few moments later, a man emerged from an office.

Tall and dark, but Joie found his face too thin to be handsome. More hatchet-like, with a beak of a roman nose and a prominent chin, but almost no cheekbones to balance it.

"Oh, shit," the man said as they made eye contact.

"Indubitably," Bandi said. "Can you two come into my office? These ladies would like to chat without yelling. I've sent Genevieve upstairs for a bit."

"Sal, what's going on?" Camilla asked.

"It is complicated," he said, tugging Joie gently to the right and into an office that would be big enough for everyone.

She let him. This was hopefully where she could get answers.

Whether or not it would protect her from Kehoe later remained to be seen.

Joie waited next to Bandi's desk as he sat, making sure he didn't touch the phone. There was nothing she could do about the receptionist, except hope that the woman would wait fifteen minutes. It would probably all be over by then. She and Ernesta could depart. Wiser, but probably still confused.

The female, Camilla, arrived first. Joie directed her to the far chair. Franco came next, and Joie sat him down closer. Ernesta stood just in the doorway, back far enough to track the outer chamber like an expert spy.

Or burglar. Joie had been trained as both. Apparently so had her companion.

Franco was studying her from a meter away. She let him.

"How bad of a security breach do we have?" he asked the room, glancing back and forth between her and the alien boss.

She looked at Bandi.

"On the one hand, as bad as it can possibly get," the man sighed again. "On the other, these ladies aren't looking to destroy the organization, or they would have approached everything differently. Am I correct, Miss Daring?"

Joie nodded, unwilling to trust her tongue. Humans would have reacted to the situation…*differently*. More paranoid. Something.

"How did you find us?" Camilla asked.

Bandi laughed.

"The gods that nobody is willing to admit to believing in decided to play a sour, black practical joke on us," he replied. "I was walking down to get some pastries at the shop and saw Captain Daring herself standing there, staring at me. I panicked. She grabbed me. I am not hurt. They are being hunted by Taylor Kehoe."

"And Carter Faulkener," Joie spoke up.

"That one?" Bandi blanched. "He was in maximum security in that Colorado facility four months ago when I went to give him his annual physical. How did he break out? Why wasn't I told?"

"He didn't escape, Bandi," Joie said, listening as the other two gasped that she knew the man's real name. "He cut a deal with Kehoe and the two of them have been running after me and herding me, trying to get me to find Romana Pham."

"*Tyche*?" he exclaimed, using her field name. "What's happened to her? Why the hell am I not being told about these things?"

Joie shrugged.

"That's between you and TRC," she said bluntly. "If Kehoe no longer trusts you, you have other problems. Personally, he already burned me and destroyed my life, so I will never trust that goatfucker again. When we leave, you should call him and ask. Just give us six hours to get out of country, please?"

"All this and you expect us to believe you are just leaving?" Franco demanded. "Without hurting anyone?"

"That's right," Joie said. "I have no reason to at present. So, Sal here is actually Bandi Algom. Who are you? And not your cover names, please."

She still had a revolver on her hip. And close combat skills. And serious, serious anger management issues right now. She put that into her good eye as she scowled at the two of them.

Franco gulped.

"Hanni Cara," he said faintly. "This is Sora Ijynth beside me. Bandi, what the hell is going on?"

"Technology Research Command is playing a little fast and loose with things," Bandi replied. "How Daring even knew to look in La Plata concerns me, but we can chalk that up to the original operation to take down *Mithras*. Yes?"

He said that last looking directly at her, so Joie nodded.

"That should have cut the thread," Bandi continued. "And ended up instead being the only place she had to look for answers. I will own that mistake. Not like I haven't made others over the centuries. Nor you."

Centuries. Joie heard the calm certainty in those words. Nearly three hundred years old, and still only perhaps middle-aged?

"Have you seen Romana?" she asked now bluntly, overriding the murmuring from the three…*alien scientists.*

Joie had been expecting one alien and a group of humans working for him. How many other aliens were walking around on her planet, unknown because they could pass close enough for human?

She felt her place in the universe suddenly shrink by a couple of orders of magnitude.

Joie blinked as her back brain kicked in.

"Bandi, you were in Colorado four months ago?" she asked before they could answer her other question.

"That's correct," Bandi nodded. "All of the Project Herakles soldiers need to be checked regularly, because we so radically altered their DNA and gene expressions. Your Pentagon decided after six of them that the risk of them living forever and eventually going rogue was too great. That was why we created Project Cybernaut instead. You were my first, Daring."

"Did Romana ever get enhanced?" Joie queried. It had been a year. Two, if you counted severe depression. Lots of things might have happened. Had, as a matter of fact.

"She did not," he said, then paused. "Not that anyone ever told me. Some of our cyberware designs are becoming stable enough that they might be able to manufacture their own variants now. We stopped all bionetic enhancement research though."

"Would that stop Kehoe from trying it in some other lab?" Joie asked, letting Bandi Algom's words guide her somewhat randomly in questioning.

"That has to be custom tailored at a deep level," he replied. "It would not be impossible for them to do, but the error factors would be extremely high. As would the risk."

"Would they have perhaps been willing to move on from whatever test animals they had in some black lab to working on humans?" Joie asked.

Bandi shrugged in a most human manner.

"Your kind never ceases to amaze me, Daring," he said. "Or frighten me, at the end of the day."

"What if he felt the need to move beyond what the Danorak could do for him?" Joie mused, listening to the other two gasp. "Move to take control of human destiny without letting the aliens hold our leash? I presume you crossed interstellar space with some superengine that manages Faster-Than-Light travel to get here. Does he know how that system works?"

She watched all three aliens turn gray now, confirming her suspicions.

Bandi and his bosses wanted an army of supersoldiers to conquer the galaxy, but one they controlled.

Nobody, it seemed, wanted humans loose with that sort of technology. Not at their current, violent level of development.

"He wouldn't dare," Camilla said, just above a whisper.

Joie just barked a laugh. That shut the woman up.

"Lady, you got a lot to learn about humans," she said. "Ask Bandi here about the Germans. Or the Soviets."

She caught the pained look on Bandi's face.

"So, what all did you do, four months ago when you went north, Bandi?" she asked.

"Did a physical on all four Herakles graduates that survive," he said. "Two were killed in action. Only *Mithras* ever went rogue."

Joie nodded. She'd met at least two others in her time. Their size and mass tended to give them away.

"How do you inspect a man locked in a supermax cell without being at risk?" Joie asked, thinking about how Carter Faulkener would have been kept in a place with concrete walls thick enough to hold him.

"I have a portable scanner that reads all his DNA and gene expression information against the original baselines," Bandi said. "We can interpret that to estimate how he's doing. What metabolic changes we might need to introduce or retard. That sort of thing."

"And did it travel with you from Argentina?" Joie pressed.

"No, it is kept…in…Washington…" he tapered off to nothing, staring at her as his eyes got huge again. "Shit."

Joie nodded.

"What's going on, Sal?" the woman demanded.

"Taylor Kehoe has possession of the portable scanalyzer, Sora," he said, using her alien name. "Daring here is suggesting that Kehoe and his people might be able to use it when we're not around. Perhaps baseline other humans besides our original six test subjects and then experiment on them without us supervising. Yes?"

That last with him turned to look at her. Joie nodded again.

Both of the other scientists gasped.

"They might be making a new army of superwarriors," Joie said quietly. "How soon until they decide to invade South America and capture all your toys? Including your starship?"

The room fell to a silence so complete that Joie could hear the HVAC system purr quietly. The air in here was wonderfully pure. Everything about the place seemed to be calming, which was helpful, since she was here to stir shit up and hope that she could find something that would make Kehoe leave her alone.

In that, Joie was pretty sure she'd failed about as bad as she possibly could.

Then she heard a sound that her training identified as glass breaking. Remarkably similar to someone putting a fist through a glass door, in order to reach the locking mechanism and open it.

She looked around.

Ernesta had vanished.

CHAPTER 54

Taylor knew that Bouchard was going to have his ass for this, but there was nothing for it at this point. And if the General really was about to burn him, Taylor would make sure that everybody went down at the same time.

He had enough things stored in a pair of secret safety deposit boxes, independent of one another. And two different sets of lawyers that he checked in with every three months. If he missed a call, they would try to reach him. Failing that, they would each open a sealed letter with instructions.

Yeah, you all go down.

But that was tomorrow's problem. Today, he had just made the executive decision to read both Malik and Faulkener into the biggest, single ultra-secret project the Pentagon had ever created. Malik he knew he could trust. They'd learned a lot about how to pick out candidates and nurture them, after the failures of *Mithras* and Daring.

Carter Faulkener was a whole other proposition. Luckily, Taylor had had the aliens booby-trapped the son of a bitch before TRC had let him out of that cell.

They were on the street now. Mid-day crowds coming back from lunch, or headed to a late one. Perfect to vanish in.

Taylor led. Malik would follow because she followed orders. Faulkener would be dragged kicking and screaming by his own curiosity.

How often does a man get to meet his own Dr. Frankenstein, after all?

They went up the stairs to the Elliott office. Taylor had always hated the name, but the company was older than he was, so he kept his opinions to himself. They probably told anyone who asked that it translated badly out of Japanese or something.

He got to the second floor, that little balcony-patio thing that you almost had to know existed to find. Taylor walked to the door and looked in. The receptionist wasn't there, and the door was locked.

Very bad. On a variety of levels.

Had Daring taken the entire facility hostage?

"Fuck," he muttered under his breath.

"What?" Faulkener asked, looming too close.

"We have a situation," he explained. "And now both of you understand why calling the police or any other authorities would be a bad thing."

"It's locked?" Faulkener asked. When Taylor nodded, the man smiled. "I can just break the glass."

"No, actually you probably can't," Taylor smiled up at the man. "We designed it to keep you out. Specifically you, as a matter of fact."

That got a smile and a glower from the man, all in one. The sort of thing that warmed Taylor's cold soul right now.

Bouchard was going to be an ass about this. He just knew it. Tomorrow.

Taylor turned to Malik.

"You, however, can open it," he said. "Not with your fists, though."

She nodded.

"You'll want to stand back," she smiled.

Taylor moved to the far edge of the patio. If Faulkener wanted to be close, that was his fault, but the man looked around, and then scampered over quickly enough.

Freya moved to the center of the space and braced her feet. Right arm came up, palm open and fingers towards the sky.

Taylor closed his eyes. Then saw a flash of light through his lids and the crashing of glass audible anywhere within forty meters, most likely.

"I could have picked the lock," Faulkener grumbled.

"It has fourteen pins," Taylor laughed at the man. "I'd like to see you try sometime. I really would."

Most commercial locks had six these days. Good ones had eight. *Undefeatable* ones came with ten.

Fourteen was when you felt like being an asshole to the burglar.

The look of surprise on Faulkener's face was almost worth all the other shit Taylor had had to deal with.

Malik moved forward now, so Taylor started in that direction. The woman's cyberarm went through the smoking hole in the glass and she turned the locking mechanism.

That sort of thing was possible when you could shut down all the heat and pain sensors in your arm because you needed to put it into a hot stove for some reason.

She pulled the door open and Taylor got to see both of their reactions to the transparent panel being over three centimeters thick. It would stop autocannon rounds at short range, to say nothing of mere bullets. Or enhanced fists on tall assholes.

They entered. Nothing amiss in the reception area. He paused to look at his two accomplices.

"Very shortly, you are going to see things where they might decide to throw you in a small concrete box for the rest of your lives, if you ever talk about it to anybody but me or a few of my superiors," he said carefully. Mostly concentrating on the big man. *Pahket* was safe. "Questions?"

"Hundreds, but they can wait until we get back to DC," the man replied.

Good, so hopefully Faulkener wasn't going to try to run right now.

Or maybe he was. Taylor was ambivalent.

He had insurance policies in place either way. Felt like that point in the operation where everyone was about to double-cross everyone else anyway.

"Okay, so I would expect we'll find Daring down that hallway,"

Taylor said, pointing. "*Mithras*, you lead because she has a gun and you don't."

"You planning to fire that thing inside here?" the man asked Malik nervously.

Pakhet just smiled at him. The man might be bullet-proof, but these weren't bullets.

"Move," Taylor ordered. "They obviously know we're coming, and I don't have time to call in backup from elsewhere."

For a giant that weighed so much, Faulkener still moved like a ghost down the hallway. Silence itself. He reached the door at the end, placing a palm on the panel and then an ear.

Finally, he opened it and entered the main workshop where the aliens conducted experiments and built things using tools that human technology had produced.

That was the only way to keep the other aliens from realizing the truth. Human technology seemed to be rushing madly ahead, but it was all human. Anything those aliens bought or stole could be traced to a fabrication lab or a factory owned and operated by humans.

It was the bleeding edge of research that was being artificially augmented.

Secretly. Hopefully.

He followed the dangerous woman as she moved in Faulkener's wake.

The big man was in the room. Malik joined him, going slightly right where he'd gone left.

"No closer," Joie Daring snarled.

She was standing on the far side of the workshop, with Sal, Camilla, and Franco. Or Algom, Ijynth, and Cara, to use their real names.

Mithras really had stopped. So had Malik. Daring was holding a particularly-nasty looking weapon in her two hands. His brain kept muttering ray gun quietly.

She seemed to think that it was good enough to stop either of her foes.

Taylor was alone in the doorway, watching the scene. Trying to figure out how to take her down without killing her, when somebody grabbed him by his hair and socketed the barrel of a pistol in his right ear.

Fuck.

CHAPTER 55

Ernesta heard the sudden rupture of sound and moved immediately. Broken glass was never a good thing. Doubly so here.

She had seen a standard fire escape map next to the staircase that the woman Genevieve had taken, so she knew there was another staircase nearby. Quickly, she moved to it and silently flowed up to the third floor.

There was a light on in a doorway as she emerged, so Ernesta looked in. Genevieve twitched, seeing her, but didn't make a sound. Eyes like a fawn looked up at her. Ernesta smiled to reassure her and put a finger to her lips.

"I'm going to close this, just in case," she told the woman. "That way you'll be safer. Okay?"

Genevieve nodded, pale almost to white.

Ernesta reached in and pulled the door shut. This lab's secrecy was probably irrevocably blown at this point. She could use that. Just invest some money down here through a handful of blinds, and she could keep track if they remained in Argentina. Maybe they only abandoned La Plata, but there was too much infrastructure already.

Too much sunk cost to uproot everything and still manage to keep it secret.

Especially since Ernesta knew what to look for.

She moved to the top of the front stairs and peeked just enough of an eye around to watch a giant of a man move past. Then an Afro-Caribbean woman. Then an Anglo she assumed was the notorious Kehoe who was behind all of this insanity.

Forty-odd years of business meetings and financing planning sloughed off her shoulders and she was nineteen again, moving down the stairs like a billowing of smoke.

She heard the door open to where Joie had the three aliens, and peeked again. The first two had entered the room, leaving Kehoe in the doorway. Presumably where he could run if he had to.

"No closer," Joie called in a clear voice.

Ernesta was sorry that they hadn't had a chance to coordinate things. Joie might think she'd been abandoned again, like all the men in her life had done.

Hopefully, this would make up for it.

She looked back at the front door, just to make sure the three new intruders were alone, then slid up behind Kehoe before he could do anything. One hand got a good tangle into his hair and anchored him in place. Then she put Bandi's tiny pistol in his ear.

"Don't get stupid," she whispered as she moved him deeper into the room. "I'm not sure I'd ever be able to wash your brains out of my jeans, and this is my favorite pair."

He nodded, at least as much as she allowed.

Inside the room, the other two agents had turned around, caught midway by her surprise flanking maneuver.

Just like the old days.

"Everybody remain perfectly still, or this man melts," Ernesta announced to the room, mostly watching the woman. *Mithras* didn't have a weapon in hand, but the woman probably was a weapon, based on what Joie had told her.

The tableau held. Out of the corner of her eye, Ernesta saw the giant tense up to do something. Probably didn't care if Kehoe died, based on everything Ernesta had heard.

Sal McKenzie, the alien also known as Bandi Algom, opened his mouth and spoke a word.

Ernesta had been that kid who liked to read weird shit as a child and teenager, though only in private so she didn't get teased, even when her grandfather was in charge. Even the old Lovecraft and Derleth crap from the early twentieth century. *Non-Euclidean geometry* had always seemed to her to be a tacky buzzword to try to convey alienness in words. The sound that the alien emitted defied description.

Loud, yet quiet. Harmless, yet penetrating like a diamond-tipped drill bit. Polite songbird, yet terrible Harbinger of the Apocalypse.

Ernesta nearly wet herself hearing it.

The giant collapsed forward like someone had flipped off a light switch in his head. One moment tensed. The next a sack of noisy potatoes on the floor.

"Sorry," the alien announced quietly. "*Mithras* was about to overreact to the situation. The man was always unstable."

Ernesta felt Kehoe relax. Not preparing to do anything, but calming. He'd apparently had the same opinion of the giant, and with him out of the picture, maybe nobody had to get shot.

Joie had pivoted to the woman, holding something like a carbine rifle. An alien one.

Ernesta had an idea so wicked she chuckled.

"Kehoe, I know you have the tools," she said in a louder voice. "I want you to pop the woman's cyberarm off. Don't destroy it. Just disarm her."

He unconsciously turned to look at her in surprise. Or tried to. She held him in place with a snap of her wrist that was probably painful.

Hair pulling has to be done just right to be enjoyable, after all. She knew that.

"Malik, do what she says," he ordered carefully, body perfectly rigid. "Pop your arm off for now."

The woman wanted to argue. She had, however, fallen out of control of the situation before she'd even known it. Her giant ally was down. Her boss was neutralized.

Ernesta studied the woman to try to get a psychological grip on her. You could do that, given enough time and the right training. Forty years of running an illegal international smuggling operation taught you an amazing amount about reading people at first glance.

Right now, any twitch was likely to get this Malik killed. And her boss. That realization hit home.

Captain Daring had been the very best at what she did, and now the woman had recruited help.

Ernesta smiled at her in a reassuring way.

"Okay," the woman said calmly. "I am moving to the table so it doesn't fall far."

"Go ahead," Joie replied, covering her with whatever that thing was.

The woman took two careful steps forward, moving with great deliberation. Ernesta heard the clack as the various latches let go. The woman reached across her body and tugged on the now-lifeless hand, pulling it out of her sleeve. It came to rest on the table.

"Back up," Joie ordered. "Face against the wall and good arm up so we can frisk you. You too, Kehoe."

Ernesta maneuvered him to a close wall, well away from the soldier. Got him in place. Checked him everywhere. Enough to make the man flinch in embarrassment. Down the front was a good place to hide a weapon. He didn't have anything there but what God had intended.

She wasn't impressed with it.

She ended up with his wallet, his phone, a wad of local currency, and a small device she couldn't identify. About the size of a zippo lighter, done in a matte black. It had a rocker switch you had to flip to open, and a button underneath.

She wondered what it would blow up.

Then she moved to the other woman. Physically, almost a copy of Joie, in that she was tall, lean, and exuded an air of danger. Darker skin. Short, curly afro. Ernesta slipped the pistol into her own pocket and stepped close, making sure to keep out of Joie's way if her friend needed to shoot someone.

The skin felt strange under her fingertips, but that was nothing new. Ernesta knew that it had armor under it.

The woman had a phone, a wallet, and precious little else. Ernesta stepped back and wondered if both of them had hotel keys in their wallets.

She wasn't feeling mean enough to destroy their IDs and maybe strand them here.

Not yet, anyway.

Instead, she picked up the spare cyberarm and tucked it under her arm as she stepped around and covered them again.

"Okay, you can both turn around again," Joie said.

Ernesta moved to stand between Kehoe and the door. That also let her keep watch in case the sound of shattering glass had drawn bystanders from the outside world.

Now, it was all in Joie's hands.

CHAPTER 56

oie held the weapon that Bandi had handed her when they stepped out of his office, like he had expected her to protect him and the others. Except that maybe he did. They were aliens. Scientists. They had come to this planet apparently looking for human killers that they could use to take over the galaxy one of these days.

Which said a lot about the wiser folks out there who had forbidden such a thing.

Now, she had Carter face-planted. The other cyberbabe hopefully disarmed, though she had to wonder if the woman had replaced both arms at some point and Kehoe was looking to pull a fast one on them.

She kept her weapon centered on the woman's chest.

"I need you to take off your jacket and shirt," Joie said baldly. "Slowly. Carefully. But immediately."

The woman scowled, but every woman has a moment of raw annoyance when someone wants her topless. Even when it wasn't a sexual thing.

Still, she complied. The jacket hit the floor. The shirt was a long-sleeved pullover in jersey. Tight enough to flow with you, but not skin tight.

Taking something like that off one-handed was a complete bitch. Joie could testify to that. Eventually, she managed, showing off a black sports bra underneath, that was holding in an impressive chest.

Joie wondered if hers were real. Or fake like they'd done to Joie when they rebuilt her.

"Good enough," Joie said.

The shoulder was what she cared about. That seam where flesh ended and hardware began. The woman had one on the right arm, but like Joie, still had her left.

"What did you do to *Mithras*?" Joie asked the alien beside her, finally relaxing some.

She and Ernesta had the only obvious weapons in here. Whatever the hell Bandi had done was something else.

"Kehoe asked us to build in an organic switch that could turn the man off at short range, if he went rogue again," Bandi replied with a grimace that extended all the way into his voice. "Just as he has a device that can disable or destroy cyberware at short range. The effect will wear off in about an hour, and *Mithras* will have one of the worst hangovers of his life. There is a second setting that would have ended him, but the situation did not appear to warrant it."

"Is this it?" Ernesta asked, tossing something this way.

Joie caught it without looking away from the other one-armed woman. In her new hand. Blind.

Reflexes were a wonderful thing.

"That is it," Bandi confirmed.

"What's the range on the handheld?" Joie asked, smiling now at the woman across the way with her dead, gray eye.

Kehoe must have had it in his hand, hand in his pocket, back on that day. Joie hardly remembered anything except the sneer on this face and then all her systems shutting down forever.

"Approximately twenty-seven meters," Bandi said. "Sufficient for this room."

"Not interested in cooking her," Joie said, conveying sincerity with her eyes as the woman got a moment of panic in hers. "Just want to know how far it works."

"You know too much, Daring," Kehoe finally spoke up, maybe

recovering from the shock of getting out-hustled. "We need to talk about how to handle this going forward. My bosses won't like a rogue ex-agent running around. Nor a Mexican Crime Lord who knows all this. They'll get ugly if we don't sort it out before we leave the room."

"Well, I got bad news for you then, Kehoe," Joie replied. "You knocked me out of my comfortable life because you were looking for Romana. I have no idea where she is. I only came this far because we thought that maybe we could figure out why *Mithras* had to be taken down and if it was related. And why my entire life got revoked. I learned that part, but not why Romana disappeared. Nor where."

"You have two options, Daring," Kehoe called from across the room.

Workbenches separated them, but Joie had already planned to jump up atop the one in front of her if somebody decided to duck. That would let her get around quickly, as the tables were close enough together.

It helped that none of the bad guys were currently armed.

"Oh?" Joie asked. "I think I have a lot more than that."

"You can come in from the cold," Kehoe continued. "Right here. Right now. You've moved into a new part of the overall conspiracy and I'm already going to catch hell from Bouchard and others for letting *Mithras* and *Pakhet* know. You two just add to my headache."

"And if I say no?" Joie asked.

"Then you have to run, Daring," he scowled. "And there is nowhere that we won't chase you. Same with her. Shortly, I expect an order from the top to annihilate her entire organization, just as collateral damage in case she told anyone."

"But you'll protect us?" Ernesta sneered at the man. "Protect all my people? Is that what I'm hearing you say?"

Joie found it interesting, watching Kehoe turn to face her. They weren't that far apart, but Ernesta was armed.

"It wouldn't be the first such organization on a *Do Not Hit* list, Hernandez," he explained carefully. "You aren't doing anything particularly noteworthy, as far as that goes. Obrador was moving into terrorism and revolution with his arms dealing, so he had to be ended. Daring handled that. I'm willing to make a deal. You two come in and work with me, so I can tell Bouchard and a few Senators that you're deep cover agents, rather than dangerous rogues who might find a reporter and blow all this up so badly that we probably do get an early visit from the stars. People in the know live in quiet terror of that outcome, even out several centuries, because anything we do might bring them down on us today."

"Would it be so bad?" Joie asked, wondering if she'd finally turned into the sort of anti-establishment revolutionary that she used to be sent to kill.

Kehoe turned back to her. "We're a century and change ahead of where we should be. They might let us remain here, and they might decide to crash us back to the Industrial Age. Or earlier. Wouldn't take much. Couple of electromagnetic pulse detonations in the right spots. Blow up every satellite in orbit, which I'm told would be child's play for them. Throw in some computer viruses. Boom. Every computerized system in the world dies. Do you have any idea how catastrophic that would be? Food deliveries would be paralyzed overnight. Generator stations would implode. Millions, maybe billions would starve in a matter of months. That's the risk we're facing."

"No, Kehoe," she snapped. "You're playing with matches and asking me to help put out the fire you've started because it looks like you might be about to burn the damned house down. Why should I help?"

"Because I'll make your life hell otherwise," he said. Perhaps the first honest words she'd heard out of his mouth in years. "They might just kill you out of hand. Personally, I think that would be a waste. You were better than *Mithras*, and he was supposed to be the best there was."

He paused and grimaced.

"Look, I can protect you, or I can destroy you," he offered. "That's about as much leeway as Bouchard will allow me, when this is all done."

"Will you allow her and I to pretend to be your deep cover agents, even though we don't come in immediately?" Ernesta asked. "If we returned to Mexico as soon as your people calmed those shits down, and then you came and debriefed us?"

"Why?" Kehoe demanded.

"As you said, you can destroy her and end my organization, or you can protect all of us," Ernesta said, waving to the room. "I'll take Joie home with me. You sort all this shit out, including the big fellow there, then come to Guadalajara, you two, maybe you three. All six of you if you're feeling bold, but that might be hard to keep quiet, considering how the Interior Ministry leaks like a sieve."

"You're sure, Ernesta?" Joie asked. "That's far more than I originally requested, and way more than I can make up to you later."

"Joie, you have already paid your debt," the woman smiled at her. Joie felt a jolt of warmth roll through her so alien she wondered if they had been transformed when nobody was looking. "If I can get the US government to add a layer of insulation around what I do, I don't have to pay as much in bribes. That means I can abandon a few business endeavors that really cause me to need so much money."

Kehoe's attention snapped right to at those words.

"Such as?" he demanded.

"Crossing the border going north is expensive for me, Kehoe. But pretty profitable," Ernesta said. "I'll make you a deal to stop. To end my associations with all those *coyotes* and their organizations. Except for maybe the odd person who needs to be smuggled across. All the other stuff, the drugs, the booze, and all the things not paying various duties, will remain south of your territory. You protect me a little, and I become even less of a threat to you and yours. And that protection includes Joie."

Every face turned to her now. Joie actually felt a blush creep up her cheeks.

She'd gone from being alone and abandoned by everybody, to suddenly having more friends and even family than she knew what to do with. And that was before she knew she had to reach out to all her family in South Texas to apologize.

"You willing to accept some exile for a while, Daring?" Kehoe asked. "While we work all this out?"

She noted that he said *a while*, rather than forever. As if he expected to be able to recruit her back into the TRC at some point.

Get the Senate to reactivate her old commission? In spite of everything that might have to be told to certain folks to manage that?

Or just tell them that she was a deep cover agent? Pretending to work inside of a Mexican crime cartel, where she might be approached by the sorts of folks that previously would have hired Carter to do things?

"What about Romana?" Joie asked. "All this started because you lost track of her."

"I talked to Graydon in Seattle," Kehoe replied. "He doesn't know or won't tell me what he does know, but I also know that they haven't had any communications in six months or so."

Yes, she supposed so. They would have dropped all their AIs onto every email and comm number Romana had first thing. Tracked down every message she might have sent or received.

And come to a dead end.

"And?" Joie prodded.

"And Pham is still the impetus behind all this, Daring," he said. "If you come back into the fold, your long-term mission will be to find her. I can let you have some downtime to acclimate. And for me to get folks in DC to buy off on it. Then I'll come visit. Or send someone you know. One of these two, maybe. This security breach is monstrous, but it still pales while Pham is gone and nobody knows where she went or why."

"Did the other aliens contact her?" Joie asked.

"If they did, we're probably completely fucked, Daring," he snapped. "Just buying rope until they decide to hang us with it. I'm fighting in a burning house, sure, but there's also a bomb on the mantle, counting down to an explosion that might destroy everything. What's it going to be?"

Joie studied the other one-armed woman in here. Saw a sister under the skin. Kehoe was an asshole, but what she saw now was that it was probably a constitutional thing, rather than anything personal.

She turned to Bandi and the other two aliens.

"Sorry to ruin your afternoon," she apologized.

"You brought needed clarity, Captain Daring," Bandi replied.

She wasn't sure about that, but now wasn't the time to argue. Instead, she turned to Ernesta.

"You're certain?" she asked.

Ernesta nodded and smiled.

It would be an odd and awkward home, but Joie might belong somewhere again. Amy would be pissed, but that couldn't be helped. Maybe Joie could transfer her franchise number to a local one in Guadalajara?

Weirder shit had already happened this week, after all.

"Alright," Joie announced. "We'll go back to Mexico after you call off your dogs there. I'll lay low and wait for you to contact us. Then I'll start hunting Romana."

"*We* will," Ernesta stated flatly.

Joie wanted to cry, but managed to hold it for now. She'd been the lone wolf hero type for so long it was almost literary, even when she'd been occasionally paired with Romana. Now, she had whole networks of folks that had been willing to help her at the drop of a hat, without any expectation that she could ever pay them back.

Except to pay it forward for the next woman in need. The next victim running away from some man. Because it might be you.

"We will," Joie amended herself, smiling gratefully.

Ernesta surprised her by immediately turning to the door. She was still holding the cyberarm that had come off the black woman with Kehoe. And Bandi's pistol. She turned to Bandi and handed him the beam weapon he had thrust into her arms earlier.

"I don't think I will be needing this," she said.

He took it and smiled, bowing his head.

"Am I getting my arm back?" the woman asked.

"No," Ernesta replied from the doorway. "Have Bandi make you a new one. Call this an insurance policy so we can get safely away, check out of our hotel, and get to my jet. It will be available without any strike teams?"

"Can I have my phone back to call them off?" Kehoe asked in a snarky tone that sounded more like the man Joie remembered.

Ernesta grinned and emptied her pockets onto the table. Phones, wallets, change. Joie still had the little device for killing cyberware, but didn't need to do anything with it. She was keeping it.

Maybe she'd mail it back to him later. Or Bandi, since she knew the address here.

Joie joined Ernesta at the door and got handed a spare cyberarm Mark II. She recognized the model from the faint ridges where the *Sunburst* barrel would open in the palm.

Quickly, they moved to the front of the facility. Ernesta stopped at the desk to grab the phone and call someone. Turned out to be the intercom.

"Genevieve, it's safe to come out now," Ernesta said, her voice coming out of speakers everywhere.

Ernesta smiled at her and they exited into sunlight.

Maybe she wouldn't have to be alone anymore.

EPILOGUE

oie was upstairs in that same private restaurant in Guadalajara, sitting next to Ernesta on one side and all the woman's lawyer and accountant sharks around them. Lunch had just been carried away in the form of empty plates and bowls.

Joie had two arms, including the one Ernesta had gotten for her when they first reached Buenos Aires. Freya Malik was the woman who had lost her Mark II arm, at least until Joie and Ernesta had boarded the jet. Then Ernesta had boxed it up and mailed it back to Bandi.

Joie was wearing a dress today. Low cut in the front and tight through the waist, before flaring out around her knees. Blue with stars, made out of a modern material that was stretchy and sleek and cool when the afternoons were getting hot. Sleeves that covered her seam and went all the way down to her wrists. Her hair was up in a complicated braid, which was one of the first things she'd had to learn again when she had enough hands to do it.

Ernesta smiled at some internal joke as she sipped sangria poured from a pitcher on the side table. The sharks gossiped about various things among themselves. They were all well-dressed and dangerous, but at the end of the day they were really remorae. She and Ernesta were far more lethal.

One of the waitresses was coming up the stairs carrying a heavy briefcase. Anvil-case style. It dragged her shoulder down. She set it at the far end of the table as everyone fell silent.

"A man arrived with this, Señora," she said breathlessly. "And a note."

Joie watched her pull an envelope out of her apron. Like everyone working, she wore black pants, a black, long-sleeved shirt, and an apron with her name embroidered on it. Constanza handed it to Joie now, rather than Ernesta, quickly withdrawing.

Joie saw her name on the front. Or rather, *Daring*, which was all that most people called her anyway. The envelope was only sealed at the tip, so she slipped a finger under it and pulled out a single piece of heavy-stock paper. Trifolded. Almost linen by weight.

The letterhead was from *Elliott Engineered Integrated Logistics*.

Captain Daring,
Someone suggested that you might need a better arm than the
knock-off model Ms. Hernandez acquired for you. If you open
the humerus panel, you will find a note to disarm the circuitry
by removing a small board I have marked. Consider it an
apology for letting someone ruin your life before. I am still
working on a way to quietly construct replacements for your
other parts, but the lab has had to be packed up and moved to
a new location, so I have minders around constantly. This
piece was already in stock from before.
Cheers, and until I see you again,
Sal McKenzie, PhD

Joie rose from her chair and handed the missive to Ernesta without a word. She moved to the box and popped it open. Malik's arm had been so much darker than Joie's skin that they'd only briefly entertained the notion of keeping it. Ernesta had folks working on hiring someone to build her a new one. Plus, she'd been introduced to the *Pedros*, and Sarah called the woman almost daily now.

This one matched her skin tone perfectly, down to the freckles on the back she remembered in dreams and nightmares.

Joie lifted it out of the box as the sharks gasped. Ernesta was immediately at her side as Joie popped the panel in the upper arm and saw where *someone* had put a small, red bow on a chip with a note that said *Pull here.*

Joie did. It came out cleanly. She didn't do hardware, but Ernesta took it right out of her hand and handed it to one of the sharks, along with the letter.

"Research this," she instructed the man in a voice brooking no argument. He took both and vanished down the steps at almost a run.

"Do we trust it?" Ernesta asked.

Joie shrugged. She'd become much more whole in the last two weeks, home in Mexico and learning to not look over her shoulder constantly.

Joie flipped the arm over and studied the underside of the forearm. She pressed a spot her memory knew and a panel popped open. A loading bay for four ammunition disks.

Cyberarm, Mark II. XM24E4 *Sunbolt* Cyberarm rifle. She looked in the box and found a smaller box with eight fusion rifle ammunition disks in it. Four centimeters across. Half a centimeter thick. Deadly.

"I think they're serious," Joie whispered. "I'm just not sure I'm ready to pay the costs."

"You aren't alone, Joie," Ernesta said. "Keep that in mind. You've got me, Sarah, even Celeste."

Yeah, Ernesta had even contacted Mitch's mom to let her know Joie was safe. And to bring her in on what might be turning into a global conspiracy of dangerous women.

With a proper cyberarm, Captain Daring was back in the danger business. She would need it.

Pretty soon, Kehoe would walk through that door and she'd be off hunting for Romana Pham.

She could do this. Joie had more friends than she'd ever realized.

READ MORE

Be sure to read all the books in the Captain Daring series!

Revoked
Returned
Reborn

Available at your favorite retailers!

ABOUT THE AUTHOR

Blaze Ward writes science fiction in the Alexandria Station universe (Jessica Keller, The Science Officer, The Story Road, etc.) as well as several other science fiction universes, such as Star Dragon, the Dominion, and more. He also writes odd bits of high fantasy with swords and orcs. In addition, he is the Editor and Publisher of *Boundary Shock Quarterly Magazine*. You can find out more at his website www.blazeward.com, as well as Facebook, Goodreads, and other places.

Blaze's works are available as ebooks, paper, and audio, and can be found at a variety of online vendors. His newsletter comes out regularly, and you can also follow his blog on his website. He really enjoys interacting with fans, and looks forward to any and all questions—even ones about his books!

Never miss a release!
If you'd like to be notified of new releases, sign up for my newsletter.

http://www.blazeward.com/newsletter/

Buy More!
Did you know that you can buy directly from my website?

https://www.blazeward.com/shop/

Connect with Blaze!

Web: www.blazeward.com

Boundary Shock Quarterly (BSQ):
https://www.boundaryshockquarterly.com/

ABOUT KNOTTED ROAD PRESS

Knotted Road Press fiction specializes in dynamic writing set in mysterious, exotic locations.

Knotted Road Press non–fiction publishes autobiographies, business books, cookbooks, and how–to books with unique voices.

Knotted Road Press creates DRM–free ebooks as well as high–quality print books for readers around the world.

With authors in a variety of genres including literary, poetry, mystery, fantasy, and science fiction, Knotted Road Press has something for everyone.

Knotted Road Press
www.KnottedRoadPress.com

www.ingramcontent.com/pod-product-compliance
Lightning Source LLC
Chambersburg PA
CBHW060236100726
47907CB00003B/658

9 781644 702895